PRAISE FOR *IF I TELL YOU THE TRUTH*

"Bold and evocative, Jasmin Kaur's sophomore novel proves she is an unflinching writer. Tackling several tough topics, *If I Tell You the Truth* is a book that invites much-needed conversation."
—**JASMINE WARGA**, *New York Times* bestselling and Newbery Honor-winning author of *Other Words for Home*

"Timely and rare, this bold, pull-no-punches book deftly tackles immigration, rape culture and what it means to be undocumented in today's society. You'll smile, you'll cry, you'll want to burn down the patriarchy."— **SONA CHARAIPOTRA**, author of *Symptoms of a Heartbreak* and co-author of *Tiny Pretty Things*

"Weaving prose, poetry, and art, Jasmin Kaur's original voice gives us a searing insight into the lives of a mother and daughter and the secrets we keep and how they shape our lives."—**AISHA SAEED**, *New York Times* bestselling co-author of *Yes No Maybe So*

"Deftly layered with prose and poetry, Kaur tells a story of culture, courage, and heart. I was moved beyond words."—**NISHA SHARMA**, award winning author of *My So-Called Bollywood Life*

"A fast-paced story that will keep readers engaged and a thoughtful, loving examination of immigration, sexual assault, and chosen family."
—*KIRKUS REVIEWS*

PRAISE FOR *WHEN YOU ASK ME WHERE I'M GOING*

"Gut-wrenching and awe-inspiring, all in the same breath. Jasmin Kaur writes the type of poetry that you never want to stop reading. The type of poetry that makes you want to cry, laugh, stop and think, scream, and then use your own voice to tell your stories and speak your truth without apology. This book will change you."
—**LAYLA F. SAAD**, author of *Me and White Supremacy*

IF I
TELL YOU
THE
TRUTH

ALSO BY JASMIN KAUR
When You Ask Me Where I'm Going

IF I TELL YOU THE TRUTH

BY *jasmin kaur*

HARPER
An Imprint of HarperCollinsPublishers

ISBN 978-0-06-291264-0

Typography by Jordan Wannemacher
20 21 22 23 24   PC/LSCH   10 9 8 7 6 5 4 3 2 1

First Edition

for Gayatri,

whose wisdom guided

so much of this work

trigger warnings

sexual assault

police brutality

immigrant trauma

victim-blaming

domestic violence

alcoholism

depression

anxiety

This story was imagined and written prior to Covid-19. For an in-depth discussion on how the pandemic would have affected protagonists Kiran and Sahaara, please see the notes section on p. 445. If you wish to avoid spoilers about key plot points, do not read the notes section until you have completed the novel.

some stories
bury themselves so deep
within the flower bed of the mind
that the earth trembles. throbs.
when they are dug out.

Deep breath in. Deep breath out.

You've done this before. You can work through a panic attack.

Focus on something specific. Something that can bring you back down to earth.

I remember my daughter's eyes. They are oceans of deep brown, but if you catch them in the light, they are liquid amber. Round as my own and glistening with a hopefulness that is foreign to me, they are so very similar to another pair that still appears in my dreams. A pair of eyes that she will never meet, although their owner still breathes. She has a smile that digs deep into her cheeks, a smile that soothes my trembling hands more times a day than I can count. Her mess of wavy, jet-black hair is just as unruly as mine. It frames honeyed brown skin that illuminates beneath the sun and hides a tiny, rose-shaped scar just above her right ear.

And then there's her jaw.

It is a sharpened blade so unlike my rounded chin. I suppose I should confess that there are moments when the resemblance is too much. When, out of the corner of my eye, I think I see someone else hidden there: the man who has, unknowingly, placed me in the back seat of this police vehicle.

kiran

august 2001–march 2002

i wasn't exactly sure

if this could be considered
running away from home
when my parents were the ones
who put me on the flight
and waved goodbye at the terminal

go to school
study hard
come home

don't get into any trouble
in between.

when i landed
the earth did not
immediately shatter

and wasn't it dizzying
how my aunt and uncle picked me up
from vancouver international airport
and i made perfectly polite small talk
all the way to surrey

as though absolutely nothing was wrong

as though i could, in fact, be the girl
mom had always expected:

the well-behaved girl
the masked girl
the studious girl
who would go to school
and then marry the perfect man
from the perfect family
just for her mother's
nod of approval

as though i hadn't thrown up twice on the plane
and rehearsed *the phone call* exactly eleven times
(i still wasn't ready)

i'd left chandigarh
the only home i'd ever known
at the height of a humid august
with a tiny secret blossoming in my belly

and canada greeted me with chilly wind
dry as bark against my unexpecting skin
as if the earth herself needed to remind me
that nothing would be the same.

like morning sickness
choices felt foreign
to my body

my parents' demands usually
came packaged as suggestions:

biology is the best field to enter.
don't you want to be successful?

> *good families want foreign-educated*
> *daughters-in-law with homegrown morals.*
> *you should study in canada.*

imagine how easy
your life would be if you
married into the ahluwalia family.

> *go meet their son for lunch.*
> *get to know him more.*
> *the engagement doesn't*
> *need to be soon.*

why don't you marry prabh
after you finish your
university program?

when i missed my period
two weeks after ██████████
████████████████████████

that day i needed to scrub
from my mind forever

when i smuggled the pregnancy test
from a shop where no one
would recognize me

when i stared at that little +
unblinking, unmoving

something cracked
beneath my chest

i knew i needed
to make a decision
—and quick

i knew that this decision
could only come from me.

the phone call home

there was no blueprint for it
no easy way to tell my mother the truth
when we were two icy continents
who only knew each other from afar

i didn't know how to say

that the boy i thought i loved
had called me a liar

that his brother had done something
i needed to burn from my memory

that my body had become an enemy
i was forced to live with day and night

that i was terrified and shattering
and ached to be held

that i needed my mom.

so i simply spit out
the two words
she needed to know

i'm pregnant.

                                        what do you mean?

i mean—i'm
        pregnant.

                                this is why i told you
                                        to be careful
                        when you are alone with prabh!

                        it doesn't matter whether
                        you are engaged or not.

                        a man is still a man.

i hesitated for a moment.
i couldn't bring myself to tell her.

the reason

when mom asked
whether i'd scheduled the abortion
it wasn't so much a question
as it was a matter of fact

in what universe
would her teenage daughter
who had just crossed an ocean
plan to raise a baby?

she would never know
how my frost-coated heart
pined for someone
to call its own.

lost and found

between the pages of a story
i could hide from all of them
and me

but in poetry
i found a mirror

a place where light
could return to my chest

on this endless, tearful night
the sea of my stomach churned
as i searched for rest
in a bed that wasn't mine
and i tried not to shiver
thinking of the storm brewing
in my mother

slowly but surely
the star-drenched words
of hafiz and rumi
steadied my breath

asking me to trust
that stiller waters could exist
somewhere in this body.

the morning after

My thumb traced over the words printed on yellow-worn paper as a fresh tear betrayed me. Rumi's Sufi poem insisted that what I sought was also seeking me.

I wanted, so painfully, to believe him.

A fat droplet slipped through my fingers and landed directly on the ghazal. Over the months since the violation, it had almost become a ritual to cry into this book. Dried tears jutted from its pages like ribs peeking out from skin. Each tear was an emblem of a lonely night when I wanted to break free of my body. They were evidence of hurt but also proof that I could solidify and survive.

I was seeking safety. If safety was seeking me in return, I would kiss its hands in gratitude. In my eighteen years of existence, I'd never felt more alone, more vulnerable, more heart-shatteringly afraid.

Last night, my aunt and uncle picked me up from the airport and drove me to their home in Surrey. Sitting in what would be my bedroom while I was living in Canada, I made the most terrifying phone call of my life.

I told Mom that I was pregnant. *My* mom. As in, Hardeep Kaur. As in, the woman who once told me that I couldn't use tampons because they'd take away my virginity.

There was no going back, no more delaying the inevitable series of catastrophes that would arise from her only child being pregnant out of wedlock. What was going through her mind? What was she doing? Where was she sending her earth-rumbling rage now that I was no longer in arm's reach?

I dabbed at the fallen tear with my gray cotton sleeve and reluctantly closed the book's saffron cover. Its spine couldn't support me forever. Chachi had already knocked on the bedroom door twice, asking if I was ready for breakfast.

It was nearly noon.

With a sigh, I dropped *The Musings of Rumi* among the perfectly folded chunnis and jeans and hoodies sitting in my oversized suitcase. I would try to unpack later today. Perhaps it would help me settle into these new surroundings.

Right now, I had to put on a show for Chachi. It wouldn't be long before she'd return to the door, wondering if everything was okay. I'd be forced to sit with her in the kitchen and make small talk without:

a) Bursting into tears because of the cells proliferating in my abdomen and my mom's burning anger and, well, my entire catastrophic life

b) Projectile vomiting, courtesy of violent morning sickness

Two very difficult tasks, but if Mom had prepared me for anything, it was holding it together before an audience. *Composure*, she would say. *You keep your composure no matter what.* Digging through neatly packed stacks of clothing, I carefully drew out a thick black shawl that could hide my blooming stomach.

At nearly three months pregnant, I was starting to show. I mean, I didn't *think* I was showing until Mom made those putrid comments outside the security gate at Delhi Airport. In my mother's typical fashion, she went on a heated tirade about how I didn't look like a girl worthy of marriage into the Ahluwalia family. *Kiran, you need less butter on your praunté and more sit-ups in your workout routine*, she had said. At the acid of her words, I squeezed my nails into my sweaty palm, willing my tongue not to snap back. I was about to leave her and Dad's side for the first time in my life. Four years of university in Canada. Four years of oxygen. Four years to figure myself out without the fire of my parents' scrutiny hot against my skin.

I sealed up the suitcase and stood, eyeing myself in an oval mirror that hung between a worn night table and a smiling portrait of my aunt, uncle, and their two young children. At the moment, my two little cousins were off at summer camp and Chacha, Dad's younger brother, was dealing with insurance clients at his office. That meant Chachi was the only one home to see my tear-ravaged face. My insides crumpled at the thought of crying in front of her. It would almost be as bad as crying in front of my parents.

Breathe, I told myself, glaring at my quivering bottom lip in the mirror. *The more you cry, the worse your face is going to get.* My dark moon eyes were already bloodshot and swollen and utterly embarrassing.

Two sturdy knocks suddenly landed on the door. "Kiran, puth, are you coming downstairs?" Chachi called. "Breakfast is ready. Well, it's lunch now, I suppose. . . ."

Breath wavering, I dipped my tongue in false cheer. "Hanji! I'll be down in a minute!"

With one last glance in the mirror, I reminded myself of all the hell I'd already faced. An awkward conversation was nothing.

in the kitchen

chachi's sleek black braid snaked down her spine
and she glanced back from the stove
to smile and fret and remind me
that it was okay to feel

somehow
my bee-stung eyes didn't horrify her

> *it's perfectly human*
> my aunt said
> *to miss home*
> *to miss your parents*

> *never feel ashamed of your tears*

i nodded and lowered my gaze
and didn't correct her assumptions
about why i was in shambles

> *we couldn't be happier that*
> *you're staying with us!*
> *our home is your home.*

chachi was the day to my mother's night
kinder than necessary
softer than the rest of my rigid family

even if i couldn't tell her the truth
about everything hidden
beneath my tearful smile

perhaps
i could find solace in her warm embrace

biology major

orientation day arrived
before i'd even managed
to orient myself in time and space

i was a newborn to this new country
terrified of getting lost on the bus
and finding my classes on my own
and trying to make friends
when i could barely do that back home

i knew why i had to be here

i knew i couldn't stay in canada
if i didn't go to university

i knew i couldn't support a child
without a stable career

i knew i had so much more to fear than a new school

but, god, i was still terrified.

freshie

The word *no* was an art form foreign to me. I mean, I'd always loved the *idea* of saying no, but nothing made my skin crawl like the thought of disappointing people. So, of course, when Chachi asked if I could take the bus to SFU for my orientation, I ate all my nerves, dropped an enthusiastic *not a problem!*, and desperately hoped that I wouldn't end up in the wrong city.

This was the real me: the girl who pressed all her desires flat to avoid causing a stir. The girl on the phone who told Mom that she was having a baby? I didn't know her, and she certainly wasn't here with me at this school.

I knew that if I started running right now, I could catch the bus. I was sure of it. I could get the hell off this frightening, confusing concrete jungle of a campus and hide beneath my comforter, perfectly safe, perfectly alone.

Pull it together, Kiran. Isn't that what the white people say? You're stuck here.

I pried my eyes off the long walkway that led to the bus stop and turned to face a monstrously intimidating cement building, far larger than my familiar, teacup-sized college back in Chandigarh. I forced my feet forward.

The atrium was swarming with students, most gathered in a dense lineup that led to unopened double doors. I scanned the line in search of someone who I could talk to: a group of white boys in red SFU sweatshirts and matching hats chattered loudly among themselves; a tall, gray-haired woman stared idly out the window to our left; a bored-looking girl in black overalls blew an enormous pink bubble, glancing at me and then popping her gum in my direction. My heart galloped against my ribs. The last thing I wanted to do right now was stumble over my English while I asked these strangers for help.

Canada won't be so bad, Dad had said before I left home. *I'm sure you won't be the only Punjabi at your school. And even if you are, maybe it'll build some character.*

I didn't need character. I needed a thimble of familiarity.

My clenched breath unfurled when I caught a glimpse of dark-haired, unmistakably Punjabi girls poring over their French manicures. "Sat sri akaal!" I called in Punjabi, waving at the group as I approached. "Is this the orientation for new students?"

The group eyed me and then each other. A tall girl in the middle pulled the pink binder in her arms a little closer. "Yeah," she said, her English crisp with whiteness. "There's a table over there where you sign in. . . ." She pointed to two middle-aged white women sitting behind a desk to my right. I watched as a girl with side-swept bangs whispered something in her ear, eyes flashing toward me as she spoke. Was I missing something?

As I walked away, a high-pitched voice echoed loud and clear, rising, undoubtedly, from the girl I'd just spoken to. "Why are there so many freshies here?" Laughter and groans erupted behind me.

Freshies. I didn't know what the word meant but I couldn't help but feel like it was directed at me. Was I being paranoid? Maybe it was a Canadian thing that I didn't understand?

When I returned to the line, I pasted my eyes to the ground, not making the mistake of speaking again.

No one is possibly paying attention to you. You can't be the only new person here.

There was no coaxing myself out of my nerves: after the registration incident, I felt like a neon sign in this auditorium. Did my sun-marked skin glow with the word *outsider*? *Loser*? Maybe it was something a little colder.

Loud chatter swallowed the cavernous room as freshmen slowly poured in, filling the seats closest to the top before stragglers settled in near the bottom. From what I could see, most people seemed to know each other, probably arriving from the same high schools. Pulling my notebook open to a blank page, I did my best to look invisible—just as dull as an empty seat. I began to scribble a to-do list that I'd later have to tear out and hide:

Visit a gynecologist
Buy prenatal vitamins
Find a place to rent

The last item was going to be exceptionally tricky, but at least I had time on my side. It would be a few months until my stomach would bloom so large that I'd no longer be able to hide it beneath an oversized shawl. A few months before Chachi and Chacha would realize the truth and inevitably kick me out of their house. A few months to find a bedroom where I could afford the rent, go to school, and safely raise this child.

A shiver stole through my spine. Was I actually doing this?

"Rahul is trash!" someone loudly declared, and my head shot up instinctively, searching for the voice. It was coming from a brown girl with a pixie cut a row below mine. "He's always been trash. He will always be trash. Accept it. It's the truth." Her thick blue streaks were mesmerizing. She couldn't possibly be Punjabi with hair like that.

"How?!" her friend replied, toying with her raven-dark braid. "He left his family for Anjali. That's definitely not trash behavior." They were talking about my favorite movie. I pretended not to eavesdrop.

"So, he treats Anjali like shit, marries Tina, and then finds Anjali once Tina is dead? What's so romantic about that?" the blue-haired girl argued.

"Hold up. You're talking about *Kuch Kuch Hota Hai* Rahul. I'm talking about *Kabhi Khushi Kabhie Gham* Rahul."

"It's the same Rahul!"

Her friend paused, as if calculating something. Then she burst out laughing. "That makes no sense."

"It makes complete sense!" The blue-haired girl looked around as though searching for someone. My stomach jumped when her eyes locked onto me. She had spotted me staring. "What do you think?"

"S-sorry?" I stammered, warmth creeping into my cheeks. "Are you talking to me?"

"What do you think about Rahul and Anjali?"

"Oh . . . I didn't mean to eavesdrop," I mumbled. "I loved *Kabhi Khushi Kabhie Gham* but, to be honest, Rahul *was* kind of terrible in *Kuch Kuch Hota Hai*. . . ."

"See! Terrible, Simran. *Terrible*," she laughed to her friend. Her honey-brown eyes returned to mine. "I'm Joti. This is Simran."

"Kiran. Nice to meet you two," I quietly replied. My eyes wandered to the silver septum piercing dangling from Joti's slightly upturned nose.

She caught me staring again. "Like it?" She smiled.

"Oh, sorry, I didn't mean to—I think it's lovely."

"So do I . . . but my mom isn't really feeling it. She thought I was getting a koka like yours." She pointed to my more traditional nose ring, a tiny gold piece on my left nostril.

My fingers gravitated toward the piercing that Mom had chosen for me. "I . . . like yours better," I told Joti. "I think I'm gonna take this out soon."

Joti surveyed me with something thoughtful and nameless before she spoke. "What program are you in?"

"I'm majoring in biology." Hardly my favorite subject, but it always landed me the highest grades. Dad said the numbers were all that really mattered. If it had it my way, I would've applied for English. "I might do a chemistry minor as well."

"Look at that," Joti said, tilting her head to survey me. "Another bio student. Aren't we a perfect set of brown girl stereotypes?"

I peered from her glimmering piercing to her bold haircut to my own distorted reflection in her purple glasses and couldn't help but laugh. If we were a brown stereotype, maybe they needed another category.

❧✶❧

"Do you know what the word *freshie* means?" I asked Joti as we left the orientation. We had spent the first hour in the lecture hall receiving welcome after welcome by university staff. Then we were divided into groups and shown different buildings on campus. Joti told me to stick by her side during the campus tour, even though I was supposed to join the red group. I happily obliged. This place was a concrete maze and I had no idea how I'd find my classes on my own.

"It means fresh off the boat," she explained, rolling her

eyes. "Like, straight from Punjab. It's how they make fun of new immigrants around here. Why?"

Blood rushed to my cheeks once again. "Oh."

"Kiran, why?" Joti stopped dead in the center of the sidewalk. Students pushed past us on either side, but she was unbothered by their glares. "Where'd you hear that?"

I explained the incident with the Punjabi girls in the atrium. Joti's mouth fell open and fury filled her eyes. There was another emotion there. I think it was pity. "Fuck 'em," she bristled through gritted teeth. "Those girls are still stuck in high school. They don't get that their own parents were new immigrants at some point. Don't take it personally. We're not all like them. I promise."

I could feel tears threatening to form, so I changed the subject. I'd dealt with enough embarrassment today. "Where's your family from, originally?"

"We came here about six years ago," Joti said, moving along the sidewalk again. I followed at her side. "Immigrated from Jalandhar."

The surprise was plain on my face. "You weren't born here?"

"What made you think that?" she asked.

"Well, I mean . . ." I adjusted the textbook in my arms, hoping I wouldn't sound horribly presumptuous. This funny, thoughtful girl had given me the time of day. I didn't want to ruin my ridiculous stroke of luck. "I don't mean to offend you at all, but you don't seem like a lot of the other Punjabi girls I know."

"Maybe you don't know enough Punjabi girls, then," she laughed, the irony of my recent immigration from Punjab lost on neither of us. Then she went quiet for a moment, as though she, too, was choosing her words carefully.

"I was joking about the stereotype thing I said earlier. I think we're all pretty complicated. Just beneath the surface."

I nodded in agreement, hand instinctively reaching for my belly. I was no stranger to complications just beneath a cookie-cutter exterior. But, to put it bluntly, her "surface" confused me. It seemed like Joti was welcome to be herself on the outside, as boldly and as loudly as she wished. If I had come home with a septum piercing, my parents would've immediately marched me back to the jewelers to get it removed.

"I'm sorry. I didn't mean to judge you or anything. I guess I just assumed that you would have to be born in Canada for your parents to let you . . ."

"Look like this?" she finished my sentence, stifling a grin beneath pursed lips. "Don't get me wrong. My parents weren't always open to me doing this shit. The way I see it, our parents are growing with us. I'm the youngest sibling and my sister was an easy kid to raise. She never wanted to go out or dye her hair or whatever. Love her, but she was a *complete* Goody Two-shoes," Joti sighed in exasperation. "My parents were expecting me to be another Deepi. I took some getting used to."

"I suppose that makes sense. I really don't know if my parents will get used to me, though," I said, surprising myself with my honesty. My gaze shifted nervously from Joti to the whistling maple trees ahead. As their only kid between four devastating miscarriages, I was their one shot at crafting the child they wanted. The only place to pour all their hopes and rest their heavy expectations. "I'm not exactly living up to all their dreams."

My eyes remained on the earth, but I could feel her studying me. "Give 'em time. They'll come around. Trust me."

I nodded as if I believed her. "So, your dad is okay with your piercing as well?"

"My dad, um . . ." Joti's voice seemed to wither in her throat. "My dad actually passed away recently."

"Oh my god," I breathed. "I'm sorry. I'm so sorry. I—"

"Don't be." She half smiled, silencing my impending word vomit. Her eyes wandered the sidewalk and then rested on me. "You couldn't have known. And to answer your question, yeah . . . he was cool with it."

I had no idea what else to say, so I shut my mouth. I really was better off not talking.

funland

"C'mooooon," Joti moaned, pleading with her hands around mine. "I swear to you, it's not as scary as it looks. We'll sit in the middle. It's really only bad if you're at the front or the back."

I placed a weightless fluff of pink cotton candy in my mouth and let it melt to buy myself a moment to think. Joti had accepted none of my excuses to not join her on the roller coaster. The monstrous wooden structure looked terribly rickety. I wouldn't have set foot on the thing even if I was thoroughly unpregnant.

"I can't. I really can't." I shook my head. "Heights make me nauseous. I'll just vomit all over you."

"Fine." She sighed in resignation. "One day, you're gonna have to join me, though."

"One day."

When I said yes to Funland, I'd hardly been thinking about rides that would play cricket with my already-queasy stomach. I had come simply to hang out with Joti. Since last week's orientation, she had taken it upon herself to be my guide to all things Canadian. In her words, she wished she'd had someone friendly around when she first moved to Canada. It was, she said with a sparkle in her eye, the least she could do for a fellow Arundhati Roy fan. She told me that she came from a family that showed love through hospitality, through open doors. The concept was novel and intriguing and so very strange. I knew she'd get sick of me eventually, that her hospitality would soon wear thin, as everyone's did.

She'd inevitably grow tired of dragging along this new girl who constantly had her foot in her mouth.

For now, however, I'd cling to her side, lapping up any adventure she was willing to take me on.

The amusement park was teeming with children. They ran wild and giddy as uninterested adults trailed behind them, snacks in hand. On this lukewarm day, it seemed as if families were here to soak up the last drops of summer, the calm before school and work would consume them all. A teenage boy with sandy hair pushed past me on his way to the roller coaster, taking a fat chunk of my cotton candy on his sleeve as he brushed by.

"You could say excuse me!" Joti shouted over her shoulder. He nonchalantly raised a middle finger at us. "For fuck's sake. People these days . . ." I walked a little closer to her.

Standing next to Joti in a sea of white faces, I couldn't shake the feeling that I stuck out like a sore thumb. Although I'd been practicing my English in Chandigarh since the second grade, my accent was still a blaring siren that announced all the ways in which I didn't belong.

Wherever possible, I'd let Joti speak on my behalf. Six years in Canada had transformed her tone, but I could still hear warm inflections of Punjab lilting through her English. When she spoke, she'd drift effortlessly between English and Punjabi, while I'd do my best to speak solely in English. I desperately needed the practice.

"Chall." Joti grinned. "If you weren't into the darauna roller coaster, I'm sure you'll be up for this." She air-quoted *darauna*, poking fun at my fear. Joti stopped before a rusty gate that housed a giant metal diving board, just as tall as the roller coaster. At the bottom of the diving board was a pit full of spongy green cubes, each the size of a globe.

"What the hell is that?" I murmured.

"Bungee jumping. You climb to the top of the launch pad and then jump off." My eyes widened in horror and she tried to make it sound more appealing. "You don't hit the bottom! You're attached to a cord the whole time!"

"You've got to be kidding. Who could possibly enjoy that?"

Something devilish flashed in her smile. "Me."

We entered the dense lineup, where I stood by her side for moral support that she clearly didn't need. "Can I ask you something?"

"Shoot."

"Shoot?"

"As in, go for it," she patiently explained the foreign term. "Svaal puchla. Ask your question."

"What do you get from being dropped from the sky? Aren't you scared?"

"'Course I am." She reached for a chunk of my cotton candy and placed it in her mouth. "Tadh hi mein eho jehiaan cheejaan kardiaa. That's exactly why I do it."

"I don't follow . . ."

"I hate being afraid of fear. I'd much rather just face that shitty feeling head-on. I think I've always been like this but when Dad's kidneys went bad, it just made me want to . . . not hide from life. Does that make sense?" She sat down on a metal chain that divided the long waiting line for the ride. Scraped knees peeked out from the tattered holes in her faded jeans. A bald Black man stared up at me from her oversized t-shirt, his middle fingers raised. I think Joti called him Tupac.

"Makes sense." I nodded. "Can I, um, ask you something else?"

Her square jaw tilted thoughtfully. "Hanji."

I filled my lungs with air, hoping my question wouldn't point plainly to the truth lurking beneath my belly. "Have you ever been afraid of . . . people in your life finding out something about you that you *want* to share . . . but that you know they won't understand?"

She crossed her arms over her chest, smiling as if she was deeply impressed. "Damn, Kiran Kaur. You're gay, aren't you?"

"What?" I exhaled.

"That was a vague-specific question. You're not the first brown girl to go vague-specific on me."

"That's not it." I shook my head. "It's something else."

"Okay." Joti shrugged. "Well, to answer your question, yes. Hell yes. I still haven't come out to my mom because of just that."

"You're gay?" I asked, surprise renewed in my eyes.

"Uh-huh." She crossed her arms over her chest, shifting her body away from me, ever so slightly. "Kiran, you look like you've just seen a ghost. You okay?"

Heat flooded my ears. "I'm so sorry—I appreciate that you shared with me. I've just never met a—a—"

"—queer person before?" she finished my sentence. "I *promise* you have. Maybe you just didn't know they were queer." Her gaze wasn't unkind, but warmth continued to flood my skin. This was the dad fiasco all over again.

"I'm sorry. I probably sound ignorant—"

"Relax, Kiran." She softly smiled, arms loosening around her chest. "I get you. It's fine."

"Your—your mom doesn't know?" I asked. "I thought you said she's understanding . . ."

"She is, but this is gonna be . . . different, y'know? A septum piercing and blue hair aren't the same as me telling her that she's never gonna end up with the son-in-law of her dreams."

I nodded. This, I very personally understood.

"Anyways, whatever it is that you're keeping in, if it's a part of who you are, it's gonna be hard to hide forever. I'm clearly not one to talk 'cause I still haven't come out to Mom, but I did tell my dad."

"Really?" I was astonished that she could be so open with a parent. The concept felt intangible, like ether.

"Yeah. Told him I liked girls when he was in the hospital. I explained it to him, like . . . this is just the way that the universe or whatever made me. It's just a part of who I am."

"And . . . he took it well?" I asked, trying to remind myself that my parents were not all parents.

"As well as a middle-aged, conservative dad who's never heard the word *lesbian* before could take it." She shrugged. "He was confused but understanding. I guess there's something about your body breaking down that makes you . . . see past the superficial. Past people's random definitions of how things are supposed to be. Being sick made him see a lotta shit more clearly. Made all of us see more clearly."

I nodded quietly.

"When I told him, he was literally like, *Joti, I can't say I get it, but if this makes you happy, then it makes me happy. But your mom . . . puth, she's not gonna like this.*" She imitated her dad's voice with straight-faced seriousness and then broke into a sad, fragile laugh. She stared at her black Converse until she was ready to look up.

"Was he sick for a while?"

"It was a few years. Kidney failure's a kuthi, lemme just

tell you." She shook her head. "And he refused—*refused*—to take a kidney from any of us. Said he wouldn't be able to live with himself if we ended up going through the same shit and needed both our kidneys. Technically, he said he wouldn't be able to *die* with himself. The man had a fucked-up sense of humor." She smirked for the faintest moment, then her smile faded away.

I had no idea what to say that could make her feel better. "I'm so sorry, Joti."

"So am I." She paused for a heartbeat. "Can I give you a word of advice?"

"Please."

"This thing you wanna share . . . are you worried about what your family's gonna think?"

"Yeah," I murmured. "More than anything." I already knew what Mom thought and, although her reaction hadn't surprised me in the least, her silence was petrifying. She hadn't called me since I broke the news two weeks ago, and I couldn't help but wonder what was going through her mind. The process ahead was even scarier: one by one, everyone in my family would find out that I was pregnant.

"If they love you, eventually, they'll see past their own judgment. I *know* my mom isn't gonna stop loving me or something when I come out to her. She's just gonna be, like, on edge for a while. But once we get past that, we'll be cool." Joti spoke as if she was reassuring herself more than me.

"Next," drawled a bored-looking blonde girl in a red Funland polo. The sorrow tinging Joti's features slowly melted away, as if she was returning to wakefulness from a hazy dream. The ride attendant placed a helmet over Joti's head while rattling off a list of safety rules, then strapped her into a black harness that wrapped around her body like a vest. After tugging on the harness twice to ensure that it was secure, she sent her up a ladder that led to the top of the diving board.

Higher and higher she rose, waving and grinning at me without a tinge of detectable nervousness. I knew that my parents were nothing like hers, that no amount of love would allow them to see past their reputations. For a moment, however, I wondered about Chachi. About her relaxed aura. How she wasn't remotely stressed about me living with her, so different than the way Mom would grow irritable at the thought of anyone disrupting the carefully curated sanctuary of her home. Of her life.

Joti's world isn't yours, I reminded myself, envy bubbling in my stomach.

A ride attendant at the top of the metal diving board guided Joti all the way to the edge, turning her around so that she was facing away from the direction where she would jump. Then, with a joyful shriek, she plummeted toward the earth, staring fear right in the eyes, sending it a middle finger with her infectious, soul-stirring laughter.

hey, kiran?

she said, before i closed the truck door
and went back inside the house

you have a beautiful heart.
you'll find the right words for this situation
whatever this situation is
and it'll be okay.

and if it isn't
you know where to find me.

us freshies need to stick together, right?

a lovely family dinner

The last bit of cotton candy met my tongue, bliss from the warm summer day still embedded in my smile. Every time I hung out with Joti, things felt a little lighter, easier. I had never met someone whose joy seemed so perfectly weightless. It lifted her from sorrow just as easily as a rose petal caught in wind. If I could learn from her—if I could find a piece of her within me—perhaps things would be okay.

I reached deep into my purse, searching for the house key that Chachi had given me. After fumbling between receipts and transit maps and the random assortment of junk I carried in my bag, I gave up and rang the bell.

When the door swung inward, my grin still hung on my face like a snapshot, but my stomach fell so fast I thought I'd be sick. Air vacuumed itself from my body. I could hardly breathe as I took in the sight of her large, unforgiving eyes, her meticulously arched brows, her pulled-back bun, her pinned-in-place smile.

"Mom?" The word left my mouth an octave higher than normal. "What are you—why are you here?"

"Surpriiiiise!" came Chachi's singsong voice from just behind her. She smiled over my mother's shoulder without a clue that anything was wrong. Hardeep Kaur, the overbearing manager of my existence, stared at me, mouth upturned in a grin, eyes completely ablaze. My skin was scorching hot.

"Hi, Kiran." Wearing the white kurti that she'd bought from New Delhi and a mouthful of maroon lipstick, Mom took a single step toward me. She reached for an awkward embrace and my arms hung lifeless at my sides until I realized that I should hug her back: Chachi and Chacha were watching.

"Where—how did you get here?"

"Did you actually think I'd *miss* your birthday, puth?" Artificial sugar dripped from her words the way it did when she had so much more to say. Hai rabba, my head was spinning. Was it just me or was the doorway literally in motion? I managed a faint smile but couldn't come up with words.

Chachi's grin was still plastered to her face as she looked back and forth between us and said, "Well, dinner's ready. Shall we go eat?"

Needless to say, dinner was awkward. The sounds of forks and spoons clinking against ceramic dishware filled all the spaces between small talk. With my little cousin Joban off at a sleepover and his sister, Harpreet, far more interested in her picture book than anyone at the dinner table, Chacha and Chachi did their best to make conversation. Mom tried to play along; appearance was everything.

"Hardeep, Kiran's classes start soon. I think she has all her books, yes?" Chacha turned toward me, wiping a piece of spinach from his bristly mustache.

I raised my eyes from the lasagna that I'd been moving back and forth around the plate. "Yeah! Got everything I need!" I replied, way too excitedly. A bead of sweat trickled down from my armpit.

"Good," Mom said. "I hope you're cracking those books open already, Kiran. Trust me, you should get a head start on your readings. After the first week, it's going to be assignment after assignment."

Chacha raised a thick black eyebrow and laughed about how it was still summer. He insisted that I enjoy the last remnants of fun before school would begin. Mom placed a bite of cottage cheese and tomato in her mouth and politely smiled, not arguing with Chacha's point. Instead, she glanced at me in that subtle way of hers, speaking with her eyes. Her split-second glare said something like, *You heard what I said. Start studying and cut all this pregnancy bullshit.* I glued my eyes to the lasagna like I'd never seen anything more interesting.

I could draw out this meal for hours, but eventually, dinner would end. Chachi and Chacha and Harpreet would go to bed and I would be left alone in a room with Mom. A room where she would undoubtedly ask me the question burning holes into her tongue: Why hadn't I scheduled an abortion yet?

I was simultaneously sweaty, nauseous, dizzy, and close to tears. God, this pregnancy was fun.

Chacha made small talk about the confusing bus connections between Surrey and SFU. Chachi chimed in about the new SkyTrain that was being built as she cut a slice of lasagna for Harpreet. Without glancing up, Harpreet flipped to the next page of *The Rainbow Fish.*

When conversation lulled, Mom cleared her throat, coughing into her napkin before she said, "Kiran hasn't been giving you two any trouble, has she?"

"Trouble from Kiran?" Chachi gasped. "She's an angel! Too *polite*, if you ask me."

Chacha shook his head like he'd never heard anything more ridiculous. "Hardeep, we're so happy to have an older role model like Kiran around for the kids. We're hoping Joban follows in her footsteps and goes into sciences one day. Harpreet's already dead set about what she wants to do, aren't you, puth?" he chuckled. "Tell Thaee Jee what you wanna be when you grow up."

Harpreet suddenly perked up, wide-eyed with a wonder

that could only exist in a kindergarten heart. "I want to be a hole digger!" she proudly declared.

"A hole digger?" Mom's smile creased her cheeks but didn't reach her eyes. "What do you mean?"

Harpreet gleefully broke into an explanation of how she'd seen a lady in a hard yellow hat who was digging holes with a giant hole-digging machine. Everyone laughed about how she planned to dig all the way to the Earth's core and I began to tune out the conversation, grateful to no longer be the center of discussion. Every so often, I would look up to catch Mom's eyes lingering over me. How did I tell *this* woman that I was pregnant? What had I been thinking? How could I even be surprised that she'd travel halfway across the world to set me straight?

sometimes i wondered

who mom would've been
if it weren't for the miscarriages

if she had satisfied all their desires
to have a son who'd carry on
the family name

would she have always been
the mother she was
that summer day
so many lifetimes ago
when warm sun caressed our skin
when her husband and her in-laws
were nowhere in sight

when she pulled me onto her chest
and i fell asleep listening
to the sound of her steady heartbeat

the talk

Just as I hid myself beneath the covers of my blanket, the bedroom door creaked open. I lay there silently for a moment, trying to steady my breath before what was to come.

She was quiet at first. I didn't know what to do so I reluctantly peeked out from the warm safety of the blanket. Everything in my body wished to be buried in the bed's protective depths, but she wasn't just going to disappear if I closed my eyes to her. I managed to sit up. She remained standing.

"You think you can just come here and do whatever the hell you want?" Mom's whisper did all the work of an echoing storm.

"No." I stared deliberately at the night table to her left to avoid looking at her.

"You think you can embarrass our family like this after all that we've done for you? You know . . . I thought that you had some sense. That you'd be wise enough to not do something as shameful as this. But that was my mistake." She paused. "I haven't told your father." Tears stung the corners of my eyes and I blinked them away before she could notice.

Her maroon lips had faded. All the color now existed in her cheeks. "Kiran, just tell me one thing. Why? What's the real reason for all of this drama?"

"It's not drama." I refused to look at her. "Keeping the baby is . . . what I've decided to do. It's not—it's not to make a scene or something. This isn't about anyone else."

"*What you've decided to do?*" she sneered. "Is this a joke? Are you mad because you want attention? Is that it? Are you mad because we told you to go to school before you got married? Hm? Is this your way of speeding up the wedding?"

"I'm not marrying Prabh."

"WHY?!" Anger had gotten the best of her and it carried into her loud voice.

Silence.

"I was raped." I don't know why I said it. Or how I had managed to say it. I just knew that when the word left my mouth, my insides seared. Screamed. It tasted like kerosene and burned all the way out. The tears began to fall in earnest now.

Mom swallowed, but her expression remained unchanged, unsoftened. "By who?"

"His brother. Prabh's brother." I held my breath, hoping that I had been wrong. Hoping that she would believe me.

"How could that be? They're good men. They're from a good family."

The tears came to a halt. My skin was ice. Just like the day I told Prabh. I shouldn't have been surprised. I shouldn't have let my guard down.

"You can't seriously tell me that you had no part to play in this, Kiran. Unless . . . there's more to this that you're not telling me. Unless there's someone else."

"What are you talking about?"

"Who *really* got you pregnant? Did you meet some other boy? Was it—"

"There's no boy! There's no one! I HAVE NO ONE!" My whisper cracked.

"Keep your voice down! You have no one, hm? Then who the hell kept a roof over your head for the past eighteen years? Who fed you? Who sent you to school? How did you ever become so bloody ungrateful to do this to us?!"

"I'm not trying to *do* anything to you. Or hurt you. Did you not hear what I just said?"

"Yes, I can hear you," she hissed. "But I haven't forgotten what happened when you were sixteen, Kiran. Spending time with that boy without telling any of us."

The bruise of her words made me wince. How did me dating a boy in high school justify her not believing me? How did that have *anything* to do with this?!

"It was my mistake to listen to Prabh's mom," she pressed on. "You should have never been alone with him."

I said nothing. I wouldn't beg her to believe me.

"Does your chachi know? Did you tell anyone? Please tell me you kept your mouth shut about this."

My eyes met hers for the first time. "Why would I tell the family? To be called a liar?"

"Good." She breathed a sigh of relief. This was why she'd come: to save face. "We'll schedule the abortion."

Then she left the room just as suddenly as she had entered, and it was as if a tidal wave had hit me once again.

it's not a terrible thing

to be alone
when you have
at the very least

yourself

but i didn't.
but i didn't.
i'd never even
spoken to
that girl.

another universe

the palest green envy curdled within me
when i met joti's mom

her kind questions had nothing to do with
my weight or worth or achievements

her soft arms cradled a warmth
that carried into her smile

she filled the kitchen with savory laughter
and held joti like her very existence was a miracle

when she hugged me
it was as if we'd known each other forever

and i couldn't help but wonder
what life would be like if i was hers.

searching for my spine

Two days cramped in a house with Mom was enough to make me want to run to Joti's place and stay there until well past sunset. In the forty or so hours that Mom had been in Canada, she'd quietly danced around her anger when my aunt and uncle were nearby. As soon as they were out of sight, though, she'd eye me like she'd never seen anything more miserable. Whenever the house was empty, save for us, she'd hole herself up in my bedroom our bedroom as long as she was here—and make calls to abortion clinics, as if the pregnancy was hers. As if the choice was hers. When Mom hovered near me, I did my best to keep it together. I saved my silent meltdowns for the bathroom.

A tangled garden of family photos filled the otherwise blank walls of Joti's bedroom. I was transfixed by the portrait in the center. A short, turbaned man and a young, round-faced woman in a salwar kameez had their arms wrapped around two young girls. They all appeared to be caught on camera mid-laugh. Something about the picture made my heart swell and sink at once.

"Your dad?"

Joti smiled sadly. "Yep. That's Taran Singh."

"And that's Deepi?" I pointed to the little girl in a frothy pink dress standing in front of Aunty Jee.

"Yup." She was a head taller than Joti and wore her hair in a long braid. Joti, who couldn't have been older than five, had her hair in two tiny pigtails below her ears. Her gray T-shirt was emblazoned with a grinning Daffy Duck.

Joti ran her fingers over the portrait as if she was trying

to absorb the happiness that emanated from the preserved moment. Then she shook her head and returned to the room. On her bed was a hot bowl of buttery popcorn, two unopened cans of root beer, and an elaborate array of DVDs and VHS tapes.

"Are you feeling Bollywood or Hollywood?" Joti asked.

I pushed aside Kate Winslet's and Leonardo DiCaprio's sappy faces on the *Titanic* DVD and reached for *Kuch Kuch Hota Hai*. Kajol, my favorite Bollywood star, smiled next to Shah Rukh Khan, the bane of Joti's existence. "I thought you hated this movie . . ."

"It's my sister's." She sniffed at the VHS in disdain. "But I'm up for a critical feminist viewing if you are."

Soon, Rahul and Tina appeared on the miniature TV screen resting on Joti's black dresser. Tina was lying in a hospital bed holding her newborn daughter. In a white hospital gown, with tears welling in her eyes, she kissed the newborn's forehead. With little time to live, Tina hoped that young Anjali would remember her through letters. Rahul joined his wife at the bed, refusing to look at her.

"Okay. Not gonna lie. This part is sad," Joti murmured.

"Is Rahul really so bad?" I mumbled. A lump formed in my throat as he grabbed Tina's hand.

"He's the worst. Tina, though?" She sighed. "She's worth the tears."

Ten-year-old Anjali was now on the screen preparing to give a speech. She reached into a bowl to pull out a random topic. When she froze, petrified by the word that she'd chosen, so did I.

I knew what was coming and tried to hold it together. The only word to escape her mouth was *mom*.

Tears overtook the little girl and her father delivered her speech on her behalf. He told the audience how a mother's love was incomparable. How Anjali's mother was everything. How her absence had hollowed them.

Then I did something I was beginning to hate.

I began to cry. I cried because Rahul's words felt both familiar and foreign. I cried because I wanted to be held. Because I was aching for a different life—one in which I could leave all my sorrow in my mother's lap. I cried because I desperately wanted a mother. A family. Someone to call my own.

"Kiran," Joti whispered. "You okay?" I suddenly remembered my surroundings.

"Yeah . . . um . . . that scene just gets to me." While Joti was a little teary-eyed, my cheeks were dripping wet. The salmon walls of her bedroom slid in and out of focus as I tried to blink away my hurt.

"Are you sure?" Joti paused the movie and turned to face me, features stained with worry. "If you want to talk, I'm here."

What was I supposed to tell her? Where did I even begin? I supposed I should address the elephant in the room. Or, perhaps, the embryo.

"I, um, I'm pregnant."

"Oh . . ." Her mouth formed an O shape and she blinked a few times. "Okay. That's . . . wow."

"Yeah." The words landed one atop the other, like Joti's seed of care had broken a dam in my throat. "Things have happened that have gutted me. Like, completely emptied me out and turned me into a shell and I've been so alone and confused and I know I can't ask my family for help and that's the most painful part."

Joti gently nodded, waiting for me to go on.

"I was too scared to tell my mom when I was in Punjab, so I waited until I got here. She literally flew all the way here just to set me straight. She . . . wants me to get an abortion. She's already calling clinics."

"And what do you want?"

I paused.

I thought back to the pregnancy test I took in the damp bathroom stall of a McDonald's miles from my house. Panic strangled me but so, too, did another emotion: a painful desire to love and be loved without betrayal. "So much shit has happened that's been outside of my control. The only thing I've felt sure about is the fact that I want this baby."

"What about the father?" she whispered. "Does he know?"

Joti genuinely cared. It showed in her eyes. In her hands that reached intuitively for mine. But there was something about the story that wouldn't allow me to speak. Each time I had tried to tell the truth only to be called a liar, something shifted within me. Something burned a little hotter. The story had dug itself a hiding place within the earth of my mind. Sunk deeper into a place I was too scared to reach into.

"No" was all I could say.

"Kiran, I—I can't act like I know what you're going through. But I want you to remember that your body belongs to you. Whether you choose to keep the baby or not, the decision should be yours."

"I've been trying to tell myself that." I pulled my knees close to my chest and pushed away the memory. The moment that sparked this whole sickening mess.

"What's your plan? I don't know how you're dealing with this when school's about to start . . ."

"I have some money saved up. And I can work and study at the same time. Once my stomach gets bigger, I doubt I'll be able to stay at my chachi's house. I'll have to rent a room somewhere. But the thing is, my mom is sleeping beside me for the next two weeks. There's no conversation we can have that won't end ugly. When she's decided what to do, it's like I'm not even there."

"Kiran, I say this with complete love, okay? If you really want this, you'll have to find your spine and stand up for yourself. You need to be direct with your mom and make it crystal clear that she can't decide what to do for you. If you don't, you'll be under her thumb forever."

I exhaled, the truth stinging.

"This isn't gonna be easy, but you won't be alone. I'm here for you. However I can be."

I shook my head and a cold tear dripped into my trembling hands. "Why?"

"What do you mean?"

"Why do you want to . . . help me?"

She found my hand and stilled it within her grasp. "Because I don't know what my family would've done when Dad died if we didn't have each other. We got through it because we had shoulders to cry on and ears willing to listen. Because we had support."

joti told me

that love was a heavier anchor
than the currents that tried
to force us apart

that humans were not as weak
as their weakest moments

that family could gather
to form a lighthouse
or maybe just a flashlight
when we needed them most

that i was not as alone
as i thought i was

that maybe chachi
would be there for me
if i gave her a chance
to hear my story

weighing my options

my head was a tangled mess
and maybe writing it all down
would help me unravel things.

on a fresh sheet of paper
i listed every reason to tell chachi
and every reason not to

reason to:
joti said i needed to stop
believing that everyone
would fail me.

reason not to:
this was my mess and
i was not her burden.
she didn't owe me a thing.

reason to:
her home felt like a home.
i didn't know what that was
before i got here.

reason not to:
to tell this story
was to reopen a wound
and i was so tired of
cleaning blood.

52 ❧

reason to:
what other choice
did i really have?

a cup of cha and light conversation

if mom's greatest fear
was our whole family finding out about what was inside me
i was lighting a match dangerously close to propane
when i said
chachi, can i talk to you?

the story left me in serrated glass shards
that scraped my esophagus
even though i didn't tell her everything
(the truth of the conception died in my throat)

as chachi listened
the warm cha in her hands went cold
her wrists trembled
like the story was too much to carry

and she told me that she was better off not knowing
that there was nothing she could do to help
that my chacha would blow a fuse if he knew
that my family could be torn apart by this

but for something to tear apart
i thought to myself
it would have to be together
in the first place.

spilled milk

when mom walked into the kitchen
chacha and my cousin trailing behind her
a grocery bag in each of their hands

chachi stood up way too fast
nearly taking the turquoise tablecloth with her
(i caught the cup of cha before it tipped)

she tried to busy herself with frozen pizza
and boxes of cereal and heads of lettuce
that needed putting away

her voice was shrill and high
and not at all suspicious
whenever she spoke

did you find the chili powder i needed?

how was our day? it was great!

oh, good! you got milk! i forgot to add it to the list!

mom studied chachi in that calculating way
before her gaze drifted, inevitably, to me

her back remained to chachi
when she said, sharp and exact,
bali, you just got a new job at the hospital, right?
what unit was it again?

maternity
chachi whispered
and the jug of milk in her hands
slipped through her fingers
splintering and splattering
all over the floor.

an ultimatum

"It was a mistake, Joti. A huge mistake. I shouldn't have told Chachi," I whispered into my phone. I sat on the white carpet of my bedroom, back planted against the lockless door so that I could hear footsteps climbing up the stairs. Streaks of golden-hour light poured over my toes in the otherwise-dim room.

"Shit. Shit-shit-shit. I'm sorry, dude. I really thought she would've been helpful."

"And Mom *definitely* knows I told." I shivered. "It was all over Chachi's face. She dropped a whole jug of milk 'cause she was so nervous in front of my mother."

How could I have been so stupid?

Tension had wound itself tight around every corner of the house. I was certain that Chachi would let the news slip to Chacha soon. Then Dad would hear about it. And then the tumbling inferno of this situation would be far beyond any remnant of my control, a vicious wildfire so much greater than me.

"I need to start looking for bedrooms to rent," I whispered soft into the receiver. "Do you think you can help me?"

"Just—just come stay at my place, Kiran."

"What?"

"Listen. I talked to my mom about you staying at our house. Like, renting out Deepi's old bedroom—"

"Wait, what?" My heartbeat thrummed in my ears. "You talked to your mom? When?"

"A couple days ago. After our movie night."

I sat up a little straighter. "Why didn't you tell me?"

"I didn't wanna get your hopes up if she wasn't cool with it."

"And . . . is she?" I held my breath.

"Yeah. I explained the situation to her and—"

"What? What did you say?" My eyes bulged in panic as realization dawned on me. "Joti, you weren't supposed to tell her about the pregnancy!"

"I'm sorry. I'm so sorry. I just needed to tell her what happened so that she would . . ."

"Feel sorry for me?"

Silence sat between us for a few long seconds. "No, Kiran." She swallowed. "So that she would understand what was up and know why you need to be in a safe, supportive place." She paused, her exhale audible. "She's with you, Kiran. She wants you to come stay. We were trying to rent the room, anyways. No one feels sorry for you, trust me."

"Are you sure?" I asked, eyes watering, fear casting long shadows on this tiny thread of hope. "Completely and positively sure?"

"I'm sure. We're ready when you are."

"Okay." I nodded into the now-dark bedroom. "I'm going to think through this."

As I made my way downstairs for dinner, Joti's offer spun in my mind. My eyes glazed at the thought of her kindness. And her mom's. I knew that no family was perfect, that Joti's life was far from easy. But there was still a twinge of envy within me. She and her mom almost seemed like friends. The thought of Mom and me having a heart-to-heart (or talking about anything besides school, work, marriage, and my appearance) was unthinkable.

A memory from Chandigarh fluttered in my eyes. In the spring, Mom had been chatting on the veranda with Naseeb Aunty. She told Aunty that she didn't know how she'd deal with my doli, the part of a South Asian wedding when the bride officially leaves her parents' home for her partner's. Nothing was more awkward than the image of Mom crying as if she'd lose something in my departure.

When I stepped into the kitchen, the lights were out. Confused, I fumbled in the darkness for the light switch.

"SURPRISE!" came a chorus of voices. Mom, Chacha, Joban and Harpreet stood behind the table decorated with pink and blue balloons. A white, sprinkle-covered cake sat before them.

Chachi placed her hands on my shoulders from behind and said, "Happy birthday, Kiran!"

"I—what? You guys didn't need to do this," I gasped, fresh tears threatening to form. Guilt flooded my veins, injecting me with the word *selfish*. Maybe I didn't deserve these people— any of them. Maybe I was everything that Mom had named me. My family sang "Happy Birthday" loud and melodic, and Chacha told me to make a wish.

I wished for help. For a clear path. For just one thing to be easy.

That night, I lay staring up at the white-stucco ceiling. Mom's back was to me. She grazed my shoulder with each inhale.

"Everything that we've done has been because we want what's best for you," she murmured.

My breath was the only noise in the bluish darkness.

"Daughters are like diamonds. They're precious. They must be protected from those who want to steal them. Or damage them. That's why we only wanted you to talk to Prabh. Their family . . . we've known them all our lives. They're respectable.

They would make your life so easy. And yet . . . you choose to go and do this."

I didn't dare to speak.

"I know you told Chachi. She told me everything. And I hope she doesn't say anything to your chacha."

My ribs pressed into my emptying lungs, my last molecule of faith in Chachi disappearing.

"You're nineteen now," Mom continued. "I suppose that means you can make your own choice. But you need to understand something very clearly. Maybe it was my fault for not being clear before. After everything your father and I have done, after every opportunity we've afforded you—if you do this, you will have no place in our home. You won't humiliate me with lies and call yourself my daughter."

I turned onto my side and waited for deep slumber to draw her to another world.

dear mom,

I'm writing this because I figure you all
should know where I went. I don't know how
much you want to know. I don't know how
much you care. I don't care whether you'll
ever believe me. But I'm gone with my friend
and I suppose this tells you the decision that
I've made. Do what you need to do to save
face. Tell everyone I went back to Punjab.
Tell them I went to a different school. Just
know that everything will be a lot easier for
both of us if you don't come after me. I'm
sorry that I couldn't be the daughter you
wanted me to be.

Kiran

this isn't a poem.

instead it's an obituary
for the girl i used to be

the girl who belonged to
everyone but herself

the girl who swallowed
her heart and bit her tongue

the girl who would have
never dared to run.

the vaginal exam

when was the last time you had a pap smear?
the doctor asked with kind eyes

i don't—i don't know what that is
i replied, cheeks reddening

a pap smear is an examination of your cervix
to check for any abnormalities?
she ended her sentence like a question

you're going to go . . . inside?
i asked

she nodded and i nodded
but my lungs were coiled tight

she touched me with cold metal
between my legs
and i pulled away
muscles seizing, heart pounding

she stopped
looked up at me
breathed long and slow

asked
kiran, are you okay with this?

*are you uncomfortable with
your vagina being touched?*

are you feeling safe?

*would you like to just sit awhile
and breathe?*

three months

i'd been trying not to count all the missing pieces
but i'd be lying if i said i didn't look at my phone
hoping for a call (just one)

i knew this silence
was only making my heart heavier
so i gathered what i was grateful for
and held them close

joti was one
her mom was another
and the thought of this baby
was all the rest

six months

according to a book joti found in the library
babies begin to dream at twenty-six weeks
and i wondered what could cross her mind
before she had encountered this world

i passed all my science exams
learned way too much about chemistry
and each cell that formed her body and mine

but i couldn't yet explain this cocktail
of everything i felt:

two teaspoons of hope
three tablespoons of fear
six dashes of sadness
and a monsoon of

alone

whatever this was
i hoped she was the antidote.

nine months

dear daughter,

it's strange talking to a being who you haven't yet met.
how odd it is to love a person you've only felt.

but i've known you far longer than i've known myself
and the thought of a lifetime with you is a journey
i hope i'm worthy of.

my heart already swells for all the days when you'll soar
and breaks for all the days when you'll sink.

but i will be there, my love.
it will be my greatest honor to be there.

ਸਹਾਰਾ / sahaara (n)

a pillar, a refuge, a shelter, a source of support.

when sahaara came
when they placed her delicate, honey-warm body against me
skin still blue and caked with blood and bits from my womb

all the pain of the last ten or twelve or god knows how many
hours evaporated   melted   into thin air

all the heartbreak of every empty chair in this hospital room
fluttered away   like my chest was no longer a closed cage

all the worry about tomorrow halted
as if love was an antidote for time
and this moment could stop the hands of a clock

in that hospital room, on that sun-drenched day

nothing existed in the world but this beautiful being
crying and yawning and resting on my skin

and nothing was as musical as her soft heartbeat
synced to the beat of mine
that sounded so much like the word *home.*

the social worker

something in my gut told me
to say nothing to the social worker
that would give away my fear

curly red hair
and ice-blue eyes
that seemed to see right through me
she asked us where the car seat was

said sahaara couldn't leave the hospital without it
said i seemed quite young
asked about resources and support
and whether i needed any help

and a crackling mountain of panic
melted to water
when joti entered the room out of breath
with the car seat we'd forgotten in the car

i promised that i had
all the help i needed.

on the perfect mom

according to a magazine at the grocery store
every new mom *needed* organic baby diapers
needed a self-rocking swing
                    needed a lactation massager
needed a traveling high chair
& no one seemed to know that i just wanted
to rock her to sleep once without worrying
            that i was doing everything wrong.

our paths diverged

Joti reached for her fourth cup of coffee. I would've grabbed another if I wasn't breastfeeding. We sat on the living room carpet in an elaborate nest of textbooks and cue cards and fluorescent highlighters and color-coded notes. Joti's exhaustion-riddled eyes flitted across diagrams of oligomeric proteins and actin filaments and microtubules. We were supposed to be studying for the bio-chem exam, but Sahaara needed a feeding.

"Actin filaments are important to cells because they . . ." Joti read from a green cue card and then glanced up at me.

"They . . . they maintain the integrity of the—ouch! Sorry. I don't think Sahaara's latched on properly. Shit, my nipples feel like they're gonna fall off." I placed a pinky between my nipple and Sahaara's gums to break her latch. My newborn erupted in shrieks and I quickly placed her back on my breast. There was quiet once more.

Joti placed the cue cards on the carpet. "Why don't you take a break, Kiran? Let's try again when she's asleep."

I shook my head. "No point. She's gonna start crying as soon as I put her down."

Joti's mom was sitting on the plastic-protected sofa, sipping cha and observing our futile attempt at exam prep. "Kiran, what's happening with your other courses?" she asked.

My back stiffened with worry. I'd passed my first semester with a near-perfect GPA. This semester, I was hanging on by threads. "Two of my professors are letting me finish the semester from home, by correspondence. And one said I can't get credit for the classes I miss but I can come for the final exam. And, yeah, you already know about bio-chem. . . ." If it weren't for Aunty Jee offering to babysit Sahaara while I took the bio-chem exam, I'd fail the course.

"Hmm—" The landline rang and Aunty Jee leaned over to get the phone. "Kidhaan, Deepi? How was your day?" Aunty Jee stood up and gave Joti an oddly pleading look. I caught a grimace on Joti's face before she busied herself with chemistry notes. Aunty Jee disappeared into her bedroom but her muffled voice carried through the paper-thin walls.

"What's going on?" I asked, confused by Joti's sudden discomfort. "Did I miss something?"

"Nope, nothing at all," she said, swiftly returning to the subject of school. "Your chem class is on Monday afternoons, right?"

"Yeah. Same time as your bio class."

"And if you don't pass?"

"Then . . . I'm officially in violation of my student visa rules. If I'm not a full-time student, I could lose the visa. I need to be in at least four classes a semester."

This was a brick to my chest. What would happen if I violated the visa rules? Would the university report me to immigration? Would I randomly receive a knock on the front door while I was breastfeeding Sahaara? Could they send me back to Punjab and keep Sahaara here?

To violate the rules was to enter a black hole. I had no clue what I'd encounter.

"I could find a babysitter."

"But money's pretty low, right?"

Another brick. "It is," I mumbled. "Wish I could take a semester off. Just one."

"I know we can get through this," Joti said, "but we'll need to be realistic. It's gonna be an uphill battle from here."

"Graveyard shifts."

"Huh?"

"By the summer, maybe—hopefully—Sahaara will sleep through the night. And then I can find overnight work. And then maybe I can save up enough for another year of school?" I knew how ridiculous I sounded. International student fees were horrific, and we weren't allowed to work more than twenty hours a week.

"Joti." Aunty Jee emerged from her bedroom. "Your sister wants to talk to you."

"Mom . . . I'm not. You already know this."

"Joti. *Please*." She couldn't say no to the desperate plea in her mom's voice and got up to grab the phone.

"Hi—yup—I'm good—yup—that's good—okay—see ya." She passed the phone back to Aunty Jee as quick as she'd picked it up and returned to her sea of notes. Aunty Jee shook her head and said her goodbyes to Deepi.

"What's going on?" I asked. "Are you and Deepi not talking?" Joti's sister, Deepi, had visited over winter break and she'd been nothing but sweet. Even though we'd never met before, she had surprised me with a set of bibs and bottles for Sahaara. I couldn't imagine why Joti would be upset with her.

"It's nothing."

Nervousness deepened the lines on Aunty Jee's forehead. "Joti, this has gone on for long enough. You're increasing my blood pressure with all this drama. We need to talk about it." She crossed her arms, pulling her purple sweater closer to her body.

"That's a little dramatic, Mom," Joti mumbled, worry betraying her soft brown eyes.

"Kiran, Joti is upset with Deepi because—"

"—because she was being an asshole about you staying with us."

The silence was awkwardly punctuated by kirtan pouring out of Aunty Jee's radio. My throat went dry. "Oh," I eventually mumbled.

Aunty Jee slowly sat down on the sofa, eyes pleading and apologetic. "Deepi and I had a long talk about all this silly business. I think she understands now."

"Sure she does," Joti said under her breath.

"Joti, gall sunh meri! Oh nu samaj aa gayee hun," Aunty Jee insisted. "You two need to talk this out. You both owe each other apologies."

"*I* owe her an apology? After what *she* said?" Joti fumed, a cue card crumpling in her fist. "Mom, she owes Kiran an apology, if anything."

"What did Deepi say?" I slowly asked, terrified of the answer.

Joti glanced from me to her mom. "She was worried about what taking you in would mean for us—"

"Joti." I sighed.

"—because of your family situation and your student visa and it was fucked up for her to even—"

"Joti . . ."

"—say any of that because it wasn't her call to make in the first place. It was Mom's."

"Joti, I don't—I don't blame her," I stammered. "She's right. You guys shouldn't have to deal with me. It's not your responsibility and I don't want to be a burden. I'll figure out—"

"Kiran, chup kar," Aunty Jee said. "I want you to listen to me very clearly, puth. Tu sunhdi aa mainu?"

"Hanji," I whispered.

"Yes, Deepi was nervous at the beginning. She didn't know how your family would react. She wanted me to think about everything before I made a decision." She sat down on the carpet with me, easing herself onto her knees despite her achy hip, resting a gentle hand on my shoulder. "Kiran, I've always trusted my intuition. It's never failed me. This life has taught me that sometimes, the most beautiful humans find themselves in painful situations. That doesn't mean they're not worth fighting for. Do you understand?"

I placed Sahaara down on an ivory wool blanket as an all too familiar feeling of guilt overtook me.

A hand I knew better than most others reached toward mine. "We've got your back, okay?" said Joti.

and so i stayed there

as the years spread and stretched and flew

unconvinced that i wasn't a burden

but knowing there were hours in the day
when joti and aunty jee were at work
and sahaara was fast asleep

when the monsters tucked away
at the back of my mind
would find me, all alone
how they wanted me

i knew that i needed
to lean on these two women
born from the selfless earth of my motherland
with hearts larger than i deserved
so that the darkness wouldn't
swallow me.

kiran

january 2005–september 2005

a very long day

The years passed by both far too quickly and in slow motion. Beneath a flurry of bills and toddler tantrums and overtime shifts, single motherhood had filled me with a cloudy, seemingly perpetual fatigue.

I wiped a fresh snowflake from a picture of me and Sahaara. She was climbing up my lap, her dimples the size of dimes, her smile the size of my heart. I'd pick her up from daycare after this meeting but every separation pinched at my chest, no matter how long or short. From her bubbling vocabulary to the way she'd remove her grandmother's reading glasses and kiss her on the forehead, I found myself in humble awe of this small, wise-hearted being.

I tucked the Polaroid into my wallet and searched for the sticky note Joti had scribbled on:

#320 1649 Simon Rd. Gateway Plaza. Foster Immigration Consultancy.

Goose bumps rose beneath my warm winter coat. Maybe one of our problems was about to be solved.

Today, Sahaara's babysitter had given me her final warning: if I was late with another payment, we'd have to find a new daycare. I couldn't plead my way out of this one. All I could do was hope that Mrs. Ikuko would pay me on time. Ever since my work visa expired, she made it seem like this was too much to ask for. Without this week's pay, I wouldn't be able to cover rent, either. That would leave me three months behind and Aunty Jee was patient, but she was also struggling.

I needed to fix my immigration papers. It was the only way I could work without fearing deadly consequences.

I crossed a street that was more pothole than cement and Gateway Plaza loomed before me in all its beige, frost-crusted glory. From kapra stores to desi banquet halls to Punjabi sweet shops, the plaza carried me home to Chandigarh in bittersweet waves of nostalgia.

I'd grab mithiyaee later, but right now, I was on a mission. As I made my way up to suite #320, both hope and nervousness blanketed me. If things went well today, everything would be different. Joti had found Foster Immigration online, one of the only immigration firms that offered free, extensive consultations. This meant I would finally get some proper advice about staying in Canada.

The office door opened with a creak and I was greeted by an empty front desk. I peeked past the counter to find a long, narrow hallway. The door at the end was slightly ajar.

A fluorescent bulb buzzed and flickered above. "Excuse me?" I called. I waited for a few minutes, unsure whether to stay or leave.

"Hi, hello!" a sunburned, middle-aged white man finally emerged from behind the door. "So sorry to keep you waiting. Secretary went home sick today. Bit of a pain." He reached out a clammy hand and I shook it. "And you must be . . ."

"Kiran Kaur." I barely smiled, adjusting the heavy tote bag on my shoulder. "My friend Joti booked an appointment to discuss my student visa?"

"Ah, yes. Right. Right. Well, come take a seat in my office. Lovely name, by the way. Kiran. Is that Indian?" He glanced back as he guided me down the musty hallway.

"Um, Punjabi."

"Ah, Punjabi. Lots of Punjabi clients that I work with. You don't sound Punjabi, though."

"Sorry?"

"Your accent. I hear the Punjabi, but it comes off a little British. How'd you learn English so well?" His strange comment caught me off guard and I stifled the urge to retort with something just as rude.

"I went to an English-language school in Chandigarh."

"No kidding, eh? No Indian clothes, either, I see? Not a bad thing. It's important to look the part when you're trying to become a Canadian, if you know what I mean." I silently took a seat in a worn leather chair. He sat down behind the desk, clasping his hands together. "So, how can I help you?"

Anxiety tightened around my parched throat. This was my first time talking to a stranger about my student visa. I'd been painfully apprehensive about divulging any bit of my story to a man I didn't know, but Joti seemed so certain that he could help. I reminded myself of Sahaara's innocent eyes, her sweet smile. I had to give this a try for her. "To make a long story short . . . I'm living in Canada on a student visa. I was going to university here, but I didn't finish my program because I had a daughter while I was still in school. Costs kept piling up and I needed to take on more shifts at work, so I couldn't finish school—"

"Odd timing to have a kid, isn't it? Middle of school and all. But go on."

I raised an eyebrow and continued. "No one from the university's really followed up with me about my missed semesters and I've started building a life here and I'm wondering if there's a way for me to stay—"

"Oh, there are definitely ways. That's the good news. The bad news is some routes may take longer than others. . . ."

Exactly what I'd been afraid of. I held my breath, waiting for him to continue.

"So, you got yourself in a bit of trouble. Not the end of the world. Your child—is her father a Canadian citizen?"

"No." The hairs on the back of my neck rose at his mention. "He's not in the picture."

"Got it. Got it. And you didn't finish school. That's not good. Raises flags for the government. Do you still have the student visa?"

I nodded. "Until August."

"You mentioned work. Do you have a work permit?"

I hesitated before I spoke. "I did. I mean, it expired a while ago . . . it's been two years, I think."

"And have you been working since?"

"No," I lied without missing a beat. My instincts told me that it would be unwise to admit I'd been working, even if he was here to help.

"Uh-huh." He leaned back in his chair, toying with a yellow stress ball and surveying me intently. His face was slightly tinged red, except for two pale circles around his eyes. He looked as though he'd vacationed somewhere tropical and never removed his sunglasses. "Your daughter was born here. That automatically makes her a Canadian citizen. It also means you have a path to citizenship. This is what I'd call 'the long route.' Once your daughter turns eighteen, she becomes eligible to sponsor you as a permanent resident. Of course, she'll need the right amount of funds in her bank account to show the government she can support you and all the paperwork and so on, but I'd say it's a fairly reliable route to take."

"*Eighteen* years old?"

"*At least* eighteen. Mind you, these things always drag on longer than folks like yourself might initially anticipate."

"That's . . ." A million different scenarios crossed my

mind. Most of them involved something going terribly wrong between now and Sahaara's eighteenth birthday.

". . . not exactly ideal, is it?" he finished my sentence.

"I can't leave until she's eighteen and then come back. I—I *really* need to stay here with my daughter. You don't understand. I can't leave Canada." My shoulders prickled with heat at the thought of returning to Chandigarh.

He cocked his head and nodded. "How old is your daughter?"

"Almost three."

"Staying here is your immediate goal, then. Not just in fifteen years when the paperwork decides to catch up. I can definitely streamline that process for you." He eased himself up from his chair and bounced the smiling yellow stress ball between his hands as he paced the room.

"That would be amazing," I said, relief flooding my voice. "Things are way more complicated than I ever imagined and I want this sorted out once and for all."

He leaned against the front of his desk, just to the right of me. Looking directly forward from my seat, all I could see were his brown pant pockets. His belt. "I can get your paperwork going, but you should be aware that the fees are going to get pricey."

The flood of relief met a wall. Of course it was too good to be true. "What would I be looking at? My friend had mentioned that you have low fees. . . ."

"Well, for a case like this, you could be getting into the thousands. But you seem like a lovely girl. *Really* lovely. So, I'm going to try to lower all those overhead fees for you. I'll do my best." He paused. "But since I'm doing you a favor, I'm going to, you know, need a favor in return."

"I'm—I'm sorry?" I stammered, my pulse suddenly and strangely picking up.

He placed a hand on my knee, winter-cold even through my jeans. He slowly slid it up my leg. "It would be absolutely terrible if, *perhaps*, someone reported your legal status. I can make all that worry go away, beautiful."

For a moment, my body was frozen in place.

"What do you say, Miss Kaur?" He slid his hand farther up my leg, grazing my inner thigh. A shot of adrenaline punched me hard in the chest. The rage and fear kicked in simultaneously. Something between a scream and a cry escaped my mouth and I stood, the heavy leather chair falling to the floor behind me.

"Hey, easy—easy, sweetheart—"

"You—you fucking—" I breathed, backing away and reaching behind me for the door handle. As soon as I found it, I bolted from the office, down the hallway, past the front counter, heart thumping and body moving with all the speed my trembling legs would allow.

I tore open the plaza doors with a force that could've cracked the glass. I ran across the parking lot, across the street, along the sidewalk. I kept running until I reached the bus stop. My heart rattled against my bones and something rose up in my throat. Without thinking, I vomited onto the snow, the ice splattered in my fear. A woman standing at the bus stop pulled her daughter closer and pretended not to see me.

Why did I go there? Why did I sit there for so long? Why didn't I run when he got so close? Why can't I breathe?!

My breath became shallow, air filling and half emptying my lungs in quick increments. The world around me twisted, trembled. I couldn't feel my body. The only thing loud and clear was the ringing in my ears.

Sit down, I told myself. I fumbled with my cell phone and tried to dial Joti's number. My fingertips would've been numb even without the snarling wind. After a few rings, the call went to voice mail. I tried again and again to reach the only person who could help me.

"Hello? Kiran?"

I couldn't get any words past my shallow breathing.

"Kiran, are you there? Is everything okay?"

"Hey," I managed.

"What's going on?"

"Um—" I begged my breath to steady. I needed to tell her what had happened.

"Hello? Is everything okay?"

"Joti, I—I went to the immigration consultation."

"How'd it go? What'd he say?"

"He, um, he . . ." Standing there in the frost, I could feel the truth transfiguring on my tongue, writhing away from my will to speak it aloud. It became a volatile creature stretching duct tape over my lips. "He said . . . after Sahaara turns eighteen, she can sponsor me to live in Canada."

"Shit. Shit! That's gonna take a while but it's better than nothing. Let's get him to start the paperwork. . . ." The rest of her words were lost beneath the ringing in my ears. Why couldn't I tell her? Why was it so much harder to speak the truth than to bury it away?

how i survived

i sealed up the nightmares
barred my mind from my tongue
slid away from the truth
grew fangs across my skin
shielded myself with fear
trusted no one but myself
held the world at arm's length
vowed to protect my daughter
by any means necessary.

august 4, 2005

i crossed an invisible line in that moment
when the clock struck midnight
and it became august fourth
and my visa expired.

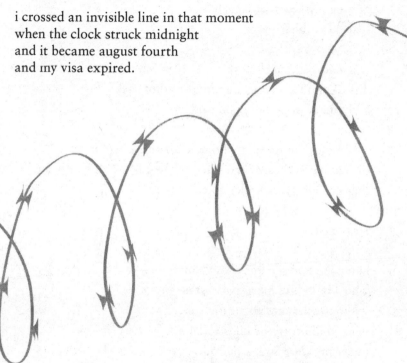

everything that happened now
would be on the other side of safety.

the tragedy of september

ikuko's grocery was closing for good
and i cleared out the last aisle
gutting my heart with each
sealed cardboard box

when day turned to dusk
mrs. ikuko handed me my final wad of cash
and said nothing but *good luck*.

that night, the woman who had become my mother
looked me in the eye and said two words
that had always sounded like a threat:

trust me.

aunty jee said she knew someone
who would hire me at her restaurant
without worrying about my papers
who would turn the question mark
under my chest into a period.
who would bring a definitive end
to one of our worries.

we'll have to tell gurinder the truth
about your immigration status
she's annoying
a bit of a know-it-all, really
but she can be trusted with this
~~aunty jee said~~
aunty jee promised

with no other options
i gave in

the unpaid bills weighed heavier
than my caution.

sahaara
august 2012–june 2019

being a kid sucked.

the grown-ups always thought
i was too little to notice
when they weren't
being honest.

grade five

august was ending and i was so very sad
grade five was coming and i hoped it wouldn't be bad

the summer was filled with swimming pool waves
rihanna and bieber were my musical faves

a new kid moved in right behind our house
the only thing that rhymed with house was mouse

his name was jeevan randhawa and he was okay
he had a lotta comic books but i had to say

i missed my friend manisha
why'd she have to move away?

this diary was for me, myself, and i
maasi could look, but no one else had better try.

grade six

i was woven by mom
who quietly said *i love you*
by asking if i'd eaten

my heart was dyed by joti maasi
who loved with pride and without a care
the only adult who knew all my secrets

i was decorated in grandma's stories
and every poem she had memorized
from bulleh shah to kartar singh sarabha
all passed down from revolutionary ancestors

but there were also tears in my cloth
gaping and frayed and worn

i'd never seen a picture
of the people who birthed my mother
even though she sometimes said i had
this woman's eyes and that man's puffy nose

my father was an empty space
a man named prabh
whose last name i didn't know

a man who doesn't matter
mom said
because family are the ones
who are there when you need them

grade seven

you and maasi usually went quiet
when i stepped into the room
but this time you asked me to sit down and listen

undocumented.

that's why you
carried sadness on your shoulders like a cinder block
couldn't find a job where you wouldn't be treated like trash
saved every penny you earned for our future
never went to the doctor, even when you ached and shivered
always said you were too busy to get your driver's license
worried so much about me switching schools
couldn't cross the border with maasi
lived in canada without your blood relatives

i'm sorry. you were too young. i didn't want you to worry.

that's what you said
when i asked why you never told me

i didn't know what to say
i didn't know how to help
i didn't know what to feel

but butterflies fluttered in my stomach for days
and i just wanted them to escape.

then came my anger

i told myself that a good daughter
wouldn't blame her mother
for a situation as overwhelming as this

but instead, frustration lapped and lashed
at everything i wanted to know
about why she was undocumented

the questions were red around the edges
before i could cool down:

why did you have to overstay your visa?

*why didn't you just go back to punjab
and live away from your family?*

*why'd you have to make things
harder for yourself?*

mom answered none of them
and barely grimaced
before she turned away
as if she couldn't face me

i didn't ask the last ones
because i knew they were more
heartbreak and hurt
than sincere curiosity

why drag me into this mess?
why even have me?

my heart crashed into the rocks

every time i asked her a question
that she didn't want to answer.

what did my dad do?
what was he like?
why didn't he want me?
why didn't he want us?

mom said
he was a bad person
and it doesn't matter
and aren't i enough?

i nodded and said nothing else
because she was sad and silent.
but the questions were eating away at me

she yelled at me
for not finishing my homework
and i just wanted to know
if he would have held me, instead.

google search

sobbing in my room after our fight
mom walked in and sat on the edge of my bed
quiet the way she usually was when distant

prabh ahluwalia
she said
that's his name

just like she did when she was angry
or wistful or simply lost in her head
she refused to look at my face
before she left the room

and i wasn't sure whether
to smile or well up in tears
as i bolted to a laptop too slow and old
to understand the urgency in my fingertips

i googled his name
and combed through hundreds of facebook profiles
until sleep tugged at my eyelids and i gave up:

all those search results
and none looked like me.

a confession

sometimes
i stared into the mirror
after everyone went to bed
studying my features
as if they were pieces
of a jigsaw puzzle
that had to be solved
with only half the box

my eyes belonged to mom.
and maybe her mom as well.

and, apparently, my nose
belonged to a man
that mom called her father.

but the golden-brown earth of my skin
and my stiletto-edge jaw

looked so very distant from
the woman who birthed me

in the stillest hours of the night
i found myself trembling
reaching for my chin
outlining it with my fingers
tracing my skin with both hands
searching for all the missing
parts of my story.

another confession

sometimes
i felt guilty for thinking
i needed more than her.

jeevan

he and i sighed at the exact same time

heavy hearts   worry in our chests
lives that felt like   a freakin' mess

despite all the holes
                              in both of our bodies
we were two pieces   of different puzzles
that happened to   fit together perfectly

a constant.   a solid.   a steadying force
in a never-resting sea   of unsureness

thank god   for friends that were family
thank whatever ran this universe
                                        for him.

welcome to eighth grade

"Jeevan! Can we just get this over with?" I said without a touch of the uncertainty thumping beneath my chest. "You're acting like I asked you to shoot me."

"Okay. Doing this." He blinked and swallowed. "This is something that is, uh, going to happen . . . now." He closed his eyes as he leaned into me and I followed his lead, holding my breath as if going underwater. His wiry braces scraped my upper lip and the cold surface of his glasses somehow landed on my forehead. He fumbled around in search of my mouth and when his dry lips finally pressed up against mine, we stayed there for a moment, no other parts of our bodies in contact. Then, like a tightly wound coil, Jeevan suddenly retracted.

Eye contact was now unbearable. "Okay. Bad idea." I grimaced.

"Yeah, no shit, Sahaara. But congratulations. We've both officially kissed someone."

"That wasn't even a kiss. You just put your mouth on my mouth."

"Yeah. That sounds like the *literal definition* of a kiss." He shook his head. "I can't believe I agreed to this. If anyone hears that we—I swear, I'll—"

"You'll what?" I smirked. "*Actually* shoot me?"

He rolled his eyes slowly and deliberately, like he was dealing with someone beyond his help. "Any other rites of passage you wanna get through today, or can we go home now?"

We shook mulch and dead leaves off our backpacks as we gathered them from the forest floor. I'd doodled dahlias and roses all over mine with a gold fabric pen. His was covered in a constellation of comic book pins and video game patches.

Throwing his backpack over his shoulder, Jeevan peered through the pine trees once again to make sure that no one at PA Jameson High School could see us. At the end of seventh grade, we realized that the fastest way home was through the hilly forest behind the soccer field. I'd only ever take the shortcut if Jeevan was walking home with me, though. The dense gathering of evergreen trees could've made for a perfect murder setting.

"Anyways, if you're serious about telling Roop you like her, you're gonna need to work on whatever that was. Because that was a mess."

"Sahaara, do me a favor?"

"What?"

"Shut up."

I wordlessly grinned. It took serious degrees of friendship to ask someone to kiss you just for the sake of getting a first kiss over with. Three and a half years had cemented us into something almost unheard of: best friends who hadn't fallen apart by freshman year.

I thought back to the day we first met, when Jeevan's family moved into the cramped basement suite of the house behind ours. My new neighbor was a comic-obsessed *boy* who was somehow snarkier than me. Who was happier lost in a book than exploring his surroundings. Not exactly ten-year-old Sahaara's cup of tea.

But times had clearly changed. Over fifth grade and the years that followed, Jeevan—and his comic books—grew on me like an itch. Beneath a sarcasm that could rival mine was a kid who was patient enough to help me master *Mario*

Kart and *Assassin's Creed* despite my butter fingers. A boy who would recount his household drama to remind me that I wasn't the only weirdo with a ridiculous family. A friend who was willing to listen to me vent or complain or simply cry until the darkest hours of a school night.

Despite Jeevan's cringeworthy kiss, he was a good guy—the best guy I knew, in fact—and I was hell-bent on helping him find love. "So, I was talking to Roop in math. Turns out she reads a lot of sci-fi. Like, dystopian stuff."

"Uh-huh?" Shards of light poured through the thick canopy of branches and across the rough terrain of Jeevan's walnut-brown cheek as he walked.

"You and Roop have so much shit in common. For example . . ." I reached deep into my denim jacket pocket in search of my iPod. "A shared taste in books. I wrote down all the graphic novels she likes. *Batgirl*'s number one on her list, Jeevan. *Batgirl!*"

"That's cool," he mumbled. His favorite comic book character, Natasha Irons, flew across the length of his fading black T-shirt. Back in elementary school, kids would've loved it. At our new high school, however, we couldn't breathe the wrong way without getting shit from randoms in the hallway. All the more reason why a girl who read his favorite books warranted much more than an uninterested "that's cool."

"Are you even listening?"

"Are *you*? I told you . . . I'm not that into her," he grumbled, scratching the wide curve of his nose. "You're the one hyping this up. She barely talks to me in person and she never even added me on Snapchat."

"She follows you on IG, though, right?"

"Yeah."

"Does she comment on your pictures or just like them?"

He scoffed, shoving his lanky arms into his pockets. "You need to get over this, bud. 'Cause I already am."

Sunlight hit me square in the face as we emerged from the forest to make the quick journey to our respective houses. Jeevan's house, which shared its backyard with mine, was off-limits ever since I told Mom about the way his parents fought.

"Wanna come over today?" I asked.

"Dad's working late. Gonna just go home and enjoy the quiet."

"Suit yourself." I shrugged. We turned our backs to each other and made our separate ways down the sidewalk.

When I got inside, I immediately scoured the pantry for Oreos. The iced side of a cookie had just grazed my tongue when muffled voices reached me. They weren't yelling but one of them sounded distressed.

My mom was crying.

I dropped the Oreos on the counter and tiptoed down the hallway, hoping the wooden floorboards wouldn't creak beneath my feet. Before I knocked, I placed an ear to Mom's bedroom door, trying not to breathe as I listened.

Mom spoke beneath sobs. "And Chachi said, 'Your mom told me to tell *you* to come but not to bring Sahaara.' Because it wouldn't look good or some utter crap like that. She didn't even have the decency to tell me herself." It was hard to decipher Mom's words between her tears, but the mention of her mom—my biological grandmother—made my stomach jump. Mom never talked about them. Or to them.

"I'm so sorry, Kiran. I'm so sorry," Joti Maasi murmured.

"And what am I supposed to do, Joti?" Mom sobbed. "It's

not like I can even go there. How would I get back in the country?"

As soon as I knocked, the room went silent. "It's—it's me," I stammered. "Can I come in?"

After a stretch of hushed whispers, Maasi pulled open the door.

The sudden sight of Mom wiping away tears was a tsunami against my body.

I'd never seen her cry before.

"What's going on?" I asked, panic rising to my throat.

"Why don't you sit down, Sahaara?" Maasi gestured to the bed and I sat, the squeak of the mattress the only noise in the room. "So, your mom got a phone call from her chachi—"

"The one who lives in Surrey?"

"Yeah." Maasi sadly nodded, taking my hands in hers. "And she had bad news. Your mom's dad—your nana—he was in a car accident near Delhi. He . . . didn't make it."

"Oh," I whispered. I had no idea what to feel for a person I'd never met before. Whose name Mom rarely even mentioned. But the anguish dripping down Mom's face was enough to make me tear up. Mom kept wiping her cheeks, but she couldn't curb the downpour.

"Are you okay?" I sniffled because I didn't know what else to say. Immediately, I regretted it. Of course she wasn't.

The water glazing her skin renewed its force, answering my question.

"What did they say about me?" I asked.

Mom looked from me to Maasi and they spoke to each other with their eyes. "What do you mean?" Maasi eventually said.

"I heard you guys through the door. They said something

about not bringing me."

"Sahaara, let's talk about this later, okay?" Maasi delicately replied. There was fine china in her voice.

"But—"

"*Later*, Sahaara." She enunciated each syllable, almost glaring.

I nodded, not arguing further, and wrapped my arms around Mom. We sat quietly like this for what could've been either a moment or a lifetime.

"I think I just need to be alone," Mom whispered into my shoulder. Her words reverberated into me and I eased myself away.

"Okay," Maasi said. "Can I call the restaurant and let them know you're not coming in?"

"No. No." Mom shook her head, sitting up a little straighter. "I can't miss work. I just need some time alone. I'll get it together." Maasi and I both knew better than to try to convince her. She was far too stubborn to listen to either of us and to be honest, her jerk of a manager would've made a big deal about her missing a shift. Maasi gingerly closed the door behind us as we stepped into the hallway.

She pulled out her iPhone and quickly sent a text. "Why don't we go for a drive?" she said with a feather-light smile. I followed her outside, my head a fuzzy blur of questions.

When I slunk into the passenger-side seat of her truck, Maasi asked whether I wanted to go to Dairy Queen or Menchie's to get my mind off things. The tears instantly welled up again. "Can you just tell me what's going on? I'm so sick of how you guys keep me in the dark about shit. Like I'm some little kid who can't handle the truth."

The blonde tips of her hair barely grazed her shoulders as

she shook her head, mouth opening and closing as if she was wrestling her thoughts. "Okay," she finally sighed, drawing her car keys from the ignition. "You're right, Sahaara. You're not a little kid anymore. And it's not that we think you are. Your mom just feels that . . . this stuff shouldn't stress you out."

"Well, guess what?" I fumed. "I'm stressed out."

"So, you know why your mom stopped talking to her parents, yeah?"

"Because of me."

"It wasn't—it wasn't because of *you*. They had expectations of your mom, like, expectations about who she'd marry and how her life would go. And when she stopped listening to them, they . . ."

"Turned their back on her."

"Yeah." The cold knowledge sat with us for a heartbeat. "Kiran's chachi phoned. The one who she lived with when she first came to Canada. She told her about the accident and it's—it's never easy hearing news like this. But it was extra shitty that her mom wasn't the one who called."

Anger burned in my veins. What kinda asshole was *so* stuck-up that they couldn't make a serious phone call to their own child? "What about the thing they said a-about me?"

"Oh . . ." She paused, resting her hands on the steering wheel. "Sahaara, you need to understand that there are some people in this world who care about their image more than anything. More than their relationships. More than family. I think that your nani's one of those people—"

"She's not my nani. Don't call her that."

Maasi nodded slightly.

"I don't get it, though." I shook my head. "Why'd I even come up?"

"She was talking about the funeral. They wanted your mom to come . . . without you. Probably 'cause your mom's family doesn't want people to ask questions about . . ." The sentence she didn't need to finish trailed away. "I'm so sorry, Sahaara. You weren't supposed to hear all that."

Without you.

These two words were needles to my insides. Sharp. Burning. Broken. "Yeah, fuck them." Jaw clenched, I reached for the door.

"Where you going?"

"Jeevan's house," I said, wiping stale tears from my chin.

"But your mom doesn't want you—"

"*I don't care.* We'll go to a park or some shit. I just wanna talk to Jeevan right now."

"Okay." She paused as though words were teetering on her lips. Instead, she slowly nodded. "Okay. Go."

I shut Maasi's truck door with an accidental thud and looked back to mouth the word *sorry*. This wasn't her fault.

When I reached Jeevan's house, I clicked open the backyard gate and flew down the cement stairs to his basement suite. Three knocks and the door swung open.

"Hey, friend—whoa. You okay?" Jeevan's tone changed the instant he noticed my eyes. He hastily shut the door behind him. "What's going on?"

I tearfully shook my head, unable to speak.

"Is it your mom? School? Family stuff?"

"Mom. Family," I managed. "Can we go to the park?"

"Yeah, let's go. One sec, lemme get my jacket." He

disappeared inside his house and quickly returned, pushing the door open with one hand and putting on his black Nikes with the other. From somewhere inside the house, Jeevan's mom asked him where he was going and who he was going with.

"Jameson Park with Sahaara! I'll be back soon!" he hollered, locking the door behind him. "Okay, let's go."

I didn't speak until we sat down on the far bench near the pine trees where we had kissed just an hour ago. A lifetime ago. "My mom's dad died."

"Oh. Shit. I'm so sorry, dude." He shifted his body toward mine.

"I never met him. He was just this . . . big, blank space that I always wondered about. You know how my mom is. She acts like her other family—her biological family—doesn't exist. But I feel so messed up." My cheeks were wet, but I didn't bother wiping them. We'd both seen each other cry enough times for the embarrassment to have run dry. "I've never seen my mom cry before. She's always the one holding it together and it almost felt . . ."

"Scary?" he offered.

"Yeah." I gulped, eyes on the unkempt grass beneath my black flats. "Exactly."

"I think it's 'cause parents are supposed to be the strong ones. Seeing them cry is all upside down and shit."

A piney wind blew toward us. I thought back to the time when Mom told me about her papers. Times when I would ask about her family. Those days when her manager would phone while she was at home, just to yell at her for shit she didn't do right at work.

Her hurt never broke through.

"Her dad was in a car accident and her *chachi* told her about it. Her own mom didn't even call."

"You're joking . . ." He frowned. "People really have no sharam."

"Right? And they *specifically* asked her to come to the funeral without me. Like I'm some sort of bastard embarrassment to their family."

A grin tugged at the corners of Jeevan's mouth and he did everything in his power to resist it.

"Whaaat?!" I raised my brows.

His smile cracked. "Bastard embarrassment?"

"It's not funny!" I laughed through tears.

"Nah, for real, though," he said. "Who cares what these people think? They're irrelevant."

"Just feel so bad for my mom," I mumbled.

"I feel you. It was rough when my nana jee died. Even though I only saw them in Punjab a few times. It was especially hard on Mom 'cause she felt guilty for being all the way in Canada. She regretted not going back home more often."

I wondered what Mom carried in her heart. Was she haunted by guilt for not being in Punjab? Did she want to travel to Chandigarh and leave me behind? In the past few years, she had begun to open up in tiny increments, but she was still, in so many ways, a mystery.

And what did that make me?

Two elderly women wearing flowery salwar kameezes strolled past Jeevan and me. They gave us the "aunty look," probably suspicious of a boy and girl sitting alone together. I tilted my chin away from them and stared into the dancing evergreen branches. When the coast was clear, Jeevan nudged me.

"Sahaara?" he murmured.

"What?"

"It's gonna be okay." He had no idea whether it actually would be, but I didn't mention that aloud. Instead, I rooted myself into his soft chest and buried my face in his shoulder. He planted a lanky arm around my back.

"Sorry . . . I'm getting snot all over you," I mumbled.

Instead of hitting me with the kind of sarcastic jab that defined our friendship, he said, "It's cool. Let it out, bud." A petal-soft quiet grew between us. "And I dunno what a 'bastard embarrassment' is, but I promise that's not what you are. I . . . feel sorry for your mom's family. Imagine never knowing the dopest living person to come from your genes." His body shook with soft laughter and I trembled with him. "You mean the universe—the *cosmos*—to the ones who care about you. Isn't that what matters?"

the anxiety came
heaviest at night

heart thumping out of my chest
stomach twisting in every direction
eyes wet and swollen
pillow damp with all my fears

maybe this is why mom didn't want
me to know about the burdens
on her shoulders.

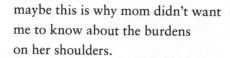

sahaara, can we talk?

just as i was about to escape
mrs. alvarez blocked my way out
of her classroom with a worn
copy of *romeo and juliet*

i nodded because what else
was i supposed to do
when a teacher wanted to talk?

the room was entirely empty
save for me and her

before i could rehearse a good
answer to the inevitable question
of why i wasn't paying attention
in class, mrs. alvarez said

> *you've been distracted*
> *lately, huh?*
> *anything you wanna discuss?*

a chorus of
don't cry, don't cry, don't cry
pounded in my head.

(what was more embarrassing
than getting emotional in front
of a teacher?)

a river threatened to flow
and i stared at my sneakers
until my eyes were satisfactorily dry.

just dealing with stuff at home.
i don't really wanna talk about it.

> all it took was an
> *oh, sahaara. i'm really*
> *sorry to hear that. is it*
> *something that's making*
> *it hard to focus in class?*

for my voice to crack

it's really hard for me to pay attention
when my head is all over the place
i managed between sniffles and
tears wiped on kleenex

> mrs. alvarez asked
> *what grounds you?*
> *what pulls you back down*
> *to earth when your worries*
> *carry you away?*

i shrugged
and then said
art, i guess.
i'm nervous most of the day
but when i'm drawing,

nothing's on my mind
but my sketchbook.

her matte black lips became a
crescent moon and she nodded
in an almost-knowing way.

so art is what grounds you.
this is your only homework
for today:

research anxiety and grounding.

grade nine

each wispy stroke of cerulean paint
danced over the sky blue & navy

a new brush
thin & precise
dipped in eggshell white
traced slowly & carefully
over the ridges of my waves
foam & bubbles came to life

& in this moment
i was floating on a warm ocean
my fears, somewhere on
a distant shoreline.

the wounded deer

sitting at the back of mr. kim's art class
i pored over frida kahlo's painting
reflecting on the question written on the whiteboard

what does this painting say to you?

i studied frida's almost-serene face
placed atop the body of a deer
stabbed through with exactly nine
blood-drenched arrows

deer-frida rested in the forest by the sea
somehow elegant in her suffering

and i wondered how long
we must distract
and paint
and survive

until our sorrow would finally and forever
wash away.

grade ten

so jeevan made it onto the basketball team and
i was sitting in the stands watching them practice.

and rhea climbed up the bleachers just to ask
me about shit that i didn't want to answer.

why were you crying in the bathroom stall?

wasn't a conversation starter but i answered,
just 'cause i felt   confrontational that day:

*because i'm in pieces over shit that will never
bother you. because i should've found a job
already so that i can pull my weight at home.
because at any given moment my whole life
could fall apart.*

    damn, she said. *that sucks*

learner's permit

guilt crushed my shoulders when i asked and she said yes.
she was stronger than the shell of any car and i didn't want to
imagine all the collisions her body & mind & heart
had faced.

mom and i locked eyes. my heart skidded against my ribs.

are you sure about this, mom?

> *you've been practicing
> for this test for weeks.
> you're leaving here with
> your learner's permit,
> okay?*

the woman at the counter snapped at us like a neck
i need two pieces of id from you

my medical care card and student id
landed on the counter

and are you her parent or legal guardian?

> *her parent. here's my
> birth certificate and care
> card. and my daughter's
> birth certificate.*

she inspected our documents
and we braced ourselves for impact
your medical card is out of date.
i'll update that for you.

> oh, i'll—i'll do that
> *another day,*
> mom stammered.

you can't access medical services until it's updated.

> *right, yeah, i'm just running*
> *late today. i'll come back*
> *tomorrow for that.*

her glare traveled from mom to me to the long line
of people waiting impatiently behind us.
take your learner's test at the booth to your left.

grade eleven

mrs. suderman asked the question as if
it was not a bullet aimed directly at my chest

why might immigration be a bad thing?

lorraine bishop's hand shot up with no safety

too much immigration means less jobs for canadians.
and we don't know what values immigrants are .
bringing into canada. more immigration
could lead to more terrorism.

and i wanted to say so many things but anger clenched
my jaw and anxiety held my tongue. and no one else
interjected so she went on

i don't think it's right that real canadians have less
opportunities than immigrants.

and all i could see was the moment when
her immigrant ancestors first placed their feet
on ~~north america~~ turtle island
and claimed it as theirs and theirs
alone

and all i could hear was the word
undocumented
leaving mom's lips like a curse
she desperately wished
to be freed from.

sahaara

august 2019–january 2020

an introduction

"It's kinda trippy, huh?" I said as we made our way up the grand staircase, a romantic Bollywood tune echoing around us. "How the *hell* are we graduating in nine months?"

"Tell me why I feel like it's gonna be a long-ass year. . . ." Jeevan sighed as he adjusted his black tie.

"What do you mea—OHHH SHIIIIIIT—" My long phulkari chunni caught itself between my heel and the final step of the staircase and I plummeted, face-first, toward the blue carpet. My palms hit the ground just before an arm swooped around my waist and shoulders.

For a moment, I lay there in a daze, my heels hooked around the final step of the staircase and Jeevan's arms around my torso, as if I was doing an absurd push-up with his support.

"Ouch. Ouch-ouch-ouch! Oh, shit! My ankle," I hissed, ignoring the kids in the lobby who'd frozen midway through a game of tag to gape at my pitiful existence.

"Crap. Hold on, I got you." Jeevan helped me sit upright on the stairs and quickly moved down a few steps to examine my ankle.

"This *would* happen to me," I groaned.

"Your ankle isn't swollen or anything . . . try to move it?" His saucer eyes were brimming with concern. They were visible, for once, without the barrier of his thick glasses. He'd worn contacts to his future sister-in-law's reception on Roop's insistence. It was their first time together at a family function and, according to his girlfriend, first impressions were everything.

I rotated my ankle and it throbbed, but it definitely wasn't broken. "I think I sprained it."

"Here." Jeevan offered me a hand and helped me up. "Let's get you to a seat. I'll go find some ice."

Jeevan eased me into a chair, and I tried to pivot my ankle again. When I shrieked like a newborn, a pair of aunties lobbed a curious look in my direction. I wouldn't be moving anywhere—let alone dancing—for a while. I'd gotten this pink phulkari suit tailored for an evening of cute selfies on the dance floor with Jeevan and Roop. Busting my ankle in a pair of far-too-tall heels was just my luck, though. I made a mental note to never wear them again.

"You sure you're good?" Jeevan called over the deafening bass of a Jasmine Sandlas song. He passed me a ziplock bag full of ice cubes that he'd gathered at the bar, a dose of motherly worry on his face.

Roop came up behind him, impatiently batting her falsies. "Sahaara, you're cool, right?" Like me, she hadn't had plans to sit around all night. She'd been gushing about her shimmery blue lehenga for weeks and wanted to show it off.

"I'm chilling. Pinky swear!" I locked pinkies with Jeevan, proving my point with the unbreakable vow we'd used since fifth grade.

"See, Jeevan? She's fine," Roop said.

Sunny, Jeevan's friend from basketball, hovered beside the two of them, one hand shoved in the pocket of his fitted gray suit jacket and the other stroking his meticulously lined up beard. His gaze absentmindedly drifted between the three of us and the dance floor.

"How 'bout I just chill here for a bit?" Jeevan asked.

"Jeevan, I'm good! Like, honestly and truly! You guys go have fun."

"You know what?" Sunny said, pulling up a seat beside me. "I'll stay with Sahaara."

"You don't have to—" I began.

"No. Chill. I don't even wanna dance," he insisted, waving away Jeevan and Roop. "You two go do your thing."

Jeevan seemed to relax. "Okay." He nodded. As Roop led Jeevan to the dance floor, she craned her neck to tell him something, her voice drowned by the ocean of noise that washed over the party. For the stillest second, Jeevan looked back at me. He threw me a reassuring smile before Roop redirected his attention elsewhere.

I took a moment to appreciate the royal-blue pants and black jacket combo I'd styled for him. The last-minute shopping trip to find him a pair of pants long enough to fit his towering frame was a migraine. It was by the divine grace of Le Château's clearance rack that he wasn't here in a pair of pants hiked up his calves.

"So," I said, turning my attention to Sunny and crossing my arms over the table, "you come to these things often?"

"Receptions?" He laughed. "Literally every other weekend. My cousins are always dragging me out to random people's hall parties. Not gonna lie, though, the food makes it worth it." He reached for a bread pakora and coated it in a perfect glaze of mango chutney. "How 'bout you?" His almond eyes twinkled through thick lashes, something sharp and intent in his gaze.

"This is my first reception."

He leaned back in sincere surprise. "You serious? How are you brown?"

"Not a lotta receptions in my family." I shrugged. "True story: I only met the bride today, but I was hyped. This is like . . . the one thing my mom would let me go out for."

"Strict parents?"

"Something like that . . ." After reassuring Mom that I'd get dropped off at home before nine thirty p.m. and promising about fifty times that I wouldn't get into a car with anyone who'd had anything to drink, she finally granted me permission to come to the reception. Her one demand: I had to take her cell phone to the party and respond every time she called or texted. She didn't inform me, in advance, that I'd get a text every thirty minutes making sure I was still alive.

When I didn't explain further, Sunny changed the subject. "So . . . speaking of brown anomalies, how the hell are Roop's parents cool with her bringing a guy to a family reception? Do they know they're dating?"

I bit into a warm samosa dipped in Heinz ketchup (chutney just didn't do it for me). "They know they're dating . . . but my theory is that he's the tall, polite future son-in-law they've always wanted, so they can get away with stuff like this. Roop was telling me her parents are really shitty about that kinda stuff. Like, appearance and caste and all that."

"Damn. Tall and polite is all it takes, huh? Guess I'm screwed."

"I think we both are," I said with the straightest face I could muster before cracking up. Sitting in a suit perfectly tailored to his lean body, Sunny was at least a head taller than me, but everyone was short next to Jeevan. "Thanks for joining me at the loser table. Glad to have some company at this very exciting pity party."

"I wasn't tryna be a community hero." He grinned, warmth simmering in his dark eyes as he surveyed me. "Just so happens that I'm not much of a dancer. I would've happily sprained my ankle on your behalf."

"Kidhaaaan?!" a voice called from behind me and I turned around to see Mani Sidhu—a guy from my eleventh-grade bio class and one of Roop's cousins—head toward us with two shots in hand. "What you doin' here, bro?"

"Roop invited me?" Like lava cooling to rock, Sunny's demeanor shifted as Mani took a seat next to him.

"Relax, I didn't know you guys were chill like that. Here, have a drink and stop acting all bitchy." He placed a shot in front of Sunny and knocked back his own. Although Mani had the same corny-ass lines running through his fade that he did at the end of eleventh grade, he looked distinctly different. Like he'd spent every moment of summer at the gym.

"I'm good." Sunny carefully returned Mani's shot. "You enjoy yourself."

Mani's vodka-reddened eyes roved between me and Sunny, calculating. "Oh, shit. I'm interrupting, aren't I?"

"Nooo!" Sunny groaned, but it was already too late.

"My bad, my bad." Mani patted him on the shoulder with a knowing look and stood just as quickly as he'd sat down. "You do your thing, bro."

Sunny looked like he could've punched him in the head as he sauntered off to the buffet.

Do not go red. Play it cool, woman. "Nice friend you've got there."

"He's—ugh—I'm sorry. Ignore him, please." Sunny, an image of unperturbable nonchalance every time I'd encountered him at school, had suddenly gone even redder than me.

I looked away to see the newly wedded bride tap the mic on the podium, her gold sari sparkling. The music melted but boisterous chatter from the tables persisted until the lights dimmed.

Beneath a whisper of light, Sunny's eyes were still warm, electric. "You're good," I murmured into his ear. "Don't stress."

just before i left the party

sunny placed a feather-light hand
on my shoulder and leaned in close
to ask for my number

add me on instagram
i said
smooth as a fresh skating rink
(although my stomach was in knots)

god, i needed a cell phone.

grade twelve

sunny skipped basketball practice to sit with me
in the back field between the portable classrooms

he picked dandelions from the sparse grass
and threw them aside
as he asked me about my day
and my favorite painters
and the thoughts that filled my daydreams
and why it was that i read so much rumi

somehow
whenever i looked away
i could still feel his eyes
peeking out from beneath the rim
of that purple raptors hat
warming the nape of my neck
flushing my cheeks red
planting wildflower seeds
beneath my chest

halloween

There were moments when no world existed beyond the edges of my canvas. Graceful hours when rhythmic brushstrokes glided color effortlessly against woven fabric. When cyan pigment danced into iridescent violet, and it would also wash over my sweaty palms, my racing heart. Sometimes, my chest went lavender as I painted, the burnt umber of my anxiety only an under-layer beneath the masterpiece of my body.

Unfortunately, this was not one of those times.

Colors were only soothing so far as the images they gathered into. Mr. Kim had asked for an "honest self-portrait." Of course, he wasn't just looking for an ultrarealistic oil painting of my face. He wanted nuance. He wanted metaphor. He wanted every goose-bump-raising and gorgeous symbol I could conjure to explain who I was.

So much fun when my identity was a question mark.

I peered from the reference pictures of me and Mom to the Frankenstein face on my canvas ready for paint. With my pointed jaw and sharp cheekbones, one half of the face was distinctly me. The other half was Mom. Our two faces fused together in a strange symphony, our differences jarring. Although our moon eyes and puffy noses were nearly identical, her round chin was my polar opposite. My end of the smile reached deep into my left dimple, unapologetic and loud. Hers was thinner. Gentle and smirkish, as it was in real life. When Mom smiled, it was always as if she was reining it in.

"All right, wonderful people!" Mr. Kim called. "Fifteen more minutes of independent project time and then we come together." He placed a stack of red crinkle paper in its corresponding cubby. The rainbow-colored shelves were filled with paper, cloth, and recycled objects that could, somehow, be worked into our art. In Mr. Kim's words, the wall was an altar for creative worship. We were to seek its gifts with gratitude and leave it pristine and tidy.

Marisol's emerald eyes peeked over from behind their canvas. "How goes it?"

"All right," I mumbled, dabbing my Forsythia Yellow paint with a touch of Eggshell to find the perfect shade of sunlight. "We'll see what happens when I add color. How 'bout your painting?"

"I'm ready to throw this canvas in a dumpster. And then set the dumpster on fire." Marisol placed their paint tray on their stool and stretched their freckled, tan arms into a graceful yoga pose. The volume of Mr. Kim's Jorja Smith album suddenly increased a notch: his reminder that it was quiet work time.

My pocket vibrated. I awkwardly attempted to pivot my body away from the teacher so he wouldn't confiscate my phone again. After months of begging in eleventh grade, Mom had begrudgingly allowed me to have Maasi's old smartphone. Sans data, but still. *What do you need data for?* Mom had said. *The phone's just for calling home.*

Sunny: What u doing tonight?
Sahaara: Not working today. Sooooo . . . homework. ☺
Sunny: Damn. Living on the edge lol
Sahaara: In class. Will msg u after.
Sunny: Wanna go to Mani's house tonight?
Sahaara: No lol

Sunny: He's having a Halloween party

Sahaara: Definitely no. Even if I wanted to, my mom would say
     no. Wanna come over n watch scary movies tho?

Sunny: To your house? 0_0 Would your mom be cool with
     that?

Sahaara: Possibly lol. Cuz Jeevan's coming over and she's
     cool with him.

Sunny: Oh. Lol. Got it.

Sahaara: So is that a yes or . . .

I watched as Sunny's typing bubble appeared, disappeared, and reappeared once more. At the sound of Mr. Kim's heels clacking in my direction, I hastily pocketed my cell.

"Sahaara, you done texting?" He raised a precisely filled-in brow.

"Oh—um—sorry—I was just—I got a message," I floundered. "Won't do it again. I promise."

"You know the policy." He extended an open palm. "Come grab it from me at the end of the day." I shut my gaping mouth and passed him the phone. With a curt nod, he turned his attention to my easel. "Talk to me about your piece. You're combining your portrait with your mom's, yes?"

"Yeah. I think I'm gonna paint a swirling night sky on my side and a sunrise gradient on Mom's to highlight how we're different, but we're also connected."

"Interesting use of contrast." He adjusted the cuff of his floral blazer as he studied my painting-in-progress. "And how does this connect back to the question of self? How does this give me an honest portrait of *you*?"

I blinked. How was I supposed to explain the weird-ass relationship I had with my face, with all the confusion it represented? "My mom raised me as a single parent and . . ." My voice lowered to a murmur only Mr. Kim could hear. "I don't know much about my father. Never seen a picture of him or anything so . . . sometimes my features make me wonder about where I came from."

Mr. Kim, a totalitarian when it came to his art studio but a softie at heart, lightly clasped his hands together. "You know, Sahaara, art can be a place of illumination, but sometimes it'll draw us through a dark tunnel first."

"What do you mean?"

"I get the sense that you have more digging to do with this painting. Don't get me wrong—your night sky and sunrise concept sounds spectacularly *aesthetic*, as you kids would say. But our inward journeys aren't always sunshine and cosmic skies, are they?"

"I suppose not . . ." I shrugged.

"Just sit with this one a little longer, kiddo. Let your ideas bloom and sprout wings and don't be afraid of where they take you. We have your mom in the portrait. And you. But what about all those unseen bits? The tricky stuff. The grim unspoken."

I knew what Mr. Kim was edging toward: the artwork needed more vulnerability. I could do it, but there was no way I'd be showing this painting to Mom.

No sooner had I walked into the house than my phone lit up with a text from Jeevan.

Jeevan: Can't make it tonight
Sahaara: WHYYYYYYY D:
Jeevan: My dad. Sorry. I'll explain later.

Sahaara: Is everything ok?

Jeevan: Yeah I'm handling it

Well, there go our plans, I thought, taking a seat at the bottom of the stairs.

Sahaara: Jeevan can't come over tonight so we can't do the movie thing ☹

Sunny: LOL shit. Tbh I wasn't tryna third wheel with u guys anyways

Sahaara: Third wheel?

The front door flew open and Joti Maasi stepped inside wearing her favorite lilac scrubs.

"Hey! I thought you were at the hospital today."

"Had to go home early and I couldn't drive all the way to my place," Maasi murmured. "I feel like shit . . . pretty sure I've got a fever." Ever since my aunt moved into her own apartment, things were quieter around the house. I missed our gossip sessions over warm cha and tense rounds of bhabhi. She was a ray of light and living without her sucked.

I touched two fingers to her forehead. Maasi's skin was a furnace radiating heat. "Yeah, you're burning up. Should I make you something?"

"Nah." She slowly undid her sneakers, each movement labored. "Sleep is the antidote."

My phone glowed once again. Another message from Sunny.

Sunny: Like . . . I just wanted to chill with u alone

As I read and reread the text, my whole body blushed. *Be chill, Sahaara.*

"Oooh, why you smiling, huh? Is it Jeevan?"

"Maasi, please," I groaned at her willful ignorance. "You know we aren't like that."

"Well, I ship it."

"*Ship it?!* Seriously?"

"What? Is that not what you kids say?" She slipped off her driving glasses and dropped them in her purse.

"It is . . . it's just not something that should ever come outta your mouth."

"Look at *you* with that attitude. As if I didn't wipe your nasty ass for two years."

"Whatever." I rolled my eyes. This was what I appreciated about our relationship: we could joke around without getting offended.

In the kitchen, Maasi plunked her purse on the counter and scoured the medicine drawer for Tylenol. As she knocked back a tablet with a swish of water, I wondered whether I should tell her about this thing sprouting within me for Sunny. She was nothing like Mom. She'd be excited that I liked someone— *happy* for me, in fact. Cheeks stitched with a grin I couldn't help, I threw caution to the wind. "On another note, there *is* a boy."

"Whaaaaat?!" she gasped. "Details, please. Come with me . . . I'm gonna lie down." I followed her down the hallway, carrying her purse to help her aching arms. The lights were out in Bibi Jee's bedroom, but sunlight still combed through thin, yellowing curtains.

"I love that smell," Maasi murmured. "It makes me miss Mom." Wispy notes of sandalwood incense hung in the air, although Bibi Jee had left for her Punjab trip two weeks prior. Something between a grunt and a loud exhale escaped Maasi's lips as she eased herself onto the spongy mattress. "Okay. I'm ready. Drop all the juicy deets, please."

I shook my head at her endearing corniness as I took a

seat at the edge of Bibi's bed. "So, his name is Sunny. He's always been around—like, floating in the vicinity because he's Jeevan's buddy from basketball—but we only got to know each other this summer. He's the furthest thing from what I expected."

"Acha? How so?"

"Like, at school, people see him as a Jack—"

"What's a Jack?"

"You've never heard of Surrey Jacks?"

She scoffed loudly. "You *do* remember I immigrated here from Jallandhar, right?"

"Okay, valid. They're this stereotype of brown guys from Surrey. People assume they fight and drink and sell drugs."

"So basically, the general stereotype that white people have of brown men?" Maasi rubbed her temples in exhaustion.

"Essentially."

"But this Sunny guy . . . is he doing that stuff? Drinking? Fighting? Selling drugs?"

"Okay, he doesn't fight or sell drugs. And I don't think he drinks much."

"But he drinks?!" Her eyes narrowed.

"Maasi. We're in twelfth grade. People do a lotta stuff." I carefully crossed my legs on the bed, toying with a loose thread in the gray wool blanket below me. "Drinking is minor compared to some of the shit that happens."

"Do you?"

"Do I drink? I mean . . . not really." I stared deliberately at the fraying thread, twirling it between my fingers to avoid eye contact. "I've tried beer a few times with Jeevan but it's not really my thing. Tastes like piss, to be honest." Last winter,

Jeevan and I broke into his dad's beer stash while he was at work. It was a no from both of us, even after a few more attempts to acquire a taste.

"Sahaara . . ." she began in a lecture-y voice eerily similar to Mom's.

"Please don't. The reason I tell you stuff is 'cause you don't get all preachy and parental. We're getting sidetracked here."

"Fine," she sighed. "Sunny. Go on. People see him as a *Surrey Jack*." Maasi air-quoted *Surrey Jack* as she turned onto her side.

I lay down beside her and rested my hands on my stomach, one on top of the other.

"He has that rep 'cause of his friends. But he's the typa guy who doesn't open up easily. Almost like Mom, I guess. He comes to life when he gets comfortable. He's funny and quirky and thoughtful. *Really* thoughtful. He goes out of his way to make sure I'm good. Last week, I was feeling down and he skipped class to read Rumi poems with me."

"He *skipped class* for you? Sounds like Prince Charming."

"What! It was cute, okay?!" I giggled. "But in class he's, like, terminally chill. Too cool for everything." The gray ceiling fan slid away as I recalled his ink-black eyes and broom-thick lashes. He hid them beneath his purple Raptors hat whenever he could help it and I had no idea why.

"So, are you two dating or what's the deal?"

"Not dating . . . yet," I said, reaching instinctually for my cell. "But he's been flirting with me in class. And texting me. And I invited him over for a movie night with Jeevan—"

"Wait. Wait. WAIT." Her gasp dissolved into a phlegmy cough. "You invited him over to the house?"

"With *Jeevan* as well!"

"For a *date* monitored by *Jeevan*?!" She completely cracked up, the wool blanket trembling with her full-body laughter like my boy drama had cured her fever.

"Noooo! It was just supposed to be, like, a friend hangout. And if Jeevan wasn't there, Mom would never be okay with him coming over." When Jeevan and I met in the fifth grade, Mom was adamant about insisting that I only play with girls. Eventually, she realized that he was harmless. Me chilling with a boy like Sunny, though? A boy whose eyes twinkled even in my dreams? It wasn't a question. She'd absolutely lose her shit. "Sunny, um, invited me to a house party tonight."

"Are you going?"

"She'd never let me."

"Have you asked?"

"Don't need to." I gulped. "I already know the answer."

Maasi's cheek rested on her pillow. Her caramel eyes melted into me. "You're a good kid, Sahaara. And your mom really does just want the best for you. You need to give her a chance to open up, though."

I snorted. "Maasi, no offense, but it's easy for you to say that when your mom is ridiculously chill about everything." Bibi Jee was my biggest advocate, always encouraging Mom to be easier on me, telling her that I deserved to be trusted.

"*Please.* You were, like, six months old when I came out to Mom. She's chill now but back then, she planned an entire akhand paat to pray away my gay."

"But my mom's never gonna chill out," I argued. "She doesn't even listen before she says no. Maybe she'll loosen up when I'm in university or something but I'm not holding my breath. I'm not even excited to get my license 'cause I know she's not gonna let me use it."

"Baby steps are key. Show her you can be responsible at this party. And with Sunny. With time, she'll slowly start to relax. Trust me."

I offered her a skeptical look. Maasi had lived with Mom for years and witnessed her naatak-level excessiveness close up. She, of all people, should've understood that there was nothing I could do to get her to stop treating me like a kid. With a sigh, I decided to call Mom just to prove my point. The phone rang and rang but she didn't answer. "Guess she already started work—"

"Hello?"

At the unexpected sound of her voice, nerves kicked me hard in the throat. "Oh, hey. I wanted to ask you something. . . ."

"What? Is everything okay? What's going on?"

"Yeah, sorry, everything's fine. But, um, there's this party tonight at my friend's house and I was wondering—"

"A party? What kind of party?"

"Like, a Halloween party. I was wondering if I could go. I'll be with my friend—"

"No."

"Wait, but you don't even—"

"Are there going to be boys there? Drugs? Alcohol?"

"Mom! You know I'm responsible. I just wanna go there to see my friend."

"Who? Jeevan?"

"No. Someone else."

"Sahaara, no. You're not going."

"Mom . . ." I began, my groan puppy-dog sad and pathetic. Swallowing the disappointment I should've been prepared for,

I quickly regrouped. Begging would get me nowhere. "Okay. Well, can I go trick-or-treating with Jeevan?"

"Do you have homework?"

"Yeah, but I'm gonna finish it now."

"I want you back home by nine, theek aa?"

"Hanji," I agreed, knowing she wouldn't be home until at least eleven thirty.

"I'll see you at home." She cut the call.

"Trick-or-treating? Really?" Maasi said.

The corners of my lips knotted into a sheepish smile and I tilted my phone away from her as I texted Sunny.

Sahaara: I'll see you at 9. Mani's house.

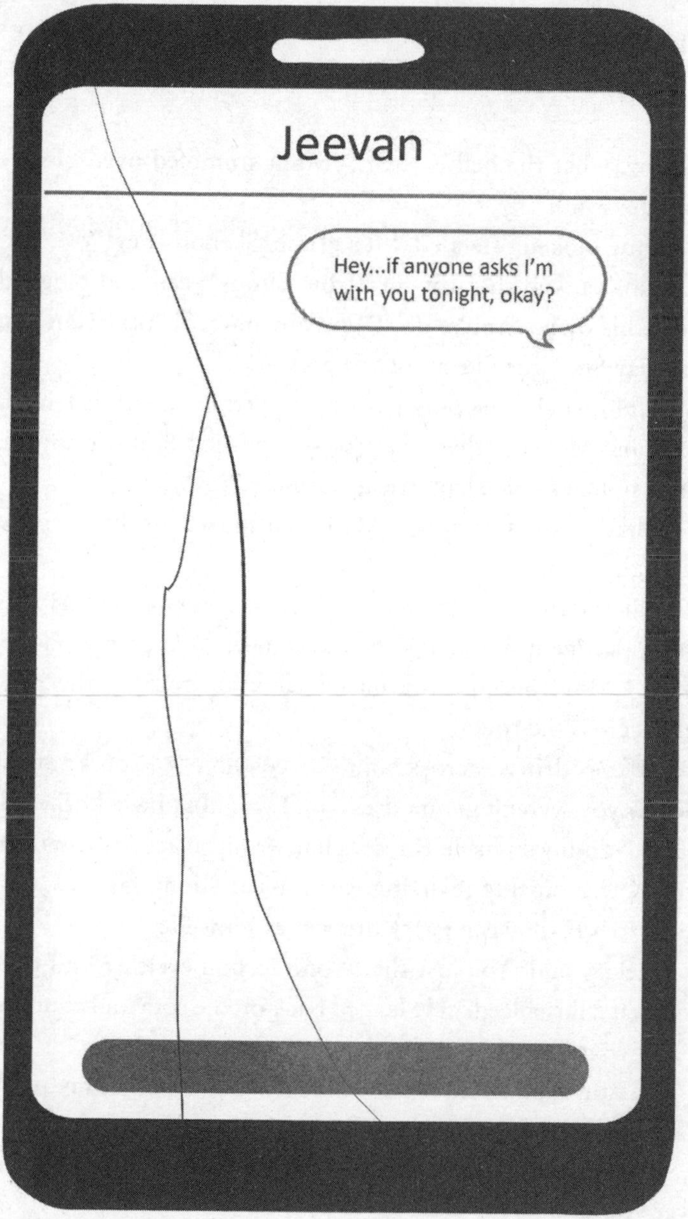
Jeevan
Hey...if anyone asks I'm
with you tonight, okay?

the house party

"Sunny, what the hell is this?!" Mani stumbled over, clearly already drunk.

Sunny looked offended. "It's grime. Skepta—hey!"

Mani yanked the aux cord from Sunny's cell and plugged it into his own. "You're not DJing anymore. Skepta? Can you just play Six Nine like a normal person?"

"Mani, you're the only person on earth who still listens to Six Nine. And I'd rather listen to good music," Sunny retorted. "Not snitches who slap little girls' asses."

"That's just a rumor," Mani murmured as he scrolled through Spotify.

Drake began to sing over the giant speakers and to Mani's disappointment, no one rushed to dance. "Watch my phone, okay?" Mani disappeared into a circle of guys by the pool table across the room.

My eyes drifted across Sunny's "costume." "You know, if I knew you weren't gonna dress up, I wouldn't have bothered, either." Sunny's purple Raptors hat was in place, as usual. In what I was quickly realizing was typical Sunny fashion, he'd come to a Halloween party dressed as himself.

"Relax, bud. You just threw on raccoon eyeliner and gave yourself a nosebleed." He leaned back on the sofa and chucked a pillow at me.

I caught it in my hands and smoothed the hem of my punk Eleven blazer. "Friends don't lie."

The *Stranger Things* reference flew over his head. "Whatever you say."

"So, Mani's parents are cool with him throwing a house party?"

"They're in Punjab."

"Ah." I nodded.

"You hungry? Should I get you a snack? Or a drink?" He rose from the sofa, motioning toward the coffee table. It was a chessboard of Crown and Coke.

"Nah, I'm good. Not hungry and I don't like drinking, to be honest."

"Oh. That's cool." He sank back into the cushiony sofa and his leg brushed up against mine, a little closer than before.

"I mean, you can drink if you want. Don't mind me."

"Nah, it's cool. I don't really drink either but . . . everyone else does. And Mani guys don't take no for an answer. My dad drinks way too much so I've never really, like, been into it."

"Yeah?" I sat up a little straighter, surprised by his honesty. "I'm really sorry."

"It's whatever." He shrugged. "I'm not gonna sit here and cry about it. But drinking loses its appeal after your dad pukes on you a few times."

"Shit. Jeevan's dad's kinda like that, too."

"Hey, why didn't he come? Isn't Jeevan, like, your chaperone?"

"Oh, shut up," I laughed, throwing the pillow back at him. "I texted him, but he didn't reply. I think he's dealing with family stuff." I checked WhatsApp again, worry beginning to bubble up in my stomach. He hadn't read my last few messages. "And he's not really into house parties and shit. Don't think I am, either, to be honest. We don't even talk to half these people at school. Why sit around with them?"

"So, why'd you come, then?" He smirked.

I couldn't help the smile that grew across my face. We held each other's gaze for just a moment too long. When I broke away, the heat of his eyes still lingered.

"And how the hell did you get outta the house?" he asked, hand grazing the edge of my dark jeans.

"Mom's at work. Told her I was going trick-or-treating with Jeevan. Maasi's knocked out cold with a fever. Bibi's in Punjab."

"Damn. *You?* Being dishonest with your parent like the rest of us normal humans?!"

Mani's playlist bounced from Drake and Posty to Fateh as people finally began to dance. Across the room, a guy I didn't recognize accidentally spilled his drink on the white carpet and shouted, "Yo, my bad, bro!" to Mani. Seemingly too drunk to care, Mani simply laughed it off.

"Could we get some fresh air?" I asked. "Crowds kinda stress me out."

"You read my mind."

I didn't realize how stuffy the basement was until the crisp outdoor breeze hit me.

"Dude, do you want my jacket? Why didn't you wear something warm?"

"I'm okay." I smiled through chattering teeth. "The blazer's thicker than it looks."

"You sure?"

Truthfully, my Eleven costume was a flimsy barrier between me and the chilly air. Goose bumps were quickly popping up across my arms. "Nope. I retract my statement. I'll take it."

He passed me his thick bomber jacket and gazed at the night sky, brown skin glowing beneath light that emanated from the party. "No stars out tonight."

"Technically, the stars are always out. We just can't see them." I bumped into his shoulder as we strolled across the grass, darkness growing as we drifted from the house.

"What you mean?"

"In the city, the lights are so bright they block out the stars. If you go to, like, a mountain, or somewhere far from light pollution, you can see the entire galaxy."

"Guess I should go find us a mountain, then." He placed an arm over my shoulder and instantly, my stomach somersaulted. If we weren't in near darkness, he would've seen my cheeks go hot red and blotchy. *Breathe*, I told myself, trying not to ruin what could be a cute moment with nervous sweating and a complete lack of chill. I channeled my inner "nonchalant Sunny" as I searched for his hand and grasped on.

"I'd be down for that," I said, voice smooth as silk and heart pulsing.

"Yeah? You, me, and a mountain, right? Not you, me, and Jeevan?"

"Just you and me," I laughed.

He turned toward the house, where deafening bass from the party broke into the outdoors. I could trace his lips, perfectly framed by his beard, under the warm light spilling from the windows. The corners of his mouth were upturned, an almost-grin. "You know, you're nothing like what I imagined."

"What you mean?" I asked.

"Promise you won't get mad?" A soft breeze carried his cedar cologne toward me and he didn't shiver, despite the wind.

"I make no promises."

"All right . . . I knew you were artsy and shit. I thought that would mean you wouldn't wanna chill with a Jack."

"You're not a Jack!" I laughed, playfully batting his chest.

"What's your beef with Jacks?" he gasped, faux offended. "I don't deny my Jack-ness. I celebrate it."

"Love that." I grinned. "Not gonna lie. I assumed stuff about you as well."

"Like what?"

"Promise you won't get mad?" I asked.

"Pinky swear." He gently grasped my wrist and locked my pinky into his, just like Jeevan and I always did. When he released my pinky, he clasped my hand in his, holding it tight.

"Back before I knew you, I thought you were just like Mani. Fighting and selling weed and shit. People kinda see you as the same person."

He loosened his grip around my hand ever so slightly.

"What's wrong?" I asked.

"Mani's annoying but . . . there's more to guys like him than just fighting and selling weed, you know? He's a person. Not just a—a Surrey Jack meme or something."

"My bad," I whispered, embarrassed to have even said something so judgmental.

"You're good, Sahaara." He threw an arm around my shoulder, drawing me closer. "Don't stress. I guess it's just a little tiring to feel like we have to live inside of, like . . ."

"A box?"

"Yeah. Exactly." Sunny said nothing further. Instead, he returned his attention to the seamless black sky. Despite his insistence that he wasn't upset, I couldn't help but feel bad. I tried to remind myself that he had his own preconceived notions about me as well. I was stirred from my thoughts when his voice, at once deep and soft, fell through the darkness. "Can I ask you something?"

"Go for it."

"What do you see in me?"

"What do you mean?"

"I mean, you're cool as hell, Sahaara. And you're mad creative. And you're going places. Why are you chilling with me?"

Sunny's vulnerability continued to surprise me, chipping away at my caution in tiny increments until I could see nothing but my mouth pressed up against his. "First of all, just 'cause you're not into abstract art, it doesn't mean you're not creative." I laughed. "And just 'cause you don't have everything figured out," I continued, "it doesn't mean you're not going places."

He opened his mouth as if gearing up to argue my point, but instead, he sighed, something recalibrating in his features. "I guess."

"And you care. A lot. Way more than you let on." A smile curled around my lips. I toyed with the brim of his hat as if my heart wasn't pounding and his mere closeness wasn't making it hard to think straight. I swallowed and said exactly what was on my mind before my nerves got the best of me. "You also happen to have gorgeous eyes. Even though you hide them for no good reason."

He cracked up. "Shit, if I knew you felt that way, maybe I'd show 'em off." He flipped his cap around and his dark eyes came into view under the moonlight. I searched for those flecks of wildflower honey that sometimes flickered beneath the sun. I wandered the constellation of beauty marks above his brow, grazing them with my thumb. For the first time, he shivered.

"You're a beautiful person, Sunny. Fuck the assumptions people make. Even mine."

"Can I ask you something else?" He released his arm from around my shoulder and turned to face me.

"Go for it."

"Would it be okay if I . . . kissed you?"

I answered with my lips, soft against his. He wrapped his arms around my waist and drew me close, the music from the house floating away. When he kissed me back, my skin was not ablaze with his touch. Instead, his mouth cooled everything down, brought time to a slow, blissful halt.

He gently pulled his lips away and stroked my cheek. "You know you're amazing, right?"

"Wait a minute," I dramatically gasped. "Are you—Sunny Sahota—catching feelings?!"

"Pleeease," he drawled, pulling me a little closer. "I don't catch feelings."

"Yeah, sure you don't." I slowly pried my eyes from his to check the time on my cell.

My heart short-circuited: Ten missed calls from Mom. Twelve texts.

Sunny glanced at the screen. "Oh, shit. Someone's in trouble."

Unlike my pulse, my fingers moved sluggishly as I tried to unlock my phone.

Mom: Where are you?

Mom: Sahaara, where are you?

Mom: You're not with Jeevan. Where did you go?

Mom: Hello?

Mom: Pick up your phone

Mom: Hello??????

Mom: HELLO????

Mom's text messages went on and on in increasing levels of freak-out. "What the hell?! It's only ten thirty. She wasn't supposed to be home for at least an hour! Shit! SHIIIIT!"

"Okay, try to calm down—"

"What should I—shit!—I should just go home now. I'll see you tomorrow." Like the Cinderella I wasn't, I made for the gate that led out of Mani's backyard.

Sunny trailed after me. "Hold up! How are you getting home?"

"With my feet," I called over my shoulder, pushing open the gate, sprinting across the driveway.

"Sahaara—just wait! It's at least a twenty-minute walk. Lemme see if I can get you a ride home."

Even through my heart-pounding panic, I calculated that he was right. "Okay, um, please be quick." Sunny zipped back into the house as I paced the driveway between a maze of cars.

How had Mom known I wasn't with Jeevan? I fumbled with my phone again as I reread her messages. Jeevan still hadn't responded.

Sahaara: Mom, I'm with my friend. I'm coming home right now.

Mom: WHERE ARE YOU?

I froze for a moment and tried to collect my thoughts. No matter what I said, I was in deep shit.

Sahaara: Sorry . . . I was trick-or-treating with my friend. It got late. Sorry. I'm coming right now.

Mom: Where are you? Who are you with? I'm coming to get you.

Sahaara: No I have a ride

The screen immediately glowed blue with a phone call from Mom. I let it ring without answering.

ਪੰਗਾ / panga / trouble

The front door swung open before I could even find my house key.

"Tu andar aaja." Mom told me to come inside without so much as a hello. "Who were you out with?" She scanned the driveway in search of said person.

"Mom, calm down! I was just trick-or-treating. I was with a girl from school." I hastily racked my brain for the best name to drop: someone whose parents Mom wouldn't know. "Rhea Gill."

"Acha? You were trick-or-treating with Rhea Gill?" Her large eyes brimmed with fury. They pierced right through my skin.

"Yes!"

"What happened to Jeevan?"

"He couldn't come. He had too much homework."

"Homework, huh?" There was a hint of laughter in her voice, as if my excuse was beyond belief.

"Yesssss!" I doubled down, committing to my lie. "He forgot about his social studies project. How's that my fault?"

"If you went trick-or-treating, where's your candy?"

Shit. I dropped the first excuse that came to me. "I was so stressed about you flipping out at me that I left my bag with her and literally ran home!"

Mom shook her head slowly, no anger dissolving. I kicked off my sneakers and flew past her to get to my room.

"So, explain to me why I'm coming home from work, sitting at a stoplight in Jeeto Aunty's car, and Jeevan and his mom pull up next to us. And I ask his mom where you are, and she says she had no idea about trick-or-treating. That Jeevan never even mentioned it to her."

I froze on the stairs without looking back at Mom. Why hadn't Jeevan messaged me? Why hadn't he given me a heads-up?

"Just explain to me why, if you were going trick-or-treating with this Rhea girl, you wouldn't have just told me that in the first place? Why'd you say you were going with Jeevan? I wasn't born yesterday, Sahaara. Where'd you actually go?"

"Fine, Mom. I didn't go trick-or-treating. I went to the party. Happy?"

"Give me your phone."

"What? Why?!" I held my phone tight in my sweaty palm, ready to defend it.

"Do I go to work for you to *lie* to me and go running off to god knows where? You want me to trust you more? And let you go out and have a phone? Whose house was this party even at?!"

Frustration welled up in my eyes and spilled over the edges. "Mom, you're not the only one who goes to work. I *literally* work my ass off after school, I take extra shifts at the bookstore *and* get all my homework done but if I want to do *one* fun thing, you completely flip out! I do this shit for *you* and you still treat me like a little kid who can't take care of herself. I DIDN'T EVEN DO ANYTHING BAD!"

From her Polaroid-still shock, I could see that the words stung. But my rage was bright crimson, too raw for remorse.

She looked just above my head as she said, "Give me the phone."

I dropped it in her hand and turned around, walking straight to my room. My nosebleed makeup now mingled with my tears and I haphazardly wiped it away, shutting the door behind me. Mom immediately pried it open.

"Sahaara, I'm talking to you! Don't just walk away from me."

"Says the woman who walks away whenever she's mad," I mumbled under my breath, getting into my unmade bed and forcefully pulling the covers over me. "Can't even look at me when I point out the truth."

"Sahaara? Hello, we're still having a conversation." The hardwood floor creaked where she paced the room.

"What's there to say?"

"You still haven't told me whose party you went to! Or who you were with."

There was nothing to lose at this point. I threw caution to the wind and told her. "It was Mani's house party, Mom. And I was there with my friend Sunny, who—oh my god!—is a boy."

"Who is this Sunny? I've never heard of him before. And who's Mani? Were his parents there? Were people drinking?"

"*I* wasn't drinking, Mom," I said from beneath the covers. "I literally just went there to hang out with my friend, and I didn't do anything bad. I'm freakin' responsible and you act like I'm gonna snort coke or something."

"Sahaara, it's not that. I obviously know you're not going to snort cocaine. And yes, you *are* responsible. But you don't understand other people, Sahaara. Not everyone else is responsible. Or has good intentions."

"Do you really think I don't have enough common sense to not do things just 'cause other people are?"

I felt the mattress sink where she sat down at the end of the bed. "I'm not talking about that. I'm talking about boys,

Sahaara. *Men*. Who is this Sunny guy?"

"He's my friend from school. And he's a good guy." She didn't need to know that I kissed him.

"And how do you know that? How do you know he's a good guy?"

"Because . . . I just do, Mom. He's Jeevan's friend from basketball and he's gone to Jameson since eighth grade and he'd never try anything weird with me."

"You don't understand, Sahaara. I'm just trying to keep you safe. Boys only care about one thing. Even if they act like they care about you. You can't just trust them . . . you never know what could happen when you're alone—"

"Yeah? And is Jeevan the same? Does he only care about one thing?"

"We've known Jeevan for years. *I've* known Jeevan for years. I've never heard of this Sunny guy before today."

"I know what you're implying, Mom. But Sunny isn't a shitty person. He's not gonna rape me or some shit."

With the covers still over my head, I felt Mom slowly rise from my bed. I peeked out from beneath my blanket to watch her walk toward the door.

"Mom. When am I getting my phone back? I have work on Friday."

She said nothing as she left the room.

trigger

breathe. distract. forget.
breathe. distract. forget.
breathe. distract. forget.
breathe. distract. forget.
breathe. distract. forget.
breathe. distract. forget.
breathe. distract. forget.
breathe. distract. forget.
breathe. distract. forget.
breathe. distract. forget.
choke. distract. forget.
choke. tremble. forget.
choke. tremble. recall.

break.
 b r e a k.
    br ea k.
        b r e   a   k.

i gathered all my
fears into a shield
& tried too hard
to protect you

i didnt know how
to apologize
for loving you

from the place
where i was
broken

so how was your night?

the next day
we both turned up at school with puffy eyes
and no cell phones.

and i broke the silence with
why don't you go first

so jeevan took a deep breath
and recalled the bullshit
right from the beginning.

he told me that
he came home from school
to the type of day that he dreaded:
dad yelling and cussing
and blaming it all on mom

he told me that
he tried to calm everyone down
but containing a fire to one spot
on a carpet was almost impossible

he told me that
his dad smashed his phone against
the tiles and held him against the wall
before his mom finally agreed
to go to her brother's house

he told me that
he returned home in the morning
relieved his dad wasn't there

and all the things
i wanted to vent about
evaporated into thin air
insubstantial before
the bruises he carried.

by the end of november
i'd already told him too much

i didn't want to be a burden when jeevan was exhausted
so when i'd catch sunny in the hallway between classes
or shooting three-pointers on the basketball court
or lying in the grass, following the clouds

something made me want to spill my guts

maybe it was the way he looked at me
like my eyes were a film he didn't bore of

maybe it was how my worries went still
each time his velvet lips tasted mine

maybe it was a weight i was desperate to unload
in arms that held me like i was more magical
than a friend

whatever the reason
i forced myself to keep the deepest secret

he knew that mom left punjab
and raised me on her own

he knew that my bibi
wasn't mine by birth

but he didn't know
mom was undocumented.

an honest self-portrait

girl with a patchwork body
a living, breathing form
fueled by questionable blood

i washed white over the canvas
and began with a blank slate

first
i built the scaffolding of my features
in soft 4h pencil outlines

soon the underlayers
then every shade of purple pigment

in murky blots and watercolor vortexes
i riddled my skin with holes

all the places where my absent dna
haunted me

i filled the dark emptiness with silver stars
begging for illumination
imagining the healing balm of clarity.

flirting with temptation

art school was a mishri-sweet daydream
a mouthwatering illusion just out of reach

even with a full scholarship
creativity would never pay the bills
or support my mom
or soften her callused palms

but mr. kim insisted that
the grant could be within my grasp
because my paintings exhaled and cried
and trembled

just fill out the form!
he said
what's the worst that could happen
if you win the scholarship?

he didn't understand
that to sniff the petals of this fantasy
was to prick myself on its thorns

why seduce myself with the thought
of something i couldn't have?

things to do when the boy
you liked couldn't make it (again)

1.   splatter fiery paint across a fresh canvas
and then water it in blues

2.   make popcorn and rewatch your favorite
netflix series

3.   make a batch of cookie dough and move
on to your bookshelf

4.   pull open your journal and write another
poem. title it: *all the reasons why i am*
enough

5.   go to the park with your best friend, jump
on a swing, and let the wind be the only
reason why your eyes water

all the reasons why i am enough

1.

2.

3.

4.

5.

selfie

wing-tip eyeliner sharper than a butterfly blade
coating chocolate ocean eyes inherited from mom
and lashes that could sweep you off your feet
rosy mauve liquid lips & glistening cheekbones
black turtleneck dress with my teddy bear coat

today and every day, i was my own woman crush

it was an unspoken rule

that at the first snowfall of winter
you were required to boomerang
the sight outside your window
and post it to your insta story
as though everyone in surrey
couldn't see the exact same shit.

in an instant
sunny replied with a picture of his own
he was standing before a white-frosted forest
fat flakes gathering in his hair
and whitening his beard

his caption read
video call me

so i did.

conversation flowed effortlessly
when i managed to hear from him, these days
(between work and family and things he said
he couldn't really talk about, i tried to be patient)

but a question had been biting at me
the way the cold inevitably
got under my gloves
what are we?
i asked.

> *what do you mean, shordy?*

i mean, what are we?
are we dating?

> his sigh became vapor
> momentarily clouding the screen
> *i don't wanna ruin us*
> *by putting labels on us.*

i don't follow.

> *we've been going with*
> *the flow and it's been good,*
> *hasn't it?*
> *we're sahaara and sunny.*
> *and being around each other*
> *feels right. natural.*

i nodded reluctantly.
yeah, i guess so.

> *honest to god, you're my*
> *favorite person, sahaara*
> *what we have is special.*
> *i don't want to change*
> *a single thing.*

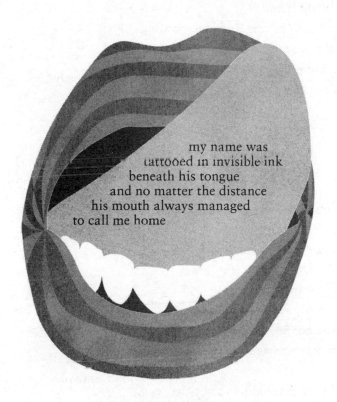

my name was
tattooed in invisible ink
beneath his tongue
and no matter the distance
his mouth always managed
to call me home

no, it wasn't written in black

but did that matter
when sunny & i knew
what we meant
to each other?

january 1, 2020

midnight struck
and maasi, jeevan, and i were sitting
on the bench outside the gurdwara
because my people were beautiful
but too many people were overwhelming

under the mellow breeze of a snowless winter night
we each took turns sharing resolutions
for the new decade

jeevan wanted to spend more time
practicing his defense skills so that
his coach would finally see him

maasi wanted to swim
cautiously with her head
before her heart dove deep
into another woman

and i just wanted this to be the year
when i could ease mom's worries.

revelations

it was nearly february when i finally found out
why sunny had been so busy

we stood at the front steps of pa jameson
where students poured from the school
like sea creatures escaping a net

sunny wrapped an arm around my waist
and promised me a perfect evening
of pastel paint and khalid
(i just needed to come up with
a waterproof excuse for mom)

a moment later
that loud guy from the basketball team
asked sunny for a deal on weed
and my throat was hooked by a fishing line
a rip curl of questions swallowing me

sunny offered no explanation on the spot
so i walked home alone
dripping salt water and pure anger

when i reached the front door
my phone pulsed with a text

i'm sorry i didn't tell you.
i promise this is temporary.
honest truth, we're having a hard time
at home. this isn't for me.
it's for my family.

why didn't you tell me?

it was a hollowing feeling
to pour (almost all) your guts out to someone
and suddenly realize they hardly trusted you
with their own truths

but i tried to put aside my concoction of hurt
when sunny opened up

i never wanted to be there
not when mani showed me the warehouse
not when his brother gave me a job
not when you looked at me
like something had shattered between us
but
the relief on my mom's face
when she took the stack of cash
and paid off the bills

reminded me why i had to

with a walnut of sorrow stuck in my throat
i remembered mom

the responsibilities and worries and work
she refused to share.

and, slowly, my frustration washed away.

sahaara

march 2020–august 2020

the unexpected blooms of spring

Jeevan and I stepped back to marvel at a towering, chiseled apple, its surface hot pink and embedded with shards of gold. "What's this supposed to be?" Jeevan grinned. "A statement about academic oppression?"

I circled the flamboyant art installation in search of some clue to explain the work. "Your guess is as good as mine," I eventually said, shrugging. "Wanna get going?"

"Yeah, down." He led us toward an echoing hallway lined with dozens upon dozens of three-dimensional, mixed-media eyeballs. Abstract art was weird as hell and I loved it.

"Any more acceptance letters?" I asked, glancing at an elaborate, protruding eyeball made entirely of yellow pencils. It glared at me, unflinching.

"Just the criminology program at UFV, so far. Let's hope I get accepted at SFU. I'm not trying to drive to Abby every day."

"Fair enough . . . the farms smell like shit. But, crim? Really?" I couldn't wrap my head around the thought of Jeevan—my velvet-soft, Akala-bumping, web-coding best friend—becoming a corrections officer or, worse, a cop. It was a heart forced into a square-shaped hole. "You sure that's what you want?"

"I dunno. Not exactly." His gaze lifted to the dark ceiling in contemplation, the black drawcords on his grad hoodie twirling between his fingers. "I mean, it'd be cool to do computer sciences, but I still haven't gotten that acceptance letter . . . mostly applied for crim 'cause Sunny said it would be easy to get in."

"Of course he did," I murmured.

"You two not cool or something?"

Another eyeball stared at me from the wall, this one composed of dried seaweed. "We're chill."

"You sure?"

I nodded, my lips pressed flat in a line. There was a weird urge within me to not talk about how everything with Sunny felt . . . sticky. Messy. Confusing. How, in the past few months, we had simultaneously become closer and more distant. When we were together in person, Sunny would vent about his deepest fears, the financial problems his family faced, his dad's constant drinking, the reasons why selling weed was a necessity—not a choice. How my mere presence made things lighter.

But his absence also weighed heavy.

Last month, he canceled on our Godfather trilogy marathon—another wasted lie to Mom about where I was going after school. He would usually give me his undivided attention during poetry class, but he would take hours—sometimes days—to reply to my calls and texts. When it came to feelings, I was a chronic oversharer, but an impulse had grown within me to protect Sunny from people who just didn't get him. After all, he was going through shit that others could hardly imagine. Keeping things from Jeevan was strange and new, though. I hated the feeling just as much as I hated Sunny's shitty communication.

Thankfully, Jeevan changed the subject without prying further. "You only applied for nursing, right?"

"Yeah, and I applied to Daphne Odjig. The art school. Mostly 'cause of the scholarship thing."

"Oh shit, yeah!" He grinned, squeezing my shoulder. "If

you get the scholarship, *please* tell me you're gonna do it."

I was quiet for a while, eyeing the circular First Nations artwork that lined this end of the gallery hallway. I knew they were Susan Point's Coast Salish spindle whorls before I could even find the artist statements. "Nursing pays really well. Maasi works, like, three days a week and makes thirty-five bucks an hour. If I do that, I'll still be able to paint and stuff in my free time, y'know?"

It was Jeevan's turn to be quiet. He removed his thick-rimmed glasses and wiped them clean on his hoodie. "What are you thinking?" I asked.

"I'm thinking . . . that nursing doesn't seem like your calling."

"Is crim *your* calling?"

"It's not. Trust me, if I get accepted into computer sciences, I'm *on* that shit. What I'm saying is, I know you're trying to be practical, but you have something really special, dude. A talent that a lotta folks would dream of. If you get the chance to follow your passion, don't let it slip through your fingers."

I watched my boots land with an echo against each of the cement stairs. "What about my responsibilities? If I made nursing money, everything would be easier. Bibi has mortgage payments she needs help with and Mom—we still aren't making enough to fix her papers."

"I feel it," he sighed. "Can't argue with that."

"Thank you for visiting Vancouver Art Gallery!" an elderly Punjabi man in a red vest smiled as we stepped outside. From the top step of the gallery, I absorbed the sight of camera-wielding tourists and yoga-pant-wearing locals wandering through downtown Vancouver.

"So glad we didn't have school today. If I had to do another close analysis of *Hamlet*, I would've gouged out my eyeballs with a rapier or whatever the hell that thing is called." I leaned on Jeevan's shoulder as I stretched my exhausted legs. "But remind me to never wear these boots again. My heels are killing me." After Jeevan delivered an irritating but expected "I told you so" lecture on wearing comfortable shoes, he said, "What's the scene tonight?"

"Psych homework. Gotta write an essay about *cognitive dissonance*. Freakin' scintillating."

"Wanna munch? It's still early."

"Food is tempting, but . . ." I checked the time on my cell. "It's five now. I told my mom I'd be back in Surrey by six thirty."

A light Vancouver breeze whipped through Jeevan's curls, carrying the buttery comfort of an Indian food truck toward us. "Call and ask if you can stay longer. There's this sushi place in Gastown—"

"Gastown?!" I guffawed. "You want me to *walk* in *these heels* to Gastown?"

"Man, I told you we were gonna be walking. Go buy a cheap pair of sneakers."

"Orrrrrr you could piggyback me all the way there." He rolled his eyes and I texted Mom since he clearly wasn't taking no for an answer.

Sahaara: Mom, is it okay if Jeevan and I eat dinner in Van?

We'll probably be an extra hour

In literally half a millisecond, Mom replied.

Mom: That's fine

"Damn. That was fast. Guess we're going to Gastown."

By the time we reached the perpetual gathering of tourists that ogled the Gastown Steam Clock (for reasons that were beyond me), I was thoroughly over our food trek. And I made sure Jeevan knew it.

"I can't feel my feet," I moaned. "How much farther?"

"You know I don't even feel bad, right?" He laughed like my suffering was comedic and I swatted his shoulder.

"Ass."

"Right there." He pointed to a neon sign two doors down. The restaurant had a line out the door.

"How the hell are they busy on a Monday?"

"They just opened. And they're supposed to be *that good*."

"We're never gonna get seats. Can we go somewhere else?"

"Let's just see." He sidestepped through a boisterous group of girls blocking the entrance and I waited outside, nursing a leg cramp. Under the evening sky, lights sparkled in the trees that lined the street. It was so pretty, it almost made up for the smell of piss that permeated the brick sidewalk.

Jeevan returned a few minutes later with a wide grin plastered to his face. "Got us a table."

"What? How?!" I followed him through the crowd and entered the dark restaurant. Glowing sculptures composed of old toys hung from the ceiling, some made of Super Soakers, others of metallic Hot Wheels and plastic Hello Kitty heads. For all my complaining, I was suddenly smitten with the artsy joint. A server covered in manga tattoos guided us past a sea of cramped tables all the way to the back. Beneath the neon light, their short white hair glowed purple and their metallic earrings, almost a dozen on each ear, shimmered and danced.

A few paces ahead, the server turned around to face us, menus in hand. "And here's your booth!"

When I turned toward the table, I nearly fell to the floor as my whole family hit me with a booming, "SURPRISE!"

"Wait—what?" I sputtered. Mom, Maasi, and Bibi were all sitting there, their smiles incandescent beneath black light.

"Happy birthday!" Bibi grinned, white bandana shimmering.

"Oh my god." My body trembled with gleeful shock and laughter. "How'd you guys—holy crap!"

Everyone moved over to make space for me and I sat down beside Bibi. Jeevan pulled up a chair. "Surprised?" he said.

"Yes! I was expecting this tomorrow. Not today. I can't believe y'all are here." My heart swelled at the sight of all the people I loved: Maasi was still wearing her hospital scrubs and Mom was supposed to be at work right now. Bibi Jee was out of the house! There was usually no convincing her to join family outings anywhere beyond the edges of Surrey. "I'm legit so happy right now," I said, eyes stinging and blurry.

"Awww, raudee aa bechari. She's crying." Bibi Jee leaned over and squeezed my face. My grandma wiped my tears with her worn fingers and kissed me on the cheek.

"Sorry—just grateful for you all—oh my god! The cake!" I hadn't even noticed the canvas-shaped cake in the middle of the table decorated with Vincent van Gogh's *Starry Night*. Two number-shaped candles were lit in the center: eighteen.

"You'll get your sushi later. Tonight, dessert comes first." Maasi's cheekbones glistened with highlight as she cleared her throat and began a chorus of "Happy Birthday." As they sang, my wish bloomed vivid and luminous within my mind's eye. I wanted this to be the year when I could finally give back to Mom for the lifetime of care she'd given to me. Across the table, she rested her chin in her roughened palm. I melted at her well-meaning eyes. The wheat-brown radiance of her skin. The creases around her smile that were slowly working their way into permanence.

I blew out the candles, sending my desperate wish into the universe, and we were momentarily thrust into darkness.

"What'd you wish for?" Maasi asked.

"New paintbrushes," I replied. Although I could've easily told her and Jeevan and Bibi the truth, it was hard to bare my heart before Mom. How strange it was to love someone more than yourself, but still hold bricks in your throat while in their presence. Perhaps it was because of her walls.

"All right, so, we need to do gifts right now because I'm way too excited." Maasi passed me a sparkly pink gift bag with a card tucked inside. "This is from me, Bibi, and Mom. Open the gift bag first."

"Aren't you supposed to open the card first?"

"Gift first!"

I plucked out the pink tissue and squealed at the cloth-bound poetry book: *The Collected Works of Shiv Kumar Batalvi*—one of Mom's favorite poets. "THANK YOOOU!" I hugged Bibi and awkwardly leaned over to hug Maasi and clasp Mom's hand.

"There's more," Maasi said, flashing Mom a look.

"Open the card, puth," whispered Mom.

I peeled open the gray envelope and pulled out the card. A folded piece of paper fell in my lap.

"What's this?" I asked.

"Read it," Mom said, voice still quiet.

"Out loud," Maasi added.

As soon as I caught a glimpse of the purple lotus—Daphne Odjig's logo—my heart stopped. "Dear Sahaara Kaur, I am pleased to inform you that you have been selected by the Department of Visual Arts to receive Fall 2020's Amplifying

the Underrepresented Scholarship and have gained entrance
into Daphne Odjig University's prestigious Bachelor of Visual
Arts Program . . ." I stopped reading and simply gaped at the
letter. "I—I got in?"

Congratulations flooded in from every side of the table,
Jeevan offering me high fives, Bibi Jee wrapping me up in a
warm hug, Maasi capturing the moment on her phone with a
video. Mom simply smiled wide, all her pride beaming from
her eyes.

I was shell-shocked, a dozen conflicting feelings rushing at
me at once. For everyone's sake, I closed my gaping mouth and
grinned, but my stomach was churning.

my grandmother's smile

stretched from ear to ear
she wore it like an embroidered shawl
stitched with her own fingers
and did not hide it in a vault
when her husband left her arms.
when they told her that widows
should no longer wear bright colors
she smiled even harder and said
i will not abandon my lover's joy
because he has abandoned his body.

my grandmother would smile
when strangers said i had inherited her mouth
she'd say *i may have gotten her lips but, perhaps,*
not her sharp, shameless tongue.

my grandmother's eyes welled with pride
when i was mistaken for her own flesh and blood
and she reminded me that it was no mistake.
that we found each other for a reason.
for unfinished business from another life.

my grandmother's deepest wrinkles creased
around her smile. if the lines on our palms
told our future, then the lines on her face carried
more stories than i had ever heard. her activist
teens in punjab melted into her outspoken twenties
when marriage and motherhood only taught her
how to shout louder

my grandmother read my face without a word
she knew that i was forcing a smile
and knew exactly why.

she reached for the letter in my lap and whispered
just quiet enough for no one else to hear

you feel guilty because you think your art
is a burden. when another job will bring
more money. but i have lived long enough
to know that the greatest burden is an
unfulfilled heart.

she said
yes, money makes us worry. but haven't we
always found a way?

for a child to sponsor
their parent's immigration

they must

1. be eighteen
2. be a canadian citizen
3. have enough income to support two people

and mom had been saving since i was born
and i had been taking all the shifts i could
but we still weren't there

for my eighteenth birthday, the gift i most wanted
was a paper promising that my mother would
no longer have to hide

but instead i was handed just a little more patience
and an invitation down a path that was never
part of the plan.

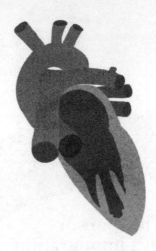

choosing one half of my heart

was the most frightening decision i ever made
left me wondering whether i should turn back
excited me and broke me all at once
was their decision as much as it was mine
only seemed right because it came from all of us

felt like stepping into forest after nightfall
with only my hands as guides

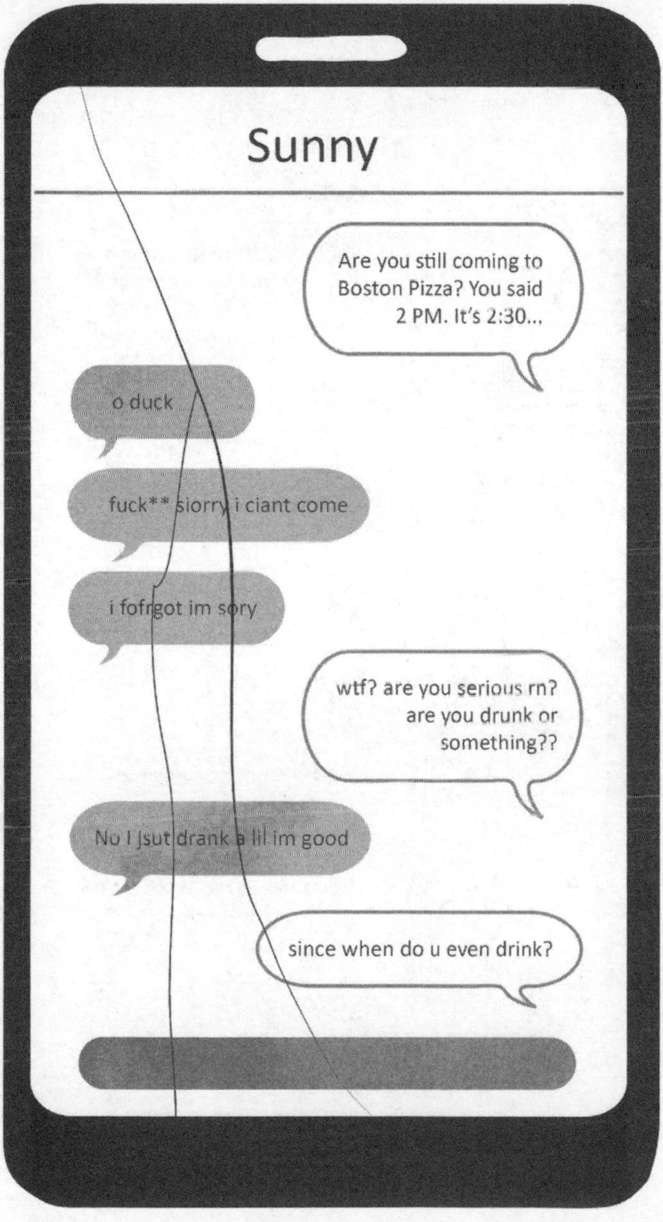
Sunny
Are you still coming to Boston Pizza? You said 2 PM. It's 2:30...
o duck
fuck** siorry i ciant come
i fofrgot im sory
wtf? are you serious rn? are you drunk or something??
No I jsut drank a lil im good
since when do u even drink?

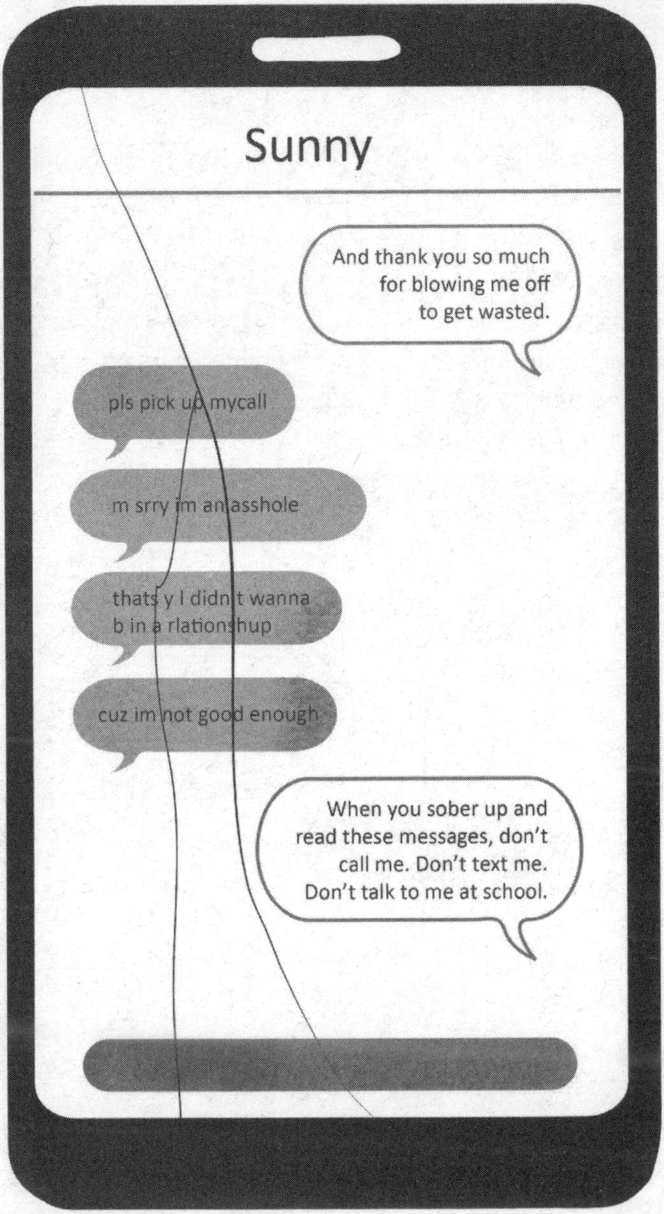
Sunny
And thank you so much for blowing me off to get wasted.
pls pick up mycall
m srry im an asshole
thats y I didnt wanna b in a rlationshup
cuz im not good enough
When you sober up and read these messages, don’t call me. Don’t text me. Don’t talk to me at school.

the doe

"Sahaara, what's wrong?" Mom walked into the living room with a wicker basket full of freshly washed laundry teetering in her arms. She placed it on the sofa and cautiously approached me. My eyes remained on my canvas. It sat flat against the coffee table amid murky paint water, fine-tipped brushes, and Bibi's Punjabi newspapers.

"Nothing." I added a blue stroke to my ocean.

"You've been crying."

"No, I haven't." I filled in the underside of the wave.

"Your eyes are red."

"I'm fine." My paintbrush slipped. The words bit at my lips, but I couldn't summon them before her. She wouldn't get why I was hurting—*devastated*—over a boy who had never even called me his girlfriend. She'd just lose her shit because I'd been chilling with him in the first place. Internally, I laughed at all the times I lied to Mom so that I could see Sunny. Was it worth it?

An old Punjabi song crackled over Bibi's radio. "*Ni ik meri akh kashni,*" Surinder Kaur crooned as Mom sat down next to me.

"Sahaara, I love you."

"I love you, too."

"You know you can talk to me, right?"

"Just like you can talk to me."

She said nothing and I continued to stare at my canvas and Surinder Kaur continued to sing. When had Mom and I become so awkward? I recalled those saffron-tender moments from childhood when I couldn't wait for her to come home from work, to sit with me in bed and tell me what she'd cooked that day and read me a bedtime story. Back in those days, I felt safest curled up in her welcoming arms, listening to her hum her favorite Neha Bhasin tunes.

"I thought about my mom today."

Brush frozen in my hand, I glanced up from the painting. "Yeah?"

I watched her without moving an inch, the way one might if they were afraid to startle a deer. Her chest rose slowly, and her exhale was audible. Her eyes were glued to the newspaper on the coffee table. "I never really had a good relationship with her, but sometimes I miss her. That's kind of strange, isn't it?" Her mouth quivered as she spoke.

"It's not strange, Mom . . . it's human." My voice was delicate as air, more surprise than sound. She never talked about her family.

"When I was a kid, I would chop sabji with her and help get the flour ready to make praunté. There was this one time when I was ten, I asked if I could flip the praunté on the stove. And she was *so* proud. Like I was growing into the woman she wanted me to be. And I was so excited to see her happy with me that I would practice making praunté and sabji and naan whenever I had a spare minute. Even when she wasn't in the kitchen. It was the same with school. I would try *so hard* just for that look of approval. I wanted Dad to be happy with me as well, but it was different with Mom."

"Why?"

"My dad just wasn't that interested in me. He dreamed of a son and when I was all he got, his disappointment never went away. Mom never actually said it, but I always felt like she needed me to be perfect to prove something to him. And the rest of his family. I was the only child she had, so . . . she had no place else to spread her expectations." She paused. "Sahaara, you know that I love you, right?"

"I know. I love you, too." I laughed softly. "So, what happened to the Goody Two-shoes? Where'd the rebel come from?"

She smiled sadly. "Just life, I suppose. Reality. There came a time—a breaking point—when I realized that I could try and try and try to make Mom happy, but it would never be enough."

At some point, the radio station had gone from old-school songs to Punjabi news. The AM 1550 host chattered away about the farming crisis in Punjab. Mom stared at the gray carpet as if she was elsewhere.

"I was upset about Sunny."

"Who?"

"That guy I went to see on Halloween," I said with the teaspoon of courage that Mom's honesty had offered me. "I . . . like him and we had plans for lunch today. I sat there at Boston Pizza for an hour, looking like an idiot all alone. He never showed up."

Whatever was on Mom's mind suddenly evaporated and her expression snapped from sad to that familiar look of anger and worry. "What? I thought you were shopping with Jeevan. Sahaara—" She paused, absorbing the way my eyes pleaded, asking her not do this right now. The cement in her tone softened. "I'm sorry. I'm just trying to wrap my head around this."

"I've liked him for a while," I admitted, unsure how much more detail to divulge.

"Didn't you say he was a nice boy?"

"He *is* nice. But he wasn't good to me, if that makes sense."

She leaned in, a fraction closer. "Wait—do you mean—did he hurt you?"

"Mom," I sighed, "the only thing he hurt are my feelings."

Her body seemed to relax, but she said, "That hurt matters, too."

"Guess so. We've got bigger stuff to worry about, though. University, the money stuff . . ." I didn't add "fixing her papers" to the list. Saying it aloud was always stress-inducing.

Mom was quiet. She stood, returning to the laundry, building tall stacks of shirts and pants and underwear.

"Ahead of Punjab's election for chief minister next year, we already have some news about potential candidates . . ." Raminder Thandi droned over the radio.

She dropped a mauve sports bra beside folded pants. "You shouldn't have to worry about money. You deserve to just be a kid. You're allowed to be sad about a boy without feeling guilty. It's—it's my fault you feel like this, that you think about crap that shouldn't be on your mind. And I'm sorry, Sahaara. I really am sorry for drawing you into my problems."

My eyes widened in disbelief. I couldn't remember the last time Mom had apologized to me. What the hell had gotten into her?

". . . former DGP Hari Ahluwalia is also reportedly considering running for chief minister . . ."

"I appreciate the apology, but—hey, are you okay?"

The sweatpants in her hands slipped through her fingers, landing in the laundry basket. She turned, swift and silent, carrying away the basket before I could tell her that she had no reason to be sorry.

just look at me

i followed you to the bedroom
where you did what you did
whenever your sorrow
was too much to carry

you hid your face
wouldn't meet my gaze
refused to stare at the being
you brought into this world

there were days when my shoulders ached
but even in the heaviest moments
i wouldn't have traded you for a lighter load

please, just look at me
i thought
so you can see how much
you are loved

coping

it had been one month and two weeks
of me refusing to look at sunny
when he passed by in the hallway
(even when i could feel his gaze
warming the nape of my neck)
and sunny trying but failing
to get my attention in class

and i was okay.
and i was smiling.
and i was counting
everything that gave me joy
besides his twinkling eyes.

my random-point-in-the-year resolution

(because new year's resolutions didn't seem to work)

was to give more of my time and heart and spirit
to the ones who cared about me
and less to the ones whose love i had to chase

i came to this resolution
on a gorgeous mid-may afternoon
at the sight of mom in my lavender maxi dress
sitting in the grass with the sun pouring gold
over her whisper-brown skin

while the smell of her home-cooked praunté
shamelessly wafted through the park
because our culture wouldn't make us shrink

mom's steady presence
promised i was whole
even when that void in my stomach
told me otherwise.

a thread of joy, severed

Mom and I climbed the cement stairs that led to the SkyTrain station. We could've avoided the train with my shiny new license but she was terror-stricken when I suggested that I try driving on the highway. I was a good driver, I swear, but every time she sat down in the passenger seat, she prayed like she would meet death. The drama.

The white Expo Line train turned up precisely on time. We found two seats in the back, where a diminutive woman eyed up the lavender maxi dress I'd somehow convinced Mom to wear. She rubbed her naked skin where soft goose bumps had risen. "Maybe I should've worn something else. I don't really like showing my arms. . . ."

Just as I was about to go off on a speech about self-love and modesty and the patriarchy, my phone vibrated with a text from Jeevan.

Jeevan: Call me please. Dad got into fight with Mom. I called the cops and they arrested him. Mom is talking to a cop rn.

Every hair on my body rose in sharp unison. "Mom, look . . ." I croaked, tilting the phone toward her.

She gasped. "Call him. Now."

"Hey. Sahaara?" I could barely make out Jeevan's words through the piercing buzz of the SkyTrain.

"Jeevan? What happened?!"

"My dad started yelling at my mom about—about some stupid shit. Like, the typical shit. And I started yelling back. And my mom—she told me to stop and just stay out of it. So I took Keerat and we—we just went to the park. Like, I tried to cool down or whatever. And—and then, like, after an hour we came back and—and—" His words were fractured like he was fighting back tears.

"And then what happened?"

"When I came back . . . fuck, man."

"What happened?"

"He had, like, fucked up her face—" His voice cracked at the last word and the phone went quiet. His silence was punctuated by sobs.

"Holy shit. Holy shit, Jeevan. Is she okay?" I barely breathed.

"We're at the hospital. She's talking to a cop in the room."

"Jeevan . . . oh my god. Are you okay? How's Keerat?"

"I'm fine. Keerat was shaking. She's sitting with Mom right now. I'm, like, numb. I can't even process what the fuck just happened."

"Okay—um—if you guys wanna stay over at our house tonight, come over, okay?" I looked over at Mom for approval and she quickly nodded, hand over her heart in worry. "And I think you should stay with your mom while she's talking to the cops."

"Shit. Yeah, I should. Okay, I'm gonna go. I'll text you."

"Love you guys."

"I love you, too."

As soon as I hung up, Mom asked what had happened. "Remember when you said you thought his dad could get violent?" I sighed. "You were right. His dad beat up his mom."

"Hai rabba." Mom shook her head. "Jeevan called the police?"

"Yeah, I think so."

"I don't know if that was a good idea. . . ."

"What do you mean?"

"The cops will complicate things. What if he doesn't go to jail?"

"Shit. That's true. . . ." My stomach sank as I imagined Jeevan's dad coming home, electric with fury. Their family wasn't safe.

"And what about Keerat? She's young. What if social workers get involved?"

"But did they really have a choice? His dad could've done way worse if they didn't get people involved."

Mom nodded sadly, hands clenched together in her lap. Heartbreak held my body just as I knew it grasped hers. All I wanted was for my loved ones to be safe and, somehow, this was too much to ask for.

The setting sun glistened through the dirty train window as the tracks curved left. I watched as Surrey bloomed before me, a city as beautiful and troubled as its people. "This is . . . *Gateway*," called the robotically calm intercom voice as the train slowed to a halt.

"One more stop," I murmured as a crowd of passengers spilled from the train. Just before the doors closed with the three chimes that signified imminent departure, two transit cops entered. The first, an older white woman with graying hair. The second, a young Asian man wearing a grimace. Mom's shoulder tensed against mine. She hugged her purse close.

"Mom, it's okay," I whispered into her ear. "I think they're just checking for payments and stuff. Try to relax." So easy for me to say when I wasn't the one in constant danger of deportation.

The Asian cop inspected each seat ahead of us, all empty save for two turbaned men chattering away in Punjabi. As he approached, his thumbs were tucked into his police belt, his arms puffed outward. In a moment of nerves, Mom caught his eye and immediately jerked her head toward the window. I could practically feel her heart thumping out of her chest.

"How are you, ma'am?" the officer asked.

She mumbled something inaudible without looking away from the window. God, I wanted to ease her panic, but I had no idea how. Her anxiousness would only make him suspicious.

"Would I be able to see both of your Compass Cards? And some ID?"

"Sure," I answered for both of us. My voice was steady, but my heart was suddenly racing as well. I handed him my transit pass and driver's license as Mom rifled through her purse. She found her Compass Card and passed it to him. He scanned both cards and nodded.

"And can I see some ID?"

"Oh, um—" Mom began.

I quickly interjected. "This is my aunt. She's visiting from Punjab. I think she left all that stuff at home."

The officer silently watched Mom's expression. Then he nodded in my direction. "Okay, let her know that she should carry her visa documentation with her." He spoke to me as if she wasn't sitting right there.

"Definitely!" I carefully stood up as the train doors opened at Surrey Central. "This is our stop. Excuse me." Mom and I slid past the cop and hurried out of the train. We squeezed our way through the crowd of commuters and didn't look back until we reached Simon Fraser University.

When the heavy glass door shut behind us, I looked at Mom: she was violently shivering.

"Mom, it's okay! We're fine. We're safe." I tried to reach for her hand, but she pulled away.

"We need to keep going," she said, throat quivering, muscles clenched. "What if he comes back? What if—"

"Mom, it's fine . . . he's not gonna come this way. Let's go home?"

Her round eyes darted across the atrium and over my shoulder. Through the glass doors of the university, the cement train station stood in plain view. "But—but he saw your license. The address. The house address."

I looked helplessly from her skittish eyes to her ticking hands. I wondered whether she was right, whether someone would be waiting at the house when we reached home. "Okay, umm . . . why don't we go sit somewhere in the university for a while? The library or . . . one of the study areas." The university tower was an Egyptian labyrinth, but I could sort of remember my way around from our twelfth-grade tour.

I guided Mom up several escalators, whooshing past uninterested students. I took a left and ran into a row of study rooms, their glass windows long and curtainless. Not what we needed. At the end of the walkway, there was a tiny room tucked into a corner, its blinds half-drawn.

"I think we're allowed in here . . ." I said. Mom shut the door behind us and began to pace back and forth.

"Try to calm down. Your breathing, remember?"

She jerked her chin at my suggestion after a few moments, as if my words were reaching her through water. She was elsewhere, drowning.

"Let's do it together. Deep breath in. One . . . two . . . three . . . four. And exhale. One . . . two . . . three . . . four."

She followed my lead and I watched her chest slowly rise and fall.

"We're safe. We're together. No one is coming. We did fine, Mom. We're okay."

"Okay." She nodded. "Okay."

"I'm gonna find a full-time job this summer. Roop was telling me that her cousins own a blueberry farm in Abbotsford. They're looking for full-time packers, like ten-hour-a-day shifts. I could work there till September and save up as much as I can before school starts. We just need to get this immigration stuff done with. Once and for all."

She didn't speak but she slowed her pace.

prom

electric by alina baraz played
& i refused to let it be sunny's song
so i reached for jeevan and he placed
a hand on the small of my back
in this long black dress
that was a sore thumb
in a sea of pastel

carry me home by jorja smith played
& i rested my head on his chest
& i didn't care who was watching
or what they thought of us
or what they thought we are

too good at goodbyes by sam smith played
& jeevan leaned into my ear
so i could hear him over the music
& asked if i would always be by his side

& i wiped the tear from his eye.

grad caps & feels

roop and i had barely spoken since she and jeevan broke up
but she swiftly turned to me in the dark auditorium
after i crossed the stage and accepted my scholarship
to say
you're going to art school?! so lucky!
my parents would think that's a waste of time . . .

black and white memories collided with her words.

the spring day on the skytrain with mom
    the cop we barely escaped
        the time i got my learner's permit
        although mom didn't have valid id
           all the bullshit she tolerated at work
           barely getting paid despite her long hours

i counted each tear-drenched night
when i was carried to dawn
with the hope of mom's pr card
finally reaching our hands

my mother wanted me in art school
more than she wanted her own breath
so i honored her wishes
accepting an opportunity
that would never again land at my doorstep

one that had, perhaps, found me in the wrong lifetime.

we didn't go to dry grad

instead, miguel played on my phone
wafting through bear creek park
with smoke that emanated
from jeevan's blunt

the sky went from golden hour divine
to breathtaking, cotton candy pink
as we sat there on our favorite green bench
and laughed about every beautiful thing
we could recall of the year
and cast away every dark memory
with the warm summer wind
as if we were just two teenagers
who were not weather-worn
beneath their skin

i'll be good by the weekend
miguel sang
as my head found its way
to jeevan's shoulder
and his arm wrapped around me
in that comfortable, easy way
that could only exist among friends
who knew each other better
than they knew themselves

things'll be good
jeevan said.
i promise.

i believe you.

this summer

wanted to be a beach
and a brand-new bathing suit

instead it was a conveyor belt full of blueberries
and a night shift in a cold warehouse

jeevan and i stood on opposite sides
of the most boring parade in history
picking out the rotten fruit before
it got packaged and shipped to wherever

when the supervisor went back to his office
jeevan flicked a blueberry at my head
and started a war he wasn't ready for

javier, a migrant worker from guaymas
with three children and a sick wife
who he called every lunch break
looked over and shook his head

said we worked like we could afford to
lose our jobs.

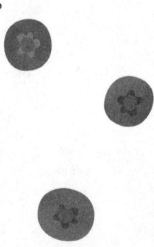

the last days of august
were slipping through our fingers

home early from work for once
mom joined bibi and me for our evening ritual
of watching the punjabi news broadcast
and poring over current affairs
with cinnamon cha in hand

there was a food drive in surrey
a unit at the hospital had been renamed
a forest fire blazed beneath the dry summer sun

and then came the news
that left the room pin-drop silent

a punjabi international student
had been arrested by border security
for working more hours
than his student visa permitted

no one needed to speak
for the same thought to be rippling
through each of our minds:

mom was working forty-three hours a week
with no work visa at all.

the fight at the restaurant

i know i shouldn't have
i know i should've held my tongue
i know there were only fifteen minutes left
until the end of this overtime shift

but i snapped

the red in her eyes could've matched her hair

and i suddenly wished i hadn't said
the pay is shit and you make your employees
work like dogs

the new cooks silently stared
eyes darting between the two of us
and returning to each other
waiting to see what would happen
and what it would mean for them

you should be grateful to even have a job
gurinder simmered
all these years you've worked here
i've given you extra hours
i gave you time off for your daughter
i never said a word to immigration

three tables sent their biryani back
and you have the nerve to be rude
to me?!

*i could get you deported
in a moment.*

i should get you deported.

Kiran

the butterflies in my stomach

have never been sweet. their wings scraped against
my insides and they were born with teeth.

most days, i could distract them with a painting
or a project or a pattern i could pick out from grass
or sky or water or cloth

but today was not most days.

when maasi and mom walked into the living room
i could already tell something was wrong

maasi's eyes were drained of their usual sparkle
and mom's hands were trembling
she looked like she'd just faced death

maasi's mind was scattered
just like the words she spit out

so that lady
    —gurinder—
the red-haired lady—their family
owns daman's, right?

she
    —she got into an argument
    with your mom and she—

—she threatened to report me.
mom finished her sentence

all the butterflies in my stomach
flapped their wings at once.
they circled my insides in an ugly
symphony and tried to claw their way
out.

an impossible woman

"We need to come up with a game plan—" I hardly managed to spit out my sentence before Mom bolted from the living room, whooshing past me and heading down the hallway, feet creaking loud against the hardwood. Maasi and I rushed after her, following Mom to her bedroom door.

"Let's brainstorm. We *need* to do something. We can't just wait around for Gurinder to screw us over."

Mom didn't say a word. Instead, she hovered at the door, fingers around the handle, back to both of us. Thick locks of black hair had unraveled themselves from her bun. Hair clips dangled haphazardly from her head like ornaments on a Christmas tree.

"Kiran, Sahaara's right," Joti Maasi began. "We need to plan for the worst-case scenario. She probably *was* just bluffing but we need to take every precaution possible here. We could reach out to a lawyer—"

"No," Mom said, voice unbending. She turned the knob and tried to vanish into the darkness of her bedroom. I caught the door before she managed to close it behind her. This conversation wasn't over just because she'd decided so.

"You try," Maasi whispered. She patted me on the shoulder and nudged me into Mom's room, alone.

Dull evening light settled into the room where Mom stood facing the window, clinging to her arms as if to stop herself from shivering. I fumbled for the light switch beside our family portrait. When she turned around, features fully visible, I startled at the sight of her. Her skin was a pale moon. She looked like she was about to be sick.

"Mom, it's okay! You're not alone in this." I reached for her arm to comfort her, but she recoiled, almost reflexively. The rejection stung.

"I *am* alone." She shook her head, back against the window. "I'm the only one who's gonna have to deal with this and the only one who can."

Seriously? I could've banged my head against a wall in frustration. Was Maasi not here, trying her best to help? Did I not even exist? "That's not the case at all. We're with you on this. I'm with you on this. If you would just listen to Maasi and talk to a lawyer—"

"—we can't talk to a lawyer—"

"—and get a different opinion—"

"—we just have to wait it out, Sahaara!" She took a step toward me, anger edging into her voice. "There's no talking to a lawyer."

"Why the hell not, Mom?" I hissed, no longer masking my exasperation. "Let's be real for a second. We're *not* ready to file the sponsorship papers—and we won't be for a long time. Not with the amount of money we're making. We need to find out what rights you have if Gurinder reports. A lawyer would help—"

"No, Sahaara. A lawyer would *not* help. Getting a lawyer involved would make things infinitely worse. It could put us in more danger. They could take advantage of—of the situation."

"That's not how things work—"

"That *is* how things work for women like me!" She grabbed my shoulders hard. "Women like me don't run into strangers who come along and miraculously make everything better. Strangers look at me and wonder what they can *take*. What benefit they can gain from my suffering. I'm not entrusting my life to some person I don't know when we've done just fine for all these years by keeping quiet."

"But Gurinder . . ."

"I'll get back in her good books," Mom pleaded. "I'll keep my head down at work. I'll take her bloody overtime shifts. I'll watch my tongue when she pushes at me. Please, just trust me. I can handle this."

financial planning

even if i worked full time
and mom didn't get fired (or worse)

the sponsorship papers
would still be a distant horizon

mom's pleading eyes
etched crimson with exhaustion
fluttered in my mind
as i imagined another life:

one that didn't feel impossible.

dead prez bumped

over my truck speakers
and jeevan sat in the passenger seat
gazing into the darkness

he was quiet just like me
because neither of us knew
what we could do for mom
if she refused to let anyone help

my vibrating phone slivered the silence

i blinked at the message
from a number i knew by heart
even though i'd deleted his name
months ago

tell me why
the nervous fluttering in my stomach
came to rest when he texted

tell me why
i barely heard jeevan when he said
are you gonna tell him off?

tell me why
the anger evaporated
just long enough for me to do
exactly what i'd promised myself
i wouldn't

of course, i responded to sunny.

my mind was a whirlpool

and i was drowning

sunny was back
and my heart was already thawing
for a boy who was only good
at goodbyes

mom was in danger
sitting in the sharp-toothed mouth
of an entire world that was ready
to swallow her whole

and i was a day away from university
wondering now more than ever
whether art school was
a catastrophic mistake

there was no way
to breathe out all this
anxiety.

a series of collisions in the parking lot

Raindrops gathered on the windshield as I waited for Mom outside the train station. Of all the joys my driver's license had bought, the greatest was being able to help her get around. I always felt like shit when she had to wait for the bus in the rain.

Over the radio, Billie Eilish bemoaned her fickle ex-lovers and my fingers itched for my phone, but I refused to text Sunny first. As if on cue, my phone vibrated.

It was Jeevan.

> Jeevan: How u feeling?
>
> Sahaara: I don't know, honestly. Just trying not to think about everything.
>
> Sahaara: My stomach is still in knots, though.
>
> Jeevan: ☹
>
> Jeevan: Like I said, we're gonna figure this out together. Right now, just try to breathe?
>
> Sahaara: Trying.

The truth was, no matter what—or who—I tried to distract myself with, nothing was working. Last Friday was red and raw in my mind. Maasi had sounded so sure that Gurinder wouldn't call immigration, that she wouldn't put her own business at risk just to get back at Mom. But the odds, however favorable, weren't enough to settle my stomach. Over the past days, I had tried to distract myself with a sketch or a new painting or a deep dive into a poetry book. The maelstrom of anxiety would only settle momentarily, though, stronger than any stupid idea about grounding.

Sahaara: Honestly, that aunty is so ridiculous. Who threatens to report an undocumented person just because they're mad about biryani?

Jeevan: Yup. So dumb. My mom knows her too. She said she just runs her mouth a lot. I wouldn't stress.

Sahaara: I know. But still. It just makes me so fkn angry that she would say something like that to my mom. Like someone else's life is a joke.

A part of me wanted to cry, but Mom would be out of the station any minute. The last thing she needed right now was the sight of me sobbing over all this. I changed the subject.

Sahaara: Anyways...don't kill me but I hung out with Sunny.

Jeevan: ...

Sahaara: He asked how you were doing

Jeevan: Lol. Did he bother asking how *you* are?

Sahaara: :/

Jeevan: Idk Sahaara. You already know what it is with him. But you do what you want.

Sahaara: What's that supposed to mean?

Jeevan: I'm sorry...that didn't come out right. I'm half asleep. Can we talk about this tomorrow?

Sahaara: Cool.

Jeevan began to type. Oh god. It was a long message. I could feel irritation swelling within me even though I knew he meant well. I didn't need a lecture right now. I needed a hug.

As I looked up in exasperation, my breath faltered. The whirring in my head, constantly reminding me of what needed doing, suddenly went silent. Even the butterflies stopped fluttering.

I forgot how to breathe as a uniformed police officer guided my mom into the back seat of his car.

"WHERE ARE YOU TAKING HER?!" came a voice that felt detached from my body. I sprinted across the parking lot as a car slammed its brakes to avoid colliding with me. The sound of his car horn only existed in the distance.

"We have concerns about this woman's immigration status. We're holding her until CBSA arrives," replied the officer, with a voice that was far too calm for the moment that was shattering my world. Head downturned, Mom wouldn't look at me. I wasn't sure if it was because of pride or shame. In Mom's case, it might have been the same thing.

I don't know when I began to cry but my words left my mouth between sobs: "That's my mom. Can I talk to her? Can you open the window?"

The officer eyed me warily and then reached inside to lower the window.

"Mom?" It's all that managed to escape my lips: the first word I learned and the only one that would ever matter. She turned and her eyes, so often guarded fortresses, filled with tears when they locked into mine. I watched as a lifetime of pain finally revealed itself across her face.

"I love you, Sahaara. It's going to be okay," she managed.

"How do you know that, Mom?"

"Just promise me you'll go to your class tomorrow." There was desperation in her voice. She was actually serious.

I laughed at the ridiculousness of this. Of everything. I laughed because I didn't know what else to do.

"Okay."

desperate measures

For eighteen years, Mom and I kept the truth of her immigration status hidden from anyone who couldn't be trusted with our lives. Mom built barbed-wire walls around her story with the belief that silence was her greatest defense. Her only option.

But here I was, standing alone in a parking lot, certain that if I had already lost everything, breaking that silence couldn't make it worse.

I hit *share* and Instagram posted my black picture and long caption. I read back my own words, wiping tears off the screen as they fell:

> *My mom is an undocumented immigrant. She's raised me as a single parent in Canada for the last eighteen years. Tonight, CBSA officers picked her up. I don't know what's happening and I don't know what to do but I can't lose her. She has worked her ass off for the last two decades just to raise me and earn her way to Canadian citizenship. She deserves to stay here. If you know *anything* about immigration and border security, PLEASE help.*

Bounding feet splashed toward me. "Sahaara!" a familiar voice called, and I was suddenly engulfed in Maasi's rain-dampened arms. "What happened?! Where'd they take her?"

"I don't know," I sobbed. "I just—I showed up at the Sky-Train and she wasn't coming out of the station but I thought she was just late and then—I saw her come out with a cop and he put her in his car. And I asked where he was taking her and he was just like—he was like, they have questions about her immigration status. And he said CBSA is coming to pick her up."

"Fuck. FUCK!" She placed a hand on her forehead and pushed back mulberry hair. "We're gonna figure this out, all right? Did he say *where* exactly they were taking her?"

"Yeah—the Immigration Detention Center. I wrote down the address. Shit! Should I have just followed the car? I wasn't even thinking."

"No, Sahaara, it's okay. Let's just calmly think this through, all right?"

I stared into her red-rimmed eyes, tears pouring from mine. "Maasi . . . what do we do?"

"We should've met with a lawyer right away. Like, right after that thing with Gurinder Aunty happened. Maybe I should've tried harder to convince her—"

"Let's just call a lawyer now," I interrupted. There was no point tearing ourselves apart over things Mom wouldn't let us do.

Within seconds, Maasi had pulled up the number for Sajjan Law Office and she was dialing. My chin tilted toward the moonless sky and I sent a desperate prayer up to whatever the hell ran this fucked-up universe. *Please, just let her be okay.*

"Hello? Oh, it's an answering machine." Maasi listened to the recording as my stomach wrung itself tight. "Hi, this is Joti Thind. I called last week about setting up a consultation for my friend who's hoping to become a Canadian citizen. My friend was taken by, um, by CBSA. Any help you could provide would be deeply appreciated. Thank you!"

"Can we leave now? To the—the detention center?" Those three words unsettled the pavement beneath my feet. Was Mom sitting in a cement cell right now? Was she being interrogated by cops? Screamed at? Being told to get the fuck out of their country?

"I'm gonna just park my car here and then let's jump into yours."

Maasi jogged across the parking lot to pay for parking and I couldn't think straight. Stillness was an impossibility when every second was sand slipping through an hourglass. I paced, endlessly circling the trunk of my car as though my motion would carry me to Mom quicker. I stared at the cement, the cars, the trees, the sky. I tried to focus on something, anything, everything, but my breath was sharp and shallow. The parking lot was a tumbling Ferris wheel propelled by my fear.

My cell phone notifications had become an almost endless buzz and I dared to look: missed calls from Jeevan, comments on my Instagram post, and a few DMs. With a deep inhale, I checked Instagram first.

Rhea Gill commented "omg ☹" on my post and Roop wrote that she was "soooo sorry." Marisol from art class commented "check DMs!" Sunny had liked the post but said nothing. No calls from him. Not even a text.

When I opened Marisol's DMs, I gasped at the flood of messages still pouring in.

Marisol: Sahaara! Omg I'm so sorry your mom was detained! I had no idea you were dealing with this.

Marisol: My cousin volunteers at All Humans Are Legal. It's this immigrant rights org that helps ppl who are undocumented.

Marisol: Hold up . . . im gonna add her to the convo

Marisol: if they're trying to deport your mom, All Humans Are Legal might be able to stop them or delay the deportation

A new conversation popped up with me, @sunandseamari, and @valeria_xoxo.

Marisol: Sahaara, this is my cousin Valeria. She's the one who volunteers at All Humans Are Legal. I screenshotted your post and sent it to her (I hope that's okay!!)

Valeria: Hi, Sahaara! I hope you and your mom are okay! Could you tell me more about the situation? My team and I will try our best to help! ❤

My fingers fumbled as I quickly typed the facts I knew like the lines on my palms. Nineteen years in Canada. Undocumented for fifteen. We were just waiting to file her sponsorship papers. We just needed a bit more money.

Valeria: Can I call you in a little while? I'm gonna see if I can get ahold of my other organizer. I just started as an intern but she's been working on cases like this for decades.

Sahaara: Yeah . . . we're gonna just drive to the immigration detention center right now . . . I'll give you a call on the way.

Valeria: the detention center at the airport?

Sahaara: yeah. fuck.

kiran

midnight, september 1, 2020

beneath a moonless sky

"P-please let me stay," I stammer. A plane tears through the night sky above me and a shiver steals through my body. When I landed at Vancouver International Airport nineteen years ago, it was a place that told me new beginnings were possible. Today, it is a portal that will return me to a cage I thought I'd escaped long ago.

The male officer chuckles without glancing back. "Ah, so you do speak." His voice is light and contemplative, like my fear is a novelty. Like it's a small excitement to an otherwise dull job. "We're actually heading to the Immigration Detention Center in the airport basement. We don't usually just throw people on flights." The woman seated beside me flashes him a look before she notices my gaze. I think she smiles but all I can see now is her clothing: it's not a typical police uniform but it doesn't matter. *CBSA* is embroidered into her black jacket and my eyes are hooked to the gun in its holster. An ugly memory begins to surface. I bite the inside of my cheek and my lungs scrape my ribs. My ribs balloon against my skin. My skin cries sweat. The air rings sharp and my mouth is metallic.

It's going to be okay. It's going to be okay. It's going to be okay. I make myself promises that I know I can't keep.

Somehow when I step inside, I can almost smell that ungodly odor from the other interrogation room. The dark place behind the veil. All those years of burying, all that work to hide from its memory, and now I am here in its dizzying reconfiguration. The other room wasn't so clean. The dampness of its concrete floor washes over me as though the time between then and now was an eyelash blinked. The sickly sourness returns, the sweat and urine trapped in that humid, windowless cage. Like this room, it was no wider than a cell, no longer than a coffin. A ringing grows in my ears, piercing louder and louder until staticky fuzz forms around the edges of my thoughts. *No. Breathe. Focus. Concentrate on where you are. Sahaara needs you to stay present.*

I study my surroundings to escape my head. To stay in my head. A black metal table rests beneath my quaking hands. Against the wall ahead of me is a large rectangular mirror. I remember the mirror from that show Joti used to watch—there was always someone standing behind the glass who could see into the room. A broken woman blinks in the fake mirror. Her eyes—my eyes—are bloodshot and puffy and exhausted. If I look at myself for a moment longer, I'm sure I'll cry again, so I guide my gaze elsewhere. The door to my left is painted a smoky gray. There's some sort of recording device sitting on a rolling cart next to the door. It reminds me of a VCR from the '90s.

The door creaks open and my heart jolts up my neck: it's the officer who was driving the car. He eases into the chair across from me but doesn't so much as glance in my direction. The details of his face are finally in focus: a thick black mustache hides his upper lip and his hairline is slightly receding. He taps his fingers on the table impatiently and doesn't bother making small talk. Every so often, he checks his phone or glances at the door. I assume he's waiting for his partner.

The cop who finally arrives is not the Asian woman who was sitting next to me in the car. This officer is Punjabi. Her auburn hair, dark against her skin, is pulled into a sleek

French braid that rests over her shoulder. She's wearing that same black polyester jacket.

"Sharon asked me to take this one," she says, and the mustached officer releases an irritated sigh.

"I'm Officer Gill. I'm with Immigration. I'm an inland enforcement officer." She extends a faint-brown hand that I struggle to shake. I want to tell myself that there could be safety in her name. That our shared ethnicity might mean she'll regard me as human. But I know power doesn't work this way. "You've already met Officer Andrews, it seems." I nod, unable to maintain eye contact. My gaze moves to my hands and stays there.

"How are you, Kiran?" she asks.

I nod as a response, eyes still lowered.

"Officer Mathews had concerns about your legal status. He said you weren't able to show him proper Canadian ID and he had some questions about your background."

I remain silent and she takes this as a cue for her next question. "Do you have a lawyer that you'd like to represent you? If you don't have one, we can assign one to you."

"No, I—I don't have a lawyer."

"So you'd like us to assign one?"

She wants to assign me a lawyer? Do they work for the police? Can I trust them? I think back to all the reasons for my silence. The men I willingly followed into danger because their names and suits and certifications lulled my instincts.

Through gnawing fear, I say yes. There's nothing else I can do.

When she places the lawyer on the phone, the two officers leave the room. He asks me just as many questions as the cop on the SkyTrain platform and I don't know which ones to answer. I reluctantly tell him about Sahaara, how I overstayed the student visa, how I've been here for nineteen years. I don't know if I should tell him why. The cement walls and officers standing just outside remind me that I can't trust anyone.

His voice is static over the phone. "And your daughter was born in Canada, correct?"

"Yes." At her mention, the lawyer's voice becomes distant and I am swallowed by my thoughts. If they deport me, I know I can rely on Joti and Aunty Jee. She'll have a roof over her head. She'll be okay.

I've lost track of his words for some time but hear him clearly when he says, "You should tell them about your daughter."

The questions come like rapid fire. So fast that there's hardly time to prepare my responses.

"So where were you coming from when you got off the SkyTrain?" Officer Gill asks.

"Vancouver."

"What were you doing in Vancouver?"

I hesitate. She can't know that I was working. "I was eating dinner."

"Who were you eating with?"

"I—um—I was with my friend. Joti." Shit. I probably shouldn't have said that.

"And where does she live?"

"Surrey."

"Was she on the train with you?"

"Yeah—she—she got off the train on the stop before—at Surrey Central."

"And how do you know her?"

"I used to go to university with her."

"Where did you study?"

"At Simon Fraser."

"And you were going to SFU as an international student? What were you studying there?"

"Biology . . . and yes. An international student." Shit. Shit. Shit. I'm spilling everything. Should I be saying all this? Fear draws all the words off my tongue and eats away any semblance of a plan.

"So, I'm guessing you were here on a student visa?"

My back hot and sweaty, I shift in the chair. "Yes."

"And that would've expired in 2004 based on what you've shared. So why didn't you return home at the end of your time in university? Did you finish your biology program?"

Although my head is lowered, their expectant gazes burn into me. If the interrogation is a test, this question is simply pass or fail. I search silently for an answer I never studied for. Each escaping second quickens my heartbeat, proving my guilt.

The male officer speaks before I find my tongue.

"Officer Mathews—the one you spoke to at the SkyTrain— he said your daughter was there to pick you up. Tell us about her. Where was she born?"

"In Canada."

"Is her father Canadian?" The churning engine that is my stomach reignites with a roar.

"No."

With the slightest upward glance, I watch him turn to Officer Gill. "Something isn't right here," he says as if I am a TV show, a topic to discuss and not a human who can hear. "I got more questions about this one."

"Hmm." Officer Gill notes something down on a piece of paper.

Officer Andrews returns his attention to me. "Is he here as well? The father?" The mention of him in *this* room is propane to my terror. The back of my neck prickles.

"No."

"So, where is he?"

"I—I don't know." *Eyes to your palms. Stay calm. Breathe.*

"Don't wanna talk about him? What's the story?" I glance up, despite myself, and there they are: two ice-pick eyes piercing straight through mine. Just like another pair once stared emptily into me, demanding that I look.

I try to tell myself that he's not the same man. That this isn't the same. But it's too late: the curtain is ripped away and I am eighteen once again.

behind the veil

and here
i imprison a truth i cannot hide from

because although the memory
handcuffs my body without permission

i wield my own pen
and all i've ever begged for is control

no one needs this poem

it is dark in my blood
and nothing to be relived

and even if i recounted
the visceral details

the gruesome retelling
was never enough evidence, anyway.

i will always be guilty.

the veil tears

"Miss Kaur? Kiran? Are you all right?" Officer Gill asks.

"I—I—I—" I heave through sobs but can't go on. The whole room is whirling.

"Can I get you some water?"

"I—can't—CAN'T—go back. He's there—in Punjab—and the election—please—please don't—please. I'm begging you. Please let me stay." I give up on words and cry into my open, thrashing palms.

"What do you mean, Kiran? Are you in danger?" Her voice is quiet. "Take your time."

I jerk my head to nod without removing my hands from my eyes.

"Are you in danger from someone in India? In Punjab?"

I nod again.

"Would you be able to explain who this person is and what danger you're in?"

I look her in the eye, not with courage but with something more brazen. Reckless and hopeless and desperate all at once. "I was raped. When I was eighteen. By my fiancé's brother. He was the DGP—the chief of police—of Punjab. Hari—Hari Ahluwalia. And—and—I didn't know what to do. I was pregnant and I was moving to Canada for school. And I thought I could start a new life here. And be safe. But my visa expired and I can't go back to Punjab. I have nowhere to go and what if—what if he finds me?—and my daughter—she's Canadian. Please. I can't leave her."

Officer Gill nods slowly as I speak. Officer Andrews crosses his arms as he surveys me intently. He says, "We have no record of you filing for asylum status in all the years you've been here." He cocks his head. "Why is that?"

"Because—because I couldn't go back. I can't go back. What if the asylum request got rejected? What if—what if—and the immigration consultant told me that my daughter could sponsor me. She's eighteen now. She's a Canadian citizen. She can sponsor me. We just need more time—we'll have the money. Please, just let me stay until she can sponsor me. For her sake, let me stay. Please."

The two officers glance at each other. "No asylum filing," the man scoffs, speaking again as if I'm not here. He folds his puffed arms tight across his chest, surveying me at his leisure.

"Regardless," she murmurs. "Could still be filed as humanitarian and compassionate grounds for the daughter."

For a moment, the officers wordlessly tussle. Arms still crossed over his chest, the man shakes his head and then curtly motions for Officer Gill to speak.

She turns her attention to me. "Kiran, based on what you've shared with us, there *may* be grounds for you to stay in Canada. It could be possible for the IRCC to offer you a path to citizenship."

"What—what do you mean?" I whisper.

"You can file your permanent resident application. We'll be doing a check-in after thirty days on the status of the application, but tonight, we'll be releasing you from custody."

At the sound of these words, I lose my breath. The relief spilling from my eyes is something I've only experienced once before in this rotting carcass of a lifetime.

It is as if I'm cradling my baby girl for the first time.

sahaara
september 2020–february 2021

if i tell you the truth

that i've dug
from the hardened depths
of this shrapnel-filled dirt
with these aching, bloody hands
would you believe me?

would you still love me?

the unspeakable

"Mom?"

My phone nearly slips from my fingers when I see her running toward us. After every reassurance that Valeria had given me, it's only the physical sight of Kiran Kaur that allows me to breathe. My feet can't carry me fast enough. There is no wall between us. I reach for her, I hold her, I cry into her arms, and she does the same in mine. She wraps herself around me and cradles my head against her chest, refusing to let go, clinging to me like we have both made it out of a burning house alive.

"What happened? What did they say?!"

"They're giving us time, Sahaara," Mom weeps. "We can file the application. There's a chance—we might—we can fix this." Every razor-winged butterfly that has ever haunted my stomach escapes as water pours from my eyes. Tomorrow, there will be lawyers and questions and forms and uncertainty, but right now, Mom is warm and near. Just as present as a human can be. The feeling that holds every inch of my skin can only be named *love*.

"Kiran," Joti Maasi whispers after she's given us our moment. She engulfs Mom in a bear hug and smiles at me over Mom's shoulder. That familiar twinkle returns to her teary eyes. "Let's get the hell out of here."

The early morning drive home is quiet. Mom is too exhausted to talk, and I do my best to keep my eyes open so that Maasi has some company. I peek at Mom in the back seat. She's pulled off her jacket and placed it over herself like a blanket. Her head rests heavily against the back window. Gratitude flushes through me at the peaceful sight of her.

"You can sleep, Sahaara," Maasi murmurs. "Don't worry. I'm fine. This day was way too fucking long."

My drooping eyelids don't take much convincing and I give in to the warm exhaustion that tugs me elsewhere. When I open my eyes, we're home.

"Mom, wake up." I gently reach for her leg and she's startled awake.

"What—oh," she says, blinking sleep from her eyes.

As Maasi groggily leaves the car, Mom's voice stops her. "Can we, um, can we talk when we get inside?"

"Of course." She yawns.

The three of us sink into the hearth of my bed. I'd forgotten to turn off the heater before I left home, so the room is deliciously toasty. Maasi sifts through the stack of immigration forms that Mom was given, eyes narrowing as she tries to decipher all the legal jargon. She mumbles something about a lawyer before she gives up and pulls the covers up to her neck.

As if she isn't seconds from slumber, she says "I'm awake if you wanna talk. Just resting my eyes . . ."

At the mention of "talking," Mom wrings her hands. She eyes the constellation of Polaroid pictures hanging above my bedpost, her chest quickly deflating. Dozens of family pictures greet me each time I get in bed. Her favorite is the one of us at my grad ceremony. She hung it there herself.

"What's wrong?" I reach for her knee and she flinches, but doesn't pull away like she usually does when she's upset.

"There are . . . things . . . that I haven't told you guys."

"What?! You? Not telling us stuff?" I gasp. "Just kidding. Go on . . . I'm listening."

"Sahaara . . ." She looks me square in the face, more fear than fatigue clouding her features. "You need to know what happened. It was wrong of me to keep you in the dark. If I told two cops tonight, I should have at least told you."

"Mom, you're freaking me out . . ." I nervously laugh, studying her pained expression. "What's going on?"

"Why do you think I stayed in Canada?"

"Uh, because your parents didn't want you to keep me? And 'cause Prabh Ahluwalia didn't want a kid out of wedlock?"

She sighs. "That's just part of the story, Sahaara. Prabh was my fiancé. My parents introduced us, and I was really nervous about him, but he wasn't terrible. He was romantic. And thoughtful. He treated me well. For a long time, he made me feel like I mattered. Like marriage would be some sort of ticket to happiness. I think . . . I think I could've loved him."

"But?" I whisper. The room is so quiet, I can hear her breath as though it's mine.

"But I was stupid. I was so stupid." Her eyes are glazed and red and I can't bear to look at them. I can deal with Jeevan or Sunny getting emotional. But Mom? The sight of my parent crying will always terrify me.

"It's not your fault he didn't want a kid. You couldn't have known he'd react like that."

"That's not it, Sahaara."

"What do you mean?"

"He's not your father."

I barely breathe. "I don't follow . . ."

"There was a party—a surprise party for Prabh. His brother and the rest of the family had planned it. I helped, too. It was at this lavish garden in Chandigarh. My parents were invited but Mom was sick, and Dad was out of town, as usual. I couldn't drive, so Prabh's brother offered to pick me up. I was dressed in this new lengha I'd bought just for the occasion. I remember being mortified that Prabh's mom wouldn't think it was nice enough. She was obsessed with appearances—even more than *my* mom and, hai rabba, that was a feat." She pauses here, gently grasping her thin wrist, slowly inhaling and exhaling as though trying to steady herself. "I was sitting in the car and Hari—Prabh's brother—he kept looking over at my lengha in the strangest way. It felt like he was leering at me the way boys would at the bus stop. And I didn't want to imagine he could do something so gross. He was going to be my brother-in-law. *I called him Jetha Jee.* But he kept staring and . . . I snapped. Asked him what he was looking at. And he said, 'You should cover your arms, your midriff. That top gives off the wrong idea about you.'"

"What the hell?" I seethe, the vein in my temple thrumming.

"He made me feel horrible. Like a piece of meat. And I asked what he meant by 'the wrong idea about me.' He started going on about how women want respect while they don't respect themselves. How they dress provocatively and behave like . . . whores. And then get upset when men harass them. And that just—that drove me over the edge. Because guys would always holler things at me. It didn't matter whether I was wearing a salwar kameez or jeans or a sari."

"So, did you tell him off?"

"I . . . I did. Sometimes I wish I didn't," she mumbles, and my skin is cold, staticky. She gazes at the darkened world outside my bedroom window and then ruefully returns to me. "He was a cop . . . so I told him that instead of blaming women's clothing for the shitty things men do, he should hold men accountable. And this . . . infuriated him."

"Go on . . ." I say, although I'm not sure if I want her to. I squeeze down on my wrist, pulse throbbing like my heart is everywhere, stomach acrid and gnashing.

"On the way to the party, he stopped at his police station. Told me to come inside because he left his suit there. I said I'd just wait in the car, but he *insisted* I join him. He said it wasn't safe for me to sit outside alone at that hour. It was around seven in the evening, so the police station wasn't so busy, but sometimes, I don't even think it would've mattered if it was. He took me to an interrogation room. I wasn't even scared at first. Just confused and irritated that he was wasting my time when I wanted to get to this bloody garden party and make sure that all my stupid centerpieces were set up correctly. And that's where . . . that's where he . . ." She swallows and breathes deep. "I can't say the word, Sahaara. It makes me dizzy. Sick. But you know what it is."

The acid in my throat already told me where this was going, but her words still punch me in the gut and vacuum the air from my lungs. I don't know what to do or say besides resist an urge to puke. I can't even cry.

"Mom . . ." I croak after a few moments. "What the fuck? What. The. *Fuck!*" Maasi flinches in her slumber but doesn't wake.

"Afterward . . . I was shocked. Frozen inside. I couldn't even process what had happened. It was like something broke within me. Like I was a jammed clock or something. And . . . I got back in the car—his car. And I went to the party. And I acted like everything was fine because I didn't want to ruin Prabh's birthday. His mom saw a tear in my lengha and she scolded me for it. I was so numb . . . I just apologized. A few weeks later, I found out I was pregnant. And I—I was so desperate. I needed something—someone—to hold on to. So I held on to you." As Mom speaks, my face burns hot and red. Rage courses through every inch of my skin. Through every goose bump and hair on my body. I want to break something. I want to break him. I want to break all of them. I don't know why I'm sitting in Canada right now when I should be in Punjab tearing the flesh off his bones.

"Did you tell Prabh?"

"I did. And he took his brother's side. Didn't believe me for a second." She draws her ivory cashmere sweater closer, as if a chill is passing through the room. Hunched forward, her waifish body shivers. Her vulnerability pours rage into me like a corrosive fuel. How could anyone dare to put their hands on her?

"Fuck him. And his brother and his stupid fucking family. We're here and they can't do shit about it." I cuss without a filter and she doesn't stop me.

"Sometimes, it feels like I can't get away from him . . ." Mom shakes her head, wiping tears with her sweater.

"What do you mean?"

"Hari Ahluwalia, Sahaara. That's Prabh's brother. The one who's running for chief minister of Punjab."

hari ahluwalia

despite myself, i google his name
and like a car crash
i cannot look away
although the sight is chilling

there i am
etched into his jawline
and his chiseled cheekbones
and his slightly protruding ears

this is why
i am restless until dawn.

tonight
i want to peel away my skin

break free my eyes

drain the blood from my veins

empty every last drop

that was placed within me
by a monster

tonight
i wonder

whether any goodness can exist

in a body made from

coldness and fear

tonight
i want to give myself back.

homage to kiran kaur's 'how i left my body'

the next morning

the veil slivers my tongue as it closes
and once more, the nightmare
is too volatile to speak aloud

i have now told the truth
exactly four times

and i don't know how
i managed to forget
the aftermath of its retelling:

the vomiting
the near-fainting
the force that flattens my lungs
and siphons oxygen from my throat

worst of all, the flashbacks.

i don't know how to explain to sahaara
why i can't tell joti the story right now.

Kiran

waking from a bad dream

What the fuck am I doing here?

If Jeevan hadn't reminded me that I could lose my spot if I didn't show up on the first day of classes, I'd still be holding Mom close, processing whatever the hell is coursing through my skin right now. Instead, I'm struggling to keep my eyes open beneath fluorescent lights, wedged between a white boy in a black beret and a girl who won't stop talking about how her *avant-garde art is completely groundbreaking.*

"I look forward to seeing you all again at the end of the week. Please remember to purchase your textbooks and complete your readings *before* our next session, as we'll be jumping right into our discussion about Les Nabis." Marianne LeBlanc speaks with a thick French-Canadian accent, surveys us through ice-blonde bangs. She is both a very distinguished art critic and the teacher of my modern art course. If my mind and body weren't still reeling from the night, I'd probably be a little more starstruck to be here.

The room is just a notch larger than one of my high school classrooms and, somehow, this calms me a tiny bit. I already miss the comfort of Jameson, the safety of its familiarity. Instead of desks, the room is filled with long rows of hardwood tables, six students crammed into each one. There isn't a single empty chair in this course with a waitlist of at least forty students desperate to learn from Ms. LeBlanc—I mean, Marianne. Apparently, we're supposed to call teachers by their first names now.

When Marianne finally dismisses us, I'm out the door before anyone has even gathered their textbooks. The stairs leading to the parking tower are down the left corridor past the Starbucks—I think? I speed walk in the direction that feels right, periwinkle canvas bag slung over my shoulder. If I leave campus now, I could be back in Surrey by three p.m. I won't miss the meeting with All Humans Are Legal.

Last night lingers in my chest. It could've been longer than a lifetime. Somewhere between the mess of Mom getting detained, me calling Valeria, Mom being released and then telling me about Hari Ahluwalia, the anxiety in my chest unraveled and tightened a thousand times over. Right now, my stomach is fluttering. Bubbling. Prickling. I am composed only of sharp edges.

When I sink into the driver's seat in my truck, I catch an accidental glimpse of myself in the rearview mirror. My whole body recoils at the sight. For years, I thought that if I ever uncovered the truth about my biological father, I'd feel a liberating sense of closure, like the missing pieces of me were complete. Instead, I awoke in a body that is more foreign than before. I am a stranger. An echo of violence.

Evidence of a crime.

Those ugly moments rise in my throat. The times when I'd get pissed at Mom for keeping me in the dark. For telling me so little about him and the rest of his family. The worst of them was in ninth grade, when Mom was lecturing me about homework. I got so goddamn frustrated with her breathing down my throat that I said I wished I knew my father because he was probably less suffocating than her. The recollection makes me wanna puke.

After all those lonely nights of wondering where I came from, here I am, more lost than ever.

Jeevan grins through the hazy glass window of the coffee

shop when I finally make it back to Surrey. Mom is right beside him, adjusting and readjusting her blue ombre shawl and marigold kurti. With Maasi working an early shift at the hospital, Jeevan canceled a counseling session to come in her place. He insisted on being here for us, despite me promising that we'd be cool on our own. My heart swells at the sight of his sweet smile and curly head of hair. Honestly, I don't know what I'd do without him.

Two women I don't recognize are seated across from Jeevan and Mom. They turn to wave at me and I feebly wave back. The younger one must be Valeria.

"Hiii, Sahaara! Nice to see you face-to-face!" Valeria stands to politely hug me. Up close, I'd recognize her anywhere. She and her cousin Marisol share the exact same watery-green eyes and penny-deep dimples. Valeria gestures to the older woman. "This is Prem, one of our senior lawyers at All Humans Are Legal."

Prem stays seated but smiles kindly and shakes my hand. With her thick Kashmiri shawl draped across her body and short, gray-streaked hair, she looks much older than Mom. I glance over at Jeevan and he fist-bumps me as a greeting. His eyes follow me as I take a seat, his features marred in concern. I smile a little harder, trying to prove that I'm good.

"How's it going, Mom?" I whisper. "How you feeling?"

"Better than yesterday, I suppose." She looks utterly relieved by the sight of me.

"Sahaara, we were just chatting with Kiran about the work we do with undocumented immigrants," Prem says. "Truly, I wish we'd met sooner. I'm so sorry that you were dealing with all this in isolation."

"Yeah. It's been . . . hard. We weren't sure where to go for help. It was scary, like, thinking she could get reported if we talked to the wrong person. So, we tried to just wait it out, until . . ."

"Shit hit the fan?" Valeria interjects, head resting on her palm.

"Basically."

"This really isn't uncommon." Prem removes her glasses and rests her folded hands on the table. "In a lot of the cases we deal with, there's so much fear about getting deported that people suffer in silence for years. And, of course, there are those who take advantage of that fear."

"Like Mom's manager," I sigh. Steam billows from cups of cha that almost smell homemade. They sit before everyone at the table except for me. Jeevan picks up an empty glass and pours me a cup without prompting.

"Right." Prem nods and takes a sip of her tea. "Kiran was saying her manager threatened to call immigration on her. Oftentimes, employers like that hire undocumented people just because they know they can pay them less and overwork them. Who would they tell if they were being mistreated?"

Eyes weary despite her smile, Mom says, "Well, hopefully at the end of all this, I'll be able to work somewhere else. I mean, as long at the PR application gets accepted."

"Yes, that's the goal." Valeria taps a thick fountain pen against the hot-pink cover of her journal. "And we're here to offer support in any way you need. We'll work with you on your application and we'll be here every step of the way."

My gaze wanders to her gray crewneck. ALL HUMANS ARE LEGAL is emblazoned across the chest in bold white lettering. The fearless declaration is badass as hell. I think back to all the years of fear and silence, to Mom's dread that the wrong person would hear about her status and shatter our future.

A new reality sinks in as my eyes rove the table. We're a group of brown people sitting in a crowded public space speaking the word *undocumented* aloud as if it won't leave us at the scene of a crime.

Prem puts on her glasses and pores over the forms that Mom brought with her, nodding occasionally. "So, when we file your PR application, we'll want to include as much information as possible to explain why you need to stay in Canada. Reasons why you couldn't go back home to Punjab, info about Sahaara. Everything that will highlight to the government why it's imperative you remain here."

Clinging to her blue mug of cha, Mom doesn't take a sip. "Can you tell them what you told me?" I gently ask. "I think it would help your case . . ." There's no way her application could get rejected if they understood what he did.

"I, um, I . . ." Mom rests a hand over her chest as though trying to soothe her pounding heart. "I can't. I can't talk about it. Not . . . again. Is there another way?"

"It's okay," I whisper, studying Mom's quaky lower lip, a bramble of questions tangled within me. Last night, she shared more than she had over the course of my entire life. It was as though she was unfurling. Stepping out of fear. Today, she's once again a locked door.

"It's all right, Kiran," Prem kindly says. "If you do feel like disclosing that information and you feel it would be pertinent to the application, we're always here. But we did want to begin by noting that you have a strong case simply because of Sahaara." The entire table glances at me and then returns to Prem. "As you have a Canadian citizen daughter, we can write about how you've made Canada your home with her for the past nineteen years. For humanitarian and compassionate reasons, you would be asking the government not to separate you."

"The officers said something about that as well . . ." Mom rests her mug on the table. "Something about humanitarian and compassionate grounds."

"Ah, okay. I thought they might," Valeria murmurs, jotting something down in her journal. "There's a really good precedent for cases like this. We just finished working on one that was pretty similar—Canadian-born child and a migrant parent. The father got his PR card a few months ago."

I watch as hope softens Mom's brow and steadies her hands.

"If our application based on these grounds does get rejected, there are other strategies we can employ." Prem serenely smiles. "But I would say that I'm . . . cautiously optimistic."

"Okay." The corners of Mom's lips slowly rise into a smile but soon fall with the gravity of another worry. "But what about the money? Sahaara isn't earning enough to sponsor me yet."

"It *should* be possible to apply with a joint sponsorship," Valeria replies.

Mom shakes her head in soft confusion. "What do you mean?"

"It isn't unusual for multiple people to sponsor an immigrant. You were telling us you live with a local family, yes?" Prem asks.

"My friend Joti—" Mom nods. "We live at her mom's house."

"Joti Maasi and Bibi Jee are like family," I add. "The only people we can really depend on."

"Would Joti be in a position to co-sponsor with you, Sahaara?" Valeria inquires.

"I think so," I say, watching tension practically ease from Mom's clenched shoulders. We both know that if there's a way Maasi can help, she'll insist on it. For my aunt, family comes before all else. "We'd have to discuss with her, but I have a good feeling she'll be on board."

"Woooonderful," Prem melodically hums, stirring her tea with a metal spoon, before taking another sip. "Kiran, there was also something we wanted to discuss with you. And there's absolutely no rush or timeline on this, but we've been debriefing all of our clients on the project, just in case they might be interested."

Mom steals a glance at me. She nods slowly and Prem takes this as her cue to go on. "There are so many people out there who have similar stories to yours—migrants who want to seek support but don't know where to go or who to trust. Fear often stops them from speaking and we want to help change this. If there ever comes a time when you feel comfortable sharing any portion of your migration story publicly, we'd love to help facilitate that."

For the first time today, the fluttering, writhing feeling beneath my skin goes still. "What do you mean?" I ask.

"We've been filming social media content with our clients," Valeria explains, "and setting up interviews with the media. My dad was super nervous about going public at first. He decided to speak on one of our panels *after* his papers were fixed, so that eased up his nerves a bit. He ended up finding it really cathartic to let everything out."

My eyes widen at the thought of Mom on YouTube or national television speaking her truth without apology, reaching across oceans with her words. Her story could make the world a safer place for undocumented women.

For victims of sexual assault.

Even if she had the security of her PR card, I'm almost certain she'd never agree. Telling this story is so painful. I can see it right now in the deep creases on her forehead, in her fiercely clenched shoulders. But, still, I can't help but imagine it. The mere thought is mouthwatering in a bloodthirsty way. I am suddenly consumed by singular image of Mom telling the world what Hari Ahluwalia did.

i google his name again

i should be drafting my modern art essay
and brainstorming for my mixed-media proposal
but, instead, i'm standing at the bathroom sink
trying to do something i haven't done in days

i'm terrified when i look up
and finally confront the truth in the mirror

i hold the picture on my phone
up to my face
studying the similarities

i see him most clearly
when i tilt my chin to the left
he lives in my jaw
in my sharp cheekbones

i stare into round, earnest eyes
inherited from my mother:

all that i can stand to face

we mail the pr application

and autumn falls into winter
and winter melts into spring

the waiting gnaws at our skin
but we have known patience for a lifetime

for days and months and years
we have lived in uncertainty
and managed to breathe in its waters

all we can do now
is hope for the best
and trust that there will be another way
if the story of me is not enough

sahaara

february 2021–june 2021

i have never known a rage like this

one that refuses to fade in the soothing arms of time

five months have passed
but i am still haunted
by the night that dug me from my body
and declared me a monstrosity

the dream is always the same.
it is a formula, by this point,
holding me in limbo
every time it replays.

mom is trembling on my bed
telling me the story
for the very first time

the walls of my room crumble
when she explains the evil that concocted me

try to hug her but she is vapor
and the walls are cement
and each of them runs red
and i am alone in a cell

i awake in cold sweats
corrosive anger dripping from my skin
a helpless fury that gives way to silent sobs.

if this
is how
the truth
has broken me
simply from hearing it recounted

how has mom felt
carrying it alone beneath her skin
for all these years?

is there a way to free us both?

the letter

"Here goes nothing," I mumble to myself. I'm sitting cross-legged on my bed, nestled within a rainbow of fine-tipped markers. Although the carpet is covered in my usual piles of dirty laundry (I swear, I'll clean up tonight), the bed is an oasis of peace. The space I need to draw this letter out of myself. With an indigo pen, I begin with the only two words I'm certain of:

Dear Mom.

A sigh. A deflated chest. Ink hovering over paper with no language to conjure.

Where do I go from here?

The letter was Jeevan's idea. Well, technically, it was his counselor's. Madhuri had him write a letter to his dad carrying all that needed releasing from his body. All that he couldn't say in person. Sitting in his room last weekend, I watched as he poured out an ocean of words, dotted, in some places, with tears. As he filled eight pages, he was more silent, more focused than I'd ever encountered him. When he was done, we took a long, wordless walk. Then we drove to White Rock and lit a tiny bonfire on the barren midnight beach. As his letter hovered just above crackling flames, I asked whether any part of him wanted to send it to the prison. He shook his head *no* and the words charred and shriveled, his tears dripping orange in the bonfire's glow. The way he saw it, healing didn't come from his abuser. He wouldn't beg his father to cry with him.

Once nothing was left of the burning altar but a gossamer

strand of smoke, Jeevan called the process "liberating." *You need to do this, too*, he said. *And don't overthink it. Don't filter yourself. Just write what comes to you. No stress 'cause the letter's only yours.*

Only mine.

Okay. I think I can do this. With a deep breath, pen meets paper once more and I let my heart take the lead.

Mom. I write to you from outside my body. Which is to say, I am a shadow of myself. I don't know who I am. I am your daughter, but isn't that only half of the truth? Right now, and ever since you told me, I have become anger. I am not angry. I have embodied my rage—so filled with it that my heart no longer knows another way.

It never should've happened. It never should've happened and the fact that you know this pain kills me. It breaks me, Mom. I always thought the word undocumented would be the only label to hold me like a rope. But now there is another five-syllable term that has pulled itself tight around my wrists.

When you told me the truth, the term sexual assault was no longer just a painful concept that existed on the peripheries of my mind. It became a wildfire I couldn't run from after double-tapping Instagram posts about rape statistics and tweeting about empowerment and hope. God damn, I am privileged, and how bloody twisted that this is a privilege.

Mata Jee, I am still only eighteen but I am so tired of this world. I am tired of a society that only demands accountability from the vulnerable and marginalized.

I'm sick of how we are only worthy of safety if we follow the correct protocol. I'm sick of how powerful men make all the protocol. Enforce the protocol. But adhere to absolutely fucking none of it. I'm sick of watching monsters and predators rise through social ranks. Hold their prestige. Become CEOs. Basketball players. Presidents. Heroes.

I dream of healing for you. A full heart and clear skies. Everything feeling peaceful and right. But most of all, I dream that accountability can also be yours. Ours. When you told me the story, I was shattered because of the burden you carried in silence for two decades. I'm so sorry that you couldn't tell me. Mom, I am young and perhaps foolish, but I know enough to know that you deserve freedom. You deserve safety and comfort and every listening ear in this world. Your story would make the mighty crumble. It would strike fear in their bloodless hearts. And what if you were not the only one? What if Ahluwalia never stopped? What if there are other girls who need to know they aren't alone? What if our voices can stop him? I love y—

"Sahaara, puth! Darvaaja khol, mail ayee ah!" Bibi's giddy voice nearly gives me a heart attack and the last word in my letter becomes a purple, thumb-shaped smudge.

"Mail?" I call, shoving the letter under my paisley duvet before opening the door. "Is it from the bookstore? I thought that was coming next week. . . ."

"No, bache." Bibi grins through wrinkle-worn, doughy cheeks. She pinches my face as she says, "Mail from the government. For Kiran."

My heart softens. I'm truly convinced that no one on earth

has a bibi cuter than mine. Ever since we mailed Mom's PR application in the fall, she's been checking the mailbox twice a day, certain we'll get the permanent resident card any day now. As always, when she excitedly comes home with a stack of letters, I remind her that the PR process will likely take many more months. At the very least, a dozen. I glance down at the pile of envelopes in Bibi Jee's hands. To her credit, there's one addressed to Mom with a Canadian flag emblazoned in the corner. It's from Immigration, Refugees and Citizenship Canada.

Hold up. The IRCC?

"Do you think—? Where's Mom?" I gasp.

"The garden."

We approach so delicately, Mom doesn't even look away from the soil. She is the closest to peace when her hands are in the earth, planting new life and nurturing it as it grows. Back turned to us, she plucks out a carrot, fully ripened and drenched in dirt.

"Mom," I softly whisper, and she startles, dropping the carrot and clutching her chest.

"Fitteh moo, tere!" Mom cracks up, returning her fallen pink chunni to her shoulders. "Since when are you two quiet?"

"We've got mail . . ." I hand her the letter, my excitement now stained with fear. Within this envelope could simply be a request for more documents. Or a rejection. Or an approval. Mom grasps the letter in both hands, her face a kaleidoscopic phulkari of emotion. First, her eyes widen in surprise. Then, the faintest smile. Slowly, her lips fall into a frown. Nervousness now hums in her trembling wrists.

"I'm not ready," she whispers, still crouched next to the vegetable plot.

I kneel down beside her, resting a hand on her shoulder. "I'm here, Mom. Whatever it is, let's just get it over with?"

The white envelope is specked with dirt as Mom tears it open. We read the letter in silence and my heart forgets how to beat.

"What does it say?" Bibi asks.

Mom's voice cracks on each word. "Dear Kiran Kaur, your application for permanent residence has been approved."

I think the letter lands on the golden-hour grass as Mom grasps me and sobs. Soon, Bibi is wrapped around us and we are all composed of water. That night, when Maasi comes over, the floorboards laugh with our giddha and the walls cannot contain our singing. We cry, we dance, we pray, we fill ourselves with gratitude, and we do not filter our joy. In this tired little home in a weary corner of Surrey, the three Punjabi women who have given me everything are smiling and safe. On this holy night, nothing hurts.

i didn't mean to find the letter

i only meant to surprise her with a clean bedroom
a tidy space, for once, where she can gather her thoughts

but here it is
crumpled at the bottom of her sock drawer

and here i am
ears ringing with her words
while a fear washes over me
thorny and jagged and entirely new:

what if there are other victims?

in all those years of drowning
limbs so exhausted with swimming
i kept my silence to survive

but what if there is another woman
lost at sea who needs my voice
like a rope
a buoy
a life raft?

Kiran

conflicted

i hover at sahaara's bedroom door
raising my hand to knock
and then returning it to my side

i am alone in the hallway
with my shallow breathing
and jumbled thoughts

if i speak out about ahluwalia i'm drawing attention to us
but if i don't speak out i'm letting him get away
but if i speak out i'm putting us in danger
but if i don't speak out i'm putting others in danger
but if i speak out i'm diving head-first into the memories
but if i don't speak out i'll be haunted by him forever
but if i speak out they could all call me a liar
but if i don't speak out they'll call another woman's
accusation baseless
but if i—

> *mom?*
> the door creaks open
> and sahaara rubs sleep from her eyes
> *what's up? why are you standing here?*

i—
       i think i—
i think i want to
       do an interview.

                    she almost staggers backward
                    in surprise
                    you wanna talk about
                    being undocumented?

and ahluwalia.

Kiran

nervousness flutters in mom's voice

when she tells me that
she wants to speak out

i reach for the right words
to calm her nerves
to solidify her resolve

~~you're challenging the status quo~~
~~you're doing this for girls like me~~
~~you'll be making the world a little safer~~

i'll be right there by your side.

speaking sach to power

"You've got this, Mom!" I beam. "You're gonna do great."

Her smile is a weak flicker before it snuffs out altogether. Mom lowers her gaze, unsure what to do with her hands. Seated on a white pleather love seat before a seamless green screen, she picks at a piece of nonexistent lint on her sweater and tries to flatten a crease in her khaki pants. Across from her is Bimal Ghatora, the host of *Chat & Chai with Bimal*. As a makeup artist blots her forehead, Bimal twirls a finger around a lock of perfectly straightened, henna-red hair, just as vivid in real life as it is on TV. Most Saturday mornings, Bibi Jee takes a seat in the living room, dunks Parle-G biscuits into her cha, and watches Bimal Ghatora interview guests on her Punjabi Channel talk show. Her guests are usually up-and-coming Punjabi singers and naatak actors. Her conversations are light and juicy. This one is going to be . . . different.

"How are you feeling, Kiran?" Bimal asks. "Not nervous, I hope."

"I'm . . . okay." Mom nods with eventual sureness. "Glad we're not doing this in front of an audience." We're sitting in a little studio in the Punjabi Channel office. Surrounding the perfectly framed sofas and green screen, there's a tangled web of cords, lighting equipment, and a serious-looking camera. If I were watching from home, I'd think Mom was lounging in a meticulously designed living room. There's even a cute picture of Bimal Ghatora's family on the side table beside Mom.

"All right, we're shooting in thirty seconds," a bushy-bearded videographer named Satinder says from behind the camera. "If you need to pause or you'd like to say something differently, we can always stop and pick up from where you'd like, teekh aa?"

Mom looks to me for reassurance and I offer her a sturdy thumbs-up. Prem stands serenely next to me, an intricate plum shawl draped across her chest today. Although we hadn't seen her in months, she was elated when she heard about the PR card and insisted on taking Mom out for a celebratory dinner at Tasty's. Over paneer sliders and sweet mango lassi, Mom repeated words that were beautiful and terrifying and so very surprising. She doubled down on her insistence that she wanted to go public about her migration story—and name Ahluwalia in the process. Perhaps it was the safety of her PR card that gave her this stunning change of heart.

On the drive to the studio, Prem and I reminded Mom that if she had any doubts about the interview, we could immediately turn the car around and cancel the whole thing without a worry. There was something concrete in Mom's voice when she told me to keep driving.

"And we're rolling in five . . . four . . . three . . . two . . ." Satinder's voice trails off and he signals the word *one* with his finger.

"Helllllllooooo, dosto! Welcome to another episode of *Chat & Chai* with me, your host, Bimal Ghatora. Today, I have a very special guest joining me. This is a woman who has braved so much just to be with us here today. A woman who *claims* that everyone's favorite progressive political candidate for Punjab's leadership race has *actually* buried a very dark past. Kiran Kaur, welcome to the show." I gag at her choice of words. *Progressive. Everyone's favorite.*

"Thank you—thank you for having me." Unsure where to look, Mom glances at the camera and then settles on Bimal.

"Now, Kiran, shall we jump right into your claims about Hari Ahluwalia? He's the leader of the Progressive People's Party of Punjab. A former police chief who's done *so* much to help Punjab's youth break free from the grips of alcoholism and drug addiction. You tell a very different story about him. Could you share?"

"Well . . ." Mom begins, "I'd actually like to begin by talking about my own experiences in Canada." Prem smiles beside me and nods in approval of Mom's redirection of the conversation. In the car, Prem said that interviewers could get pushy, that she'd cut them off if they asked anything remotely inappropriate. "My story isn't just about . . . him. It's been a very long journey for me in other ways."

"Of course." Bimal cocks her head to the side. "You've lived in Canada for about twenty years, I believe? But you were here, for most of those years, without legal status. What was that experience like?"

Mom begins to relay her story, describing how she knew very little about her rights as a young international student. When she gets to the part about giving birth to me in Canada and overstaying her student visa, she glances faintly in my direction, then returns her attention to Bimal.

"Fascinating!" Bimal flashes a Colgate smile. "But what an awfully great risk to take, overstaying a student visa, knowing your child could also be at risk. Some would, perhaps, call that irresponsible. *Why* would you make such a decision to raise a child in Canada without legal status?"

Shock registers on Mom's face. She hunches forward, like

she's been punched in the gut, and I wince with her. "F-fear," she stammers. "Crippling and paralyzing fear. When I first came to Canada, I knew I couldn't go back, because of Hari Ahluwalia. But I was so afraid of making the wrong move and getting sent back to Punjab without a question. I felt like, the less I said, the safer I would be—the safer my daughter would be—until I could figure out a certain path to citizenship."

"What were you so afraid of?" Bimal airily asks, as if they're discussing the weather.

"I guess . . . what would happen if . . . I came back with my—with my—"

"Kiran," Prem speaks up. "Are you comfortable answering this question?"

"No. No, I'm not." Mom worriedly looks back and forth between us.

"Bimal, why don't we move on to the next question, then?" Prem suggests without blinking.

"Sure, not a problem!" Bimal simpers, sickly sweet. "So, Kiran, you mentioned experiencing a great deal of confusion around gaining citizenship. How did you figure out how to become a citizen?"

"I wasn't really sure who to turn to for help—who I could trust—but years ago, I met with an immigration consultant. He offered to help but he—he tried to, um, he tried to take advantage of me just like—"

"That's *horrible*, Kiran! Can you explain for our viewers in more specific terms what you mean by taking *advantage*?"

"Oh, um . . ." Mom's voice quivers and fizzles out. Acid creeps up my throat, just as it did when she first told me about Ahluwalia. She never told me about this immigration consultant. . . .

"Bimal, she's uncomfortable," Prem says. "Move on to the next question."

Quietly, I slip past Prem and step into the hallway, searching for the washroom that the studio assistant pointed out when we came in. When I finally find it, I rip open the door of an empty stall. Hair falls into my face as I give in to my stomach's clawing urge to empty itself.

I have no clue what Mom has truly been through. I have no idea what else she could be carrying that's never been spoken aloud. But every time she shares a piece of her story, something inside me tears apart and all I want to do is help her mend. I just want to prove—to her and to myself—that this world can do more than hurt us.

helpless

there is a kind of pain that exists
when your loved one carries a hurt
too heavy for either of you to bear

when your hands don't know
how to mend their wounds
and your rage has nowhere to go

i would do anything
to reverse time
so that she would
never know suffering
like this

even if it meant
i was never born.

before i get into my bed

i crawl into mom's

i have always been softer than her
it doesn't take much for my throat to break
for fog to fill my eyes

but this time
she cries with me
and i become the mother
hugging her close
and she becomes the child
certain that the world
is only as big as the arms that hold her.

on sunday,
the world will know my truth

and in this thin blade of time
i think i have it in me to tell joti, as well

i recount the story that was buried
when we were both young and reckless
and she could only guess at the truth shivering
beneath my skin

she says

> *kiran, this was never your fault.*
> *kiran, you did your best.*
> *kiran, you have always done your best.*
> *kiran, you are whole and holy.*
> *kiran, you are deeply loved.*
> *kiran, your past doesn't define you.*

and i tell her
this body feels like a cage
and i've lived in it all these years
but it's still an unwelcome stranger.

Kiran

perspectives

On this foggy Sunday morning, a gray sky grazes the earth the way Mom's words will inevitably encounter every South Asian in Surrey. Bibi and I are huddled on the plastic-covered sofa in the living room, TV switched to the Punjabi Channel, waiting to see what unfolds with warm cha in our hands. Although I missed the end of Mom's interview in person, there hasn't exactly been much of a wait to see the rest. The studio is rushing it onto TV less than twenty-four hours after recording. Our stomachs collectively churned last night when a melodramatic thirty-second clip aired, demanding that everything tune in for "shocking!" and "explosive!" and "scandalous!" allegations. Grumbled expletives abound, Maasi hit the off button on the remote. We spent the evening playing bhabhi and discussing the petty drama in Maasi's hospital unit and trying to distract Mom's worry with laughter.

Mom's sitting in her room right now. I doubt she's gonna come out until the TV's off.

The interview begins and I listen to all the words I heard yesterday. I observe the details of my mother as she speaks: the way she skittishly squeezes her hands when she's overwhelmed or sits up straighter when she is more outrage than anxiety. A few minutes in, they move past the parts I've already seen. Bimal Ghatora asks questions about me—what it was like raising me as a single mother and the hopes she has for my future. I try not to get teary because Bibi Jee gets ridiculously worried when anyone's upset. After we left the studio, Prem said Bimal asked whether Hari was my father. She shut down the question and told Bimal that they couldn't air that part.

"Before we end, Kiran, is there any message that you'd like to leave with viewers?" Bimal asks.

"Yes." Mom looks directly into the camera with a fierceness that draws all attention away from her trembling hands. "Hari Ahluwalia is a . . . rapist, disguised as a respectable man. I'm frightened to say all this, but I'm sharing my story because I want more than a world where our daughters suffer in silence because of the same things their mothers have lived through."

Rapist.

I've never heard her say that word out loud before. She's drifted in its vicinity when describing her trauma, but it's never actually escaped her lips. Bibi Jee turns off the TV and we both sit in silence for a long moment.

"I had no idea . . ." she finally whispers. "Rabb nu patha, I knew she was strong, but I never questioned where all that strength came from. Kiran is like my own daughter. How could I not know all this?"

"Bibi, it's my mom we're talking about. She's the only woman I know who's more stubborn than you. Of course she was gonna keep all this to herself if she wasn't ready to share."

"True. That's very true." Bibi Jee sighs. "Hari Ahluwalia, though? I really don't know if that was a good idea. . . ."

"What do you mean?"

"She shouldn't have talked about that publicly."

"Bibi, she had *every* right to. People deserve to know the truth."

"But people aren't always interested in the truth, are they? Especially when it comes from the mouth of a woman. They want a thamaasha. Drama. And these dirty politicians? They always manage to come out of the mud with their hands clean."

There is a flame kindling within me and I can feel it lashing at my lips. "Isn't that exactly *why* we need to say something? This shouldn't be the world we live in."

"It shouldn't be, but it is. Your heart is in the right place, puth, but you're young. You don't understand how cold this world is yet." She removes her thick glasses and tucks her wiry silver hair behind her ears. "Let me ask you this. What are you hoping will be the result of sharing all this publicly?"

"The same thing you were hoping for when you were protesting against the genocide in eighty-four. I want justice. I want this guy to pay for his actions."

"And how successful were our protests, my love? What justice did we ever see?"

There's so much I want to say, but I pinch my tongue. How is *my* Bibi reacting like this? This is a woman who organized sit-ins and blockades when she was a student, who once swallowed tear gas for her convictions. Both confusion and frustration sting the corners of my eyes, threatening to become full-blown tears. Nothing is worse than bawling when I can't get my point across so I try to change the subject. "Gurdwara now?" I ask, unclenching my jaw.

"Hanji, let's go. Call your mom. I'll start the car."

Gently, I knock on Mom's bedroom door and peek inside. She's sitting at the edge of her unmade bed facing the window. Her head rests contemplatively in her palm. "Mom? Let's go to the gurdwara."

"Huh? Oh . . . yeah. I'll just be a minute." Hair tangled and uncombed, she remains so still, I could paint her.

"Are you all right?"

"I'm fine. I'll meet you in the car."

Mom makes it outside several minutes later wearing a beige-and-mahogany salwar kameez, hair covered with a chiffon chunni. I opted for a pair of sweatpants, a shawl, and my *Inquilaab* hoodie. Bibi impatiently taps on the steering wheel, antsy to leave before the afternoon Sukhmani Sahib prayer begins.

"Kiran, you did great on the show. God, I couldn't have gone on TV like that . . . I would've forgotten everything I had to say. You didn't seem nervous at all," Bibi Jee says to Mom, who's sitting in the back seat. My eyes widen at her sudden switch-up, but she doesn't notice.

"Really?" Mom is transfixed on something outside the dirty window. "I was shaking the whole time. Bimal kept digging for answers. . . ."

"So, she was pressuring you to tell her those things?" Bibi Jee asks.

"Not exactly, but I wasn't planning to say all that. She was really nice afterward. I suppose she just wanted the whole story—"

"But, Mom," I interject. "She said that whole thing about how Hari Ahluwalia is everyone's favorite candidate. And remember how she kept saying *allegedly* when you were explaining what he did and—"

"Sahaara, could we just not talk about it right now?"

"Oh—uh—yeah—sorry." My cheeks go apple red. I didn't mean to upset her.

at the gurdwara

i walk through the door of a teacher emanating light
shoes off, head covered with my shawl
i avoid ~~my face~~ his face in the mirror as i wash my hands

naked feet enter the darbar, the guru's court
and i touch my forehead to the earth below their throne

at the back, i cross my legs among breastfeeding mothers
and keertan-singing grandmothers
my own family sitting far ahead

here, i close my eyes to the royal blue carpet
and the guru's golden palki
letting pain drip behind the shield of my shawl

truth be told, i don't always know what i believe
but i open my palms to any peace my mother finds
in the divine
wondering if i'm worthy of this love, too

in this cold betrayal of a body
i ache for an anchor
i pray for another life
i beg for the nightmare of my dna to end.

# of course, the aunties weigh in

I'm the first to leave the darbar and head downstairs to eat. The langar hall is a white-marbled community kitchen where anyone and everyone is fed. Between long rows of Persian carpets is a competition of noise: the staticky gurdwara speakers blast keertan from the darbar while chatter in the langar hall seems to overpower it. Eventually, Mom and Bibi Jee come downstairs. They sit down beside me on the grey carpet, placing their steel trays of roti and dahl next to mine.

"Why'd you leave so quick?" Bibi Jee asks. "Looked back for a second and you'd disappeared."

"Dunno." I shrug. "Couldn't really sit still. I needed to move."

It only takes a single bite of my roti for a random, orangey-haired aunty to tap Mom on the shoulder. Her sapphire chunni slips off her head as she drops a honeyed, "Puth, are you Kiran Kaur?"

Mom quickly swallows her water. "Oh—um—hanji. Have we met?"

"You came on TV yesterday, hunna? On Punjabi Channel?" Mom's cheeks flush pink. She nods with a slight grimace.

"Achaaa, I thought it was you!" the aunty says. "Quite a controversial discussion you've started. I've never heard anything like that on Punjabi Channel before." A couple of older women eating in the row ahead of ours look up from their conversation in interest. Bibi Jee gathers maha di dahl with a piece of whole-wheat roti and simply observes.

"I didn't mean to be controversial. I was just trying to tell my story."

"Mm." The aunty nods. "It was good that you talked about it, don't get me wrong, but it's given people a lot of questions. . . ."

"What do you mean?" Mom asks nervously. The aunties across from us glance back and forth between Mom and the blue-chunnied aunty, lapping up the exchange while sipping their tea.

"Well, for one thing, puth—and I hope you don't mind—I was wondering about your daughter. And her father."

All the nervousness in Mom's expression evaporates. "*Sorry?*" she asks, clearly irritated.

The aunty doesn't clock the difference. Or maybe she just doesn't care. "You didn't really explain much about her except that you raised her alone. Did her father leave you because of the . . . *incident* with Hari Ahluwalia? Or is Ahluwalia her father? I don't want to assume that—I hope you don't mind—I just think you should have explained. Otherwise, people are going to . . . *speculate.*"

"Listen," Bibi Jee intervenes before I can even gather my thoughts, "we *do* mind your questions. And the answers are none of your business. We don't even know who you are, *bhenji.*" Bibi Jee's sarcastic emphasis on the Punjabi word for *sister* nearly makes me choke on my water. I force down the edges of my smile but anger still smokes beneath my surface.

One of the elderly aunties who had been following the exchange decides to chime in. Her circular glasses have a magnifying effect on her eyes and somehow add more drama to her words. "You know, if anyone in my family wanted to share such a shameful story, I wouldn't have let them speak a single word of it. Instead, you're mad that she has questions. Of course people are going to have questions! You think she can just go on TV and make up a story like that—a story about a good man who's helping Punjabis—and no one is going to question her?!"

Bibi Jee drops her spoon in her tray and shakes her head in disgust. Hurt and anger writhe in Mom's eyes as she stares back at the aunty. She teeters on tears, just like I do when I can't get my point across.

"Mom," I whisper. "Let's just go. It's not worth it."

hope

The spring days begin to slip through my fingers in a haze of essays and oil pastel paintings and double espresso shots. With each passing day, the reality of Mom's permanent resident status sinks in a little deeper and the relief floods in afresh. Despite all the darkness we still carry on our shoulders, one unbearably heavy burden has been lifted. Last weekend, for the first time in our lives, Mom and I crossed the border into the US. We picked up a few gallons of milk and filled up my truck with a tank of gas, both cheaper in America than in Canada. Although we quickly realized that the US looked pretty much the same as Canada, we basked in the luxury of being able to travel freely (was this what white people felt all the time?). Yesterday, when Mom walked into the kitchen after acing an interview for a job at Bibi Jee's old office, I nearly shrieked in happiness. There is no more hiding. No more tolerating hell and calling it patience. And school—usually the least of my worries—finally feels like something I have time to worry about. As I dig through my second semester and learn my way around the temperaments of my new professors, the thought of having an entire undergrad of art ahead of me becomes a promising tide that rises steadily above my sorrows.

I'm a bundle of nerves as I approach my professor at the end of our workshop. She's standing behind her laptop, a stack of essays and abstract art textbooks to her right, intently focused on something I can't see. "Rhonda, do you have a minute? I wanted to talk to you about my—"

"—*just* a moment," she says without looking up. She pulls a black pencil out from behind her ear and quickly scrawls something on a piece of paper. Something about her glasses and cutthroat demeanor reminds me of the boss from *The Devil Wears Prada*. She could be Miranda Priestly's slightly disheveled, black-haired, artist sibling. "Okay, yes, how can I help you?"

I rifle through my binder, searching for the proposal I printed out this morning. "I wanted to show you my project proposal before I submit it. I've got a copy here." She looks it over in silence while I hold my breath. She told us not to come to her about a project unless we've really thought it through.

"So, you're doing a project about undocumented people or sexual assault?" Rhonda looks me in the eye for the first time and turns my tongue to chalk.

"Yeah—well—basically—the project is about multiple topics because it's about—it's inspired by my mom. She lived undocumented in Canada but she also dealt with sexual assault—"

"The issue is this: I don't think that you'll be able to make a powerful visual statement with your painting if you're spreading your focus across two very heavy topics. You may make a better impact if you focus on one part of her experiences."

How, exactly, do I explain this to my professor? Mom's trauma doesn't fit in neat boxes. It didn't come with a one-sentence label. "My mom's experiences are all connected. As an undocumented person and a sexual assault survivor. I can't separate them because one directly caused the other. And maybe that's the case with a lot of others like my mom. Their whole lives are affected by their past. I want to emphasize that through this project. That . . . connectedness."

Rhonda surveys me thoughtfully and nods. "All right. Well, I'd like to see *that* described in more depth. Come back to me with a more detailed proposal. And then . . . I think you're on the way to a very compelling project." She smiles and her approval has me flustered. Damn. Rhonda Ross likes something I came up with?

Jeevan is parked near the bus loop scrolling through his phone when I pull open his car door and hop into the front seat, a wide grin still plastered across my face. He's wearing the vintage Vancouver Grizzlies jersey I got him for his last birthday.

"Any particular reason why you're smiling like an idiot?" he asks.

"I've got a project idea, Jeevan! A *compelling* project idea, according to Rhonda *Fucking* Ross."

"That's your art prof, right?" he asks, carefully pulling out of the bus loop. "The famous art critic one?"

"No, I only had Marianne in the fall. Rhonda's this artist who started painting when she was, like, five. The one who's an asshole but also kind of a genius?"

"I got you. So, she liked your project? Is that a big deal or something?"

"Jeevan, YES! She's so freaking critical of everything. Like, even the classics. She talks shit about the *Mona Lisa*, for fuck's sake."

"To be fair, I don't really see what's so great about the *Mona Lisa*. She's just an aunty without eyebrows."

"True."

"Anyways, that's good, man. I'm happy for you." His silver Audi slows at the crosswalk as a smattering of students pass by. "That feminist video thing was intense, huh?"

"What feminist video thing?" I ask, analyzing a fresh crack in my matte black nails.

"The news report thing . . . from Punjab."

"News report?"

"Hold up. You haven't seen it?" His deep brown eyes steal a glance at me, and I shake my head. "Shoot. Okay. Go on YouTube. Search up *Me Too Hari Ahluwalia and Kiran Kaur* or something."

Within seconds, a shit ton of videos pop up. I tap the one with the most views: three hundred and fifty thousand, so far. In the thumbnail, four Punjabi girls wearing jeans and salwar kameezes hold signs that read "#MeToo" and "Stop corrupt politicians!" and "Stop rapist leaders!"

"Protests continue in Punjab as students refuse to support Hari Ahluwalia after the brave testimony by Punjabi-Canadian woman Kiran Kaur," says a robotically calm voiceover while the screen displays a picture from Mom's Punjabi Channel interview.

Then a girl in a fuchsia salwar kameez and matching turban appears. She speaks directly into the camera, her charcoal eyes completely ablaze. "We're here at Chandigarh University on behalf of the Feminist Students Society because we want to remind the university and the whole of Punjab that Punjabi women do *not* stand by a rapist pretending to be an inspirational young leader. We don't care if people think that Hari Ahluwalia is at least better than the others. We support Kiran Kaur as survivors and supporters. Her voice has reminded us that we, too, can raise ours. And we will be here all day, protesting Hari Ahluwalia's talk at the university. Punjab's university students say *Me Too*. We say enough is enough." The camera pans out and pivots to the left, where a crowd of dozens of students of all genders stand outside a towering university building, carrying signs and linking arms.

They begin to chant, "BELIEVE THE VICTIM! BELIEVE THE VICTIM!"

"Jeevan," I gasp, lips arching into a smile, "this is sick."

"Right?" he smirks. "Trippy how word traveled so fast. One interview and look at the ripple effect."

I'm low on data but I rewind the video and play it again. And again. Each time I watch, warmth sizzles and thunders within me, a storm brewing just like the one in that girl's eyes. I know Bibi has her fears. Her doubts. I know those asshole aunties at the gurdwara tried to crush Mom's spirit beneath their own steaming-hot bullshit. But this—these young women who took my mother's words and trusted them—they fill me with all the reassurance I need. And I hope they do the same for Mom.

"Jeevan?"

"Uh-huh?" He nods, almost peeling his eyes off the road to look at me.

"You know I'm grateful for you, right?" I think back to the sight of him sitting next to Mom in the café. To all the times when he's shown up in a heartbeat. "Means a lot that you're here. For Mom and me."

His cinnamon-sharp smile warms me in a different way than the video. "Relax, bud. Would I really be a friend if I wasn't here for you through some heavy-ass shit like this?"

There's a pang in my stomach as the dying ember of another boy's smile crosses my mind. "No. I guess not."

My phone lights up with a Gmail notification and I tap it open. "Just got an email from Prem."

"What's she saying?"

"She says, 'Hi, Kiran and Sahaara, I'm forwarding a request from Nandini Rajalingam, editor in chief at *Woman*

Magazine, India.' The *hell*?" I murmur in disbelief. *Woman Magazine* is the largest editorial fashion publication in India, so popular that it's still available in print after most of the glossies went digital. What could Nandini Rajalingam—the Anna Wintour of South Asia—possibly want from us?

I scroll down and quickly skim the message. Then I reread it slowly, certain I've misunderstood Nandini's request.

"Jeevan," I whisper, glancing up from my phone. "They want to fly my mom out to Mumbai. As the guest of honor for their Women of Power gala."

despair

"So what?" She half shrugs and then slips back into the comfort of her thick winter kambal. She pulls the jaguar-print blanket over her face.

"What do you mean, Mom? This is amazing! These girls are starting an entire movement 'cause of your interview. Your words literally got all the way back to Punjab. Isn't this what we wanted?"

"Sure. Exactly what we wanted." She sighs. "I'll talk to you in the morning, all right? It's getting late."

It's five o'clock. I gingerly sink into her foamy mattress, worry gurgling in my stomach. "I don't get it. I thought you'd be happy about this."

She pulls the blanket away from her face to look me in the eye. "Sahaara, what is there to be happy about?"

"Not everyone feels the same as those aunties at the gurdwara. Doesn't this video prove that?"

"Have you seen the Global News one?"

"What?"

"Another *lovely* video about me. I was better off not even watching it."

A Google search of Mom's name and the news network leads me to a video titled "Illegal Immigrants and Refugees: The Great Debate." Five stern-looking panelists gather around a glass table. Four of them are men. All of them are white.

I skip to the two-minute mark. "So, this woman comes to Canada two decades ago, overstays her student visa, never— not once!—does she apply for refugee status—and when Immigration finds her after twenty years, she has a whole story laid out about how she was fleeing this politician in her home country. I'm sorry, I'm not buying any of it. But, of course, the crybaby liberal snowflake generation is going to lap this stuff up and our spineless prime minister will cower before them."

"Well, Mark, I see where you're coming from," a blonde-haired woman begins, "but I'd also like to point out that Canada is a place where people come fleeing barbaric practices and governments around the world. And perhaps this woman was so afraid of the complete *craziness* and lack of humanity in her homeland that she didn't know Canada was a place where she can live freely, where civilized Canadians would respect her choices over her own body instead of *barbarically* forcing her to make choices that she didn't want."

"Holy crap." I pause the video. "She's saying this shit like it wasn't *barbaric* brown women who took us into their home and supported us. Like white people have never elected predators. Does she not get how racist this is? I can't . . ." My words trail off when I catch sight of Mom's face. She stares at the wall, eyes glazed, like I'm not even in the room.

"Mom . . . talk to me." My fingers graze her palm, but she simply blinks. "What's going on? What's on your mind?"

"I've made so many mistakes, Sahaara," she whispers. "If I knew . . . if I wasn't so bloody afraid . . . I never would've put you through this. I swear, if I just listened to Joti, all of this could've ended years ago. I'm a fucking fool."

My eyes bulge at her extremely rare use of a cuss word. Then I laugh. "So, are you telling me that you're blaming yourself, when you and Maasi were literally new immigrants, just trying your best to figure out a *completely* screwed-up situation? You're blaming yourself"—I swallow the rock in my throat—"for raising me the best way you knew how? Do you understand, Mom, that I don't blame you? I blame you for nothing. None of this is your fault."

Something like desperation is etched in her features. Her eyes trace the entire map of my face and I can't help but wonder if she's searching for a forgiveness that she never needed to seek from me. She purses her lips before she asks, "Why would that magazine want me to be their guest of honor?"

"Are you kidding? How is that even a question?"

She shakes her head but says nothing more, returning to the mysterious world of her own thoughts.

"The fact that *Woman Magazine* wants you at their gala should tell you how important your story is. People are listening to you around the world right now."

Mom is as unmoved by my words as she was by the protest video. Despite my exasperation, an idea strikes. "Okay, I know you obviously don't wanna go to India or anything . . . but what if you just take the phone call from that Nandini lady? What if you hear her explain in her own words why they chose you to speak?"

She shrugs, indifferent. "None of this matters, Sahaara. None of this fixes anything."

"Please, Mom. Just try this. For me?"

depression feels like

submersion beneath two tons of water
but somehow, continuing to breathe

simultaneous static and cold and fire
in every corner of my brain

every bad moment blooming
to eclipse every good day

each person who never loved me
returning to tell me why they were right

knowing all the reasons why i should
stay alive but not believing them

this bed and these blankets growing
larger and larger until they engulf me in a safe
cocoon

sahaara sitting right at the edge
and calling to me from a faraway shore
her voice muffled by this desolate ocean

reaching for her hand
as if it is an anchor

using every bit of my strength
to hold on

Kiran

this world is
too heavy

can i put it
down somewhere?

at four in the morning

mom and bibi jee are awake
for amrit vela meditation

and i rewatch *the girl with the dragon tattoo*
learning. studying. seeking catharsis.
from the only superhero
who deserves the title

like muscle memory
i know the scenes that make me tremble
the parts i need to skip
the parts i need to rewind and play
again and again
and again

i pause at the exact moment
when lisbeth stands in the elevator
fingers outstretched
reaching for his forehead
making him cower in fear
at a woman he will never dare
to touch again

i wish i could write to her.
will her into existence.
turn her into more than words on paper
and compelling acting before a camera.
pray to her like a patron saint.
leave an offering of white peonies
and thornless roses at her feet.

i wish i could find a lisbeth
within me.

i am unraveling

Why do I exist?

The question gnaws at my skin. Digs into my bones. Claws at the aching thing beneath my chest. I get the science of it. The feelingless monstrosity of his sperm implanting in my mother. The process of his haploid cell fusing with Mom's to form the genetic code that would create me. One part him. One part her. An equal mixture, forever inseparable. And then there's the psychology. All of us begin with an emotion. A single act of love, or ambivalence—or, in my case, cruel, calculated violence—jump-starts the process that brings a human being to life. A whole living, breathing, thinking, crying, smiling, suffering person gets created because a selfish, momentary feeling passes through someone's body. But is that all I am? Am I just the mechanics of how I came to be?

Each time Mom looks away, I sneak a glance and tell myself that I can ignore the creature growling under my skin. That I can learn how to live with it, tame it, even if I never look him in the eye and force him to reckon with the truth.

But Mom's cell phone rings and my wild, reckless ideas chase away all else.

"Hello?" Mom taps the speaker button so that both of us can listen in.

"Hellooo! Is this Kiran Kaur speaking?" Nandini Rajalingam replies, her accent similar to Mom's, but a few layers thicker. There's something kind of British about the way she rolls her *r*'s.

"This is her. I'm here with my daughter, Sahaara." A tracksuit-clad woman passes by our park bench. She pushes a stroller with one hand and sips coffee with the other. We're sitting at Bear Creek because, for the third time this week, I came home to Mom curled up in bed at five p.m. Somehow, I convinced her that fresh air would lighten her mood.

"So lovely to meet you both! And thank you so much for taking my call, Kiran. I was just telling my colleagues here that I was going to be chatting with you and they were *so* excited."

Mom's eyes narrow and I can practically hear her wondering why they'd be excited to talk to her. "No problem."

"Right, so, as I mentioned in my email, our whole team here was *absolutely* blown away by the brave honesty in your interview. It's made many rounds in mainstream Indian media, as you must know, especially with the protests in Punjab and Mumbai—"

"Mumbai?" Mom's lashes flutter in surprise.

"Yes, the Me Too protest in Mumbai, yesterday. Did you not see the news?"

"No—no, I didn't. I've been avoiding the news for the last few days, to be honest. It's gotten . . . overwhelming."

"Kiran, you've captured the attention of the whole country. It's *absolutely* astonishing to see so many young women speaking up and sharing their stories because of yours. And that's *exactly* why we're so excited to invite you to the Women of Power gala. It's a title you truly deserve and it would be our *utmost* honor to host you in Mumbai in April. We'd also love to arrange an interview for *Woman*'s May issue."

"That sounds . . . lovely. And it's so kind of you to think of me. But, in all honesty, I don't think I'd be able to come to Mumbai. It would be too dangerous, considering the circumstances with . . . you know. Especially now that my face is plastered all over the news." She pauses for a heartbeat. "I haven't even been back home to Punjab in twenty years."

"Of course, I can absolutely imagine your concerns! But if we were to fly you out, your safety would be our top priority. We could arrange for security and we'd drive you to and from your hotel, if that would make you more comfortable. And, of course, since you'd be in Mumbai, you'd be a *very* safe distance from, well, the people that you're concerned about." The reckless creature within me deflates a little when she says *safe distance*.

"Mom," I whisper, and give her a thumbs-up. "See, it's safe! Say yes!"

"No," she mouths, and shakes her head. "Can you just let me think?"

"Hello? Sorry? Are you still on the line?" Nandini asks.

"Yes, sorry, Nandini, we're still here. We really do appreciate your offer, but it's—it's a lot to reflect on. I'll have to discuss it further with my daughter and get back to you."

We say our goodbyes and Mom hangs up.

"You heard what she said! They'll give us security, Mom. We can actually do this—"

"We?" Mom rises from the bench. "Are you forgetting that you have school? And even if you didn't, there's no good reason why we should go there."

For a moment, we wordlessly lock eyes, and I wonder if we're both thinking the same thing. "I can think of a few good reasons, Mom," I murmur, meeting her at eye level as I stand up.

"She wouldn't want to see me."

It takes a few seconds for me to understand. "Your mom? You don't know that. Maybe—maybe she would. Maybe she wants to reach out but she just . . . doesn't know how."

Mom turns away. "I don't think so." She begins to walk down the cement path that winds through the park garden. I follow, hurrying to keep up with her pace.

"What if we got in touch with your relatives—your chachi—and asked them to talk to your mom first, so that it's not so awkward. We'll find out how she actually feels. And if she's down, maybe we could ask her to meet us in Mumbai. I know it's far from Punjab but maybe—maybe this could actually work."

"Sahaara . . ." She sighs. "Is this why you want to go there?"

Ever since I read that email from Nandini, I've been fantasizing about what-ifs. As in, what if Mom's presence in Mumbai fuels more protests? What if we can occupy so much South Asian media that he begins to cower in fear? What if *I* can get on TV and tell people the entire truth about me? What if my existence, living proof of his rape, can become the nail in the coffin of his political career? What if we get so loud, so in his face, so all-pervasive and godlike that he can't ignore us?

What if I can break him?

If I tell her the whole truth of my bloodlust, she'll be horrified. So I only tell her part of it. "You've been here for twenty years, Mom. Twenty years of not being able to even go *near* the place where you were born. Twenty years of not traveling or getting paid fairly or getting to have a license or do normal stuff like everyone else. All because this piece of shit made you feel *this* afraid. And it pisses me off—like, right into the core of my soul—that he could have that power over our lives. Isn't it time we stopped living in fear?"

Her eyes, staring intently into mine, soften and widen at once, as if she is in awe.

questions for an absent mother

even if you take my call
these curiosities will remain my own
(i do not possess the courage, the nerve)

1. did it hurt when i left?

2. how long did it take for you to clear out my bedroom?

3. *did* you ever clear out my bedroom?

4. did you know, deep down, that i was telling the truth?

5. what did it mean to raise a daughter in a family that wanted a son?

6. did you know how much i would struggle with motherhood?

7. were you ready for motherhood?

8. was it worth it? choosing your reputation over me.

9. do you love me?

10. can this relationship mend?

Kira

we knock on the door

Before she dials, she looks to me for reassurance. Without missing a beat, I smile and nod and tuck away any sign of apprehension. The look on her face—a mixture of fear and anticipation of hurt—tells me that one of us needs to be sure about this.

"Just ten seconds of courage. Nothing to lose, remember?"

"Right. You're right. Nothing to lose."

She's sitting at my bedroom desk, too nervous to nag about the dirty laundry piled around her feet. The phone rings for what feels like an eternity and more than anything, I'm terrified for her. Her chachi seemed nice enough, certain enough, when she offered to help Mom make this call. But I just don't want this to be another blow to her already aching heart.

"Hanji, hello?" a woman answers.

Mom's lips are parted but only air escapes.

"Hello? Helloooo, can you hear me? Hello?!" The voice on the other end of the receiver is raspy and irritated. I stare at the cell phone in shock, frozen just like Mom.

She actually picked up.

"I'm here. It's me—it's Kiran," Mom spits out.

Silence.

"Hello? Are you there?"

"So you remember me now?" Hardeep says. "After all these years?"

"You—you never called, either."

"How are you doing?"

"I'm . . . good. I'm doing fine. My daughter's here . . . Sahaara." Mom says my name and it wakes me from a trance. I pry myself from the phone screen and try to offer her another encouraging smile. Her skin is a sickly, pale sky.

"Oh—um—how is she?"

"She's well. Just turned nineteen. Studying in university now."

"Ah. I see."

Another awkward silence snares. I know Mom's racking her memory for something discussion-worthy. Hardeep beats her to it. "You couldn't even come for the funeral?"

"I couldn't—I'm sorry—I couldn't leave Canada. I wouldn't have been able to come back because I didn't have my documents—" Mom's voice cracks and she takes a moment to compose herself. Heartbreaking memories from eighth grade come flooding back. The sight of Mom crying in Maasi's arms, devastated at her father's death. Crumbling because she couldn't go to the funeral. Because her own mother hadn't been the one to break the news to her. Because I wasn't welcome among them.

I still feel nothing for the stranger on the other end of the phone. But if this call brings Mom any semblance of contentment, it'll have been worth it.

"Bali said you're coming to Mumbai . . ."

"Bali?" I mouth. "Who's that?"

"My chachi," Mom whispers to me. She returns her attention to the phone. "Yeah . . . for just a few days at the end of April. It would be . . . nice to see you. I know it's far—"

"Far?" She laughs. "Kamaleeay, of course Mumbai is far. My knee hasn't been good. Your cousins have been helping me with the shopping, taking me around town whenever I need them. Those good boys, God give them long lives, so dedicated to their family. Nahi taan, I'd be stuck in the house all day. I had a surgery, did you know? Well, of course you wouldn't."

Mom pauses, breathing through the sting and swell. "I understand. I'm sorry you haven't been feeling well. How's your health?"

"I'm fine. My health is fine." Her drawling sigh is static over the receiver. "I presume you won't be coming to Punjab."

"No . . . I can't. You've probably seen the news?"

"Have I seen the news?" she scoffs. "Of course I've seen it. Who hasn't seen it? You couldn't just let me live the rest of my days in peace, could you?"

"It wasn't about you. It was about me finally being able to come forward about what I've gone through."

"Rani Ahluwalia called me after you came on the news. But I told her to just leave me alone. She knows I haven't spoken to you. That you're not some child who I can keep in line. But the embarrassment . . . didn't you think about how this would affect everyone else? This wasn't *just* about you."

"Has anybody—are you safe? Has anyone threatened you?"

"Rani was angry with me, *furious* for years. She said we humiliated her son when you canceled the engagement, when you . . . but after your father died, she softened. She knew that none of this was my fault. That I'd done the best I could. Maybe she felt bad—I don't know—but she and her family have always given me my space. So, yes, I'm safe. You're right, though. You—you shouldn't come to Punjab."

Mom's gaze drifts above my head, glazing, departing from the present. "Yeah. Okay," she eventually mumbles.

"What days will you be in Mumbai? I'll come. I'll be there."

"But . . . wouldn't it be unsafe for you if the Ahluwalias knew you were coming to see me?"

"What the Ahluwalias don't know can't hurt them."

project (re)proposal

missing a week of school was a *yes*
from all my professors
but i haven't spoken with rhonda yet
i've rehearsed the words in my head
a hundred times but they still manage
to get stuck in my throat

hi, rhonda
do you have a minute?
so basically, my mom's been selected
to speak at a gala in mumbai.
she was chosen for this really amazing
award because of an interview she
did where she was telling her story
and it wouldn't be safe for her to
go alone because of what
she's been vocal about
and i was basically wondering
if it would be possible for me
to join her for a week in
april . . .

she mulls over my words
for a fraction of a moment
and says

>   *that would cut through*
>   *our final project presentation*
>   *week*
>
>   *but i think it could be an*
>   *important learning experience.*
>   *what's your project about,*
>   *again?*

how my mom is a survivor
of sexual assault and how
that connected to her being
undocumented

>   *why not interview others*
>   *while you're there?*
>   *women who have lived*
>   *through similar situations—*
>
>   *why not connect with a local*
>   *organization in mumbai and*
>   *expand the project?*

#MENSRIGHTSNOW
One question for all of you:
Why did she wait so long to come forward?

185   10.3 k   ♡ 29.8 k

jaskaran tha god
Damn. My dad is really still pro-Ahluwalia LOL. Why am I not even surprised right now?

12   ♡ 49

j a n a n i #MeToo
#KiranKaur is a beacon of light just like her name means. Believe her.

16   43   ♡ 392

moon-less night gal
fk hari ahluwalia and all these ppl who can look past the truth so easily.

432   122   ♡ 721

Rajesh Ramachandran
LOL at all these feminazis who are trying to bring down another good man. Sad!

89   103   ♡ 548

Champagne Bhapu Jee
Can everyone shut up about this Kiran lady, already? Are y'all really so dumb you can't tell she's lying?

339   1,017   ♡ 3,210

lorde have mercy
Kiran Kaur's story is a reminder that violence against women is EVERYWHERE. Your fave #goodguy leaders can still be abusive.

34   8,204   ♡ 28.9 k

HARLEEN B
It is EXHAUSTING reading all the victim-blaming shit about Kiran Kaur.

14   2,023   ♡ 5,231

Sunny

yoo long time no talk. hope u been good.

Sooo random but i saw the interview your mom did.

lol how do you always manage to turn up completely outta the blue

Props for speaking up and all that but i was wondering if u guys are 100% sure that it was Ahluwalia

what do you mean...

like i'm not doubting ur mom or anything i just wanted to know more cuz i've heard he's a rly decent guy

the water in his eyes

"The fuck is Sunny Sahota's problem?" I swing open the door to Jeevan's bedroom and he slowly swivels around from his laptop, pulling out one of his earbuds. His face is a mixture of bemusement and confusion.

"How'd you get into my house?"

"Keerat opened the door."

"Got it. And, uh, did I miss something? Sunny?" He closes the door behind me, carefully maneuvering past an overflowing bookshelf and cramped desk to reach a springy mattress resting on the ground.

"So this asshole doesn't message me for months," I declare, plopping down on the gray beanbag pushed against the wall, "and then he turns up outta nowhere to question me on Ahluwalia? He started asking me whether he was definitely the rapist and it wasn't someone else . . . like my mom can't remember his face." Like I am not haunted by it every time I look in the mirror.

"What the hell? Why does he care so much about the guy?"

"Apparently his dad's a People's Party supporter."

"You okay?"

"I'm fine . . . just weirded out. He was half trying to be supportive and half edging into victim-blamey crap. Didn't expect that from him. In high school, he was the type to call out predators and shit." I think back to random conversations about Six Nine and Harvey Weinstein and R. Kelly. Sunny always initiated the discussions. Sunny was always on the right side.

Jeevan scratches his scruffy chin. He rests his square jaw

in his palm. "People are disappointing as hell when their own heroes turn out to be monsters. The mental gymnastics are fucked. He might've said all that but remember that MMA fighter? We were shooting hoops once, and he started talking about how he wasn't sure about the allegations 'cause the victim dropped charges."

"Wow. Wooooow."

"Don't let him get to you, though. For every person like that, there's someone else who believes Aunty Jee."

Not letting it get to me is way easier said than done. Mom stopped watching the news reports weeks ago, but Jeevan and I couldn't disconnect if we wanted to: her story is all over Instagram and Twitter and TikTok (although the TikToks disappear quick 'cause they're political). Brown activists are writing about how shitty Hari Ahluwalia is, just as I'd hoped they would, but desi meme accounts are posting about it, too. Even if the memes make fun of him, the comment sections are grotesque and heartless. Hundreds of random people debating whether or not Mom is telling the truth, as if our lives are just a fun topic of discussion.

Meanwhile, the piece of shit himself hasn't said a word. I wonder what it would take for him to speak.

"I should get going," I mumble. "Gotta start packing for Mumbai."

"Can we, um, can we talk about that? Why bother going out there? Just an unnecessary risk, isn't it?"

"It's gonna be fine. We won't even be near Punjab."

"But, Sahaara, these politicians play by their own rules. You don't know what they're capable of. Don't you remember that HJ Party MLA?"

"What're you talking about?"

"There was a whole case last year where this HJ Party guy tried to *murder* a girl who accused him of rape. He ended up killing her uncle."

"But, Jeevan." I swallow. "There will literally be sixteen hundred kilometers of distance between us and him. And we'll have security. And no one out there even knows we're coming—"

"Except your grandma?"

"She's not my grandma."

"Sorry . . . what do I call her?"

"Hardeep."

He touches the back of his neck, his chuckle tentative and unsure. I know how rude it is to refer to elders by their first names, but Hardeep doesn't deserve much respect, in my opinion. "Okay . . . what if *Hardeep* snakes you guys out to the Ahluwalias? Given all the shit she put your mom through, I wouldn't put it past her to tip them off about your mom being there."

"She'll keep her mouth shut. Trust."

"How do you know that?"

"Jeevan, think about it. Why would she say anything about us when the Ahluwalias would get pissed off at her for even talking to my mom?"

Nervous laughter tremors in his Adam's apple as he pushes back thick curls. "This sounds like a naatak. How is this real life?"

"You're telling me."

"Sahaara . . . just . . . *why* do you want to do this?"

"For my mom." I say this with a self-assuring nod. "It's been twenty years since she's seen Hardeep. And yeah, I think she's a bitch and she doesn't mean shit to me, but my mom still deserves to see her. And figure out their shit. And not live the rest of her life feeling guilty, regretting the fact that her relationship was destroyed because of . . . me." At the last word, I go radio silent. My existence is at the root of so many things that have hurt Mom. Her overstayed visa. Her severed connection to family. Her struggle to even speak to her mother. I am the thread that binds it all together.

"But . . . you can't actually blame yourself for that. Your mom made her own choices. . . ." Jeevan joins me on the ground. He rests a heavy arm around my shoulder and I lean into his chest, that familiar scent of lavender detergent wafting from his black hoodie.

I remain a still portrait and he continues. "Why go to Mumbai now? Why not at least wait till all this shit in the news dies down?"

"It's because of the magazine. There's no way Mom would even think about going if we weren't gonna have security. And what if he gets elected?"

"Shit . . . yeah. The election," Jeevan murmurs. He leaves his arm around my shoulder and pulls out his cell phone with the other. Instantly, he finds what he's searching for. "It's in the middle of May."

"We'll be back *way* before then." I poke his cheek. "And we'll be fine. I promise. Pinky swear."

He scoffs but locks his pinky into mine. "You're something else, man. Seriously." As he draws me a little closer, I welcome the warmth of a body far kinder to me than my own. "If I could just keep you right here, I would. But I already know you're not gonna listen to me, so you better text me every hour so I know you're good. And . . ." Jeevan reaches over my lap and rifles through a red Nike shoebox sitting under his desk.

"Take this." Delicately, he rests a black folding knife in my hand. "Keep it on you wherever you go. Doesn't matter if you have security."

The flat, textured body of the knife is more than half the length of my hand. I run my thumb along the rough handle. Along the smooth ebony edge of the blade that peeks out.

"Promise you'll always keep it on you?"

"Promise. But, uh, two questions. One, how do I even open this? Two, if someone actually attacks me, what's stopping them from grabbing it from my scrawny ass and using it against me?"

"Trust me. If someone attacks you, it's better to have *something* rather than nothing. Only pull it out if you really need it, obviously. And you open it like this." He reaches into my hand and places the dull, protruding edge of the blade between his thumb and index finger. He pulls out the blade and extends it backward until it clicks in place. The razor-thin side glints beneath light pouring in through a slit in the gray curtains. "I got it sharpened, so don't touch the edge," he says, passing it back to me.

Twisting and dancing between my fingers, the hair-fine rim glows silver on the otherwise black surface. No doubt, it's sharp enough to cut through skin. "Knife is deadly. Noted."

"And you close it like this. See this metal thing?" He points to a bumpy steel strip tucked inside the handle. "That's the lock. You just push it to the left and then you can fold the blade back in." He patiently watches me fumble with the metal lock and attempt to close the knife. After a few tries, I finally get it.

"You learn quick." He grins.

"You gotta teach me how to use it, though."

"I mean . . . I assume you just grip it tight, point, and stab. Can't be that complicated. We can watch YouTube videos, if you want."

"So, you're telling me you keep a sharpened blade but don't actually know how to use it?"

"The reason I bought it is kinda gone to prison at the moment, so . . ."

I have to lean back a degree to take in his gentle face. There they are, his kind chestnut eyes, usually hidden behind his black-rimmed glasses. His thick lips that quiver as easily as mine. "You think you could've actually stabbed him?"

"If he was about to kill us? I dunno. Maybe. If it was between stabbing him and watching him beat the shit out of my mom again . . . maybe. He's just as strong as he looks. I could never hold him back."

Since the ninth grade, Jeevan's only been getting taller and bulkier, but his dad is six-foot-something with a rage that can plow through anything. Sometimes, I wonder about the shit he's witnessed, the violence he's known close up, the danger he's just barely scraped through. What has it done to his nectar-soft heart?

"It's all over now. He's gone."

"Not if my mom lets him back in the house, again." Jeevan sniffs. He leans back against the wall and stares up at the ceiling, a tear slipping through his eyelashes and gliding down his cheek. Something fierce and protective roars within me at the sight. How could anyone hurt this honeycomb of a boy? How could he hurt anyone else?

"Honestly, just let my bibi talk to your mom. She's ruthless. She'll convince your mom she'll be fine without him."

He shakes his head and the tear drips off his chin. "If all

this shit wasn't enough to show her why we're better off without him, I doubt anything else will."

I think of Mom. "Sometimes, a person just needs to know they're not alone to find their courage. She needs a reminder that all of us have her back."

"I appreciate the fuck outta you. You know that, right?"

"I appreciate you, too." I reach for a tear resting on his scruffy cheek and wipe it away with my thumb. "When did we become so corny, though?"

"We've always been this corny." He laughs. My hand still rests on his cheek. For a moment, our eyes hover over each other's, the space between us filled only with the sight of his dew-covered lashes. With the smell of hoodie. Of his skin.

Then my hand is on the neck of his hoodie and his soft mouth is pulled to mine. And his hands are on my back. My neck. And every inch of skin where his hands land becomes electric. Becomes a dizzying, gorgeous confusion of both him and me connected and inseparable and alive. And nothing exists but this beautiful boy who has always been close and far.

And just like that, he pulls back, hovering dangerously close to me and then farther away. "What just happened?" he whispers, cheeks still damp.

"I don't know," I reply, my voice water-soft.

"I don't want this."

"What do you mean?"

"I don't want you *like this*."

"Like what?" I stare into eyes that I know better than any other. Eyes that suddenly can't meet mine.

"Feeling sorry for me and—"

"Jeevan, I don't feel sorry for you. I'm—"

"—confused and fucked up 'cause of what Sunny said."

My body, still leaning into his and reeling from his touch, pulls away for the first time. "This wasn't because of him."

"Sahaara, I've known you longer than anyone. I've seen how rattled you get every time he turns up. It's like, no matter how shitty he is, you always want him to be someone he's not. This wouldn't have happened if he didn't text you. You're confused."

Irritation wells within me. He's wrong. I don't know what just happened, but it felt . . . right. "I—I—no. I'm not confused."

"Dude . . . in all these years, you've never wanted me. And now, *this* randomly happens?"

"But you didn't, either."

"Haven't I?"

Those two words constrict my throat. And seemingly his as well. For a moment, he just blinks, as if he didn't mean to say that aloud. "I—um—I can't do this right now. I can't be your blanket."

"My *blanket*? Jeevan, really?"

"I think I just need to be alone right now," he murmurs without moving from his place on the ground. "I've got a lotta shit to figure out. I'm sorry."

"I'm sorry, too."

how do you know
it's real?

does it count if the sparks are different?

if there's still a ghost of another boy
somewhere within you
made only of apricot-sweet memories
pink
      juicy
            no sign of the bruising or the rot?

does it count if you want his lips
just like you want to escape from your own flesh?

if his mouth makes you forget yourself
and this is how you manage to breathe?

is it love if it makes you feel something
just when you thought you'd always be numb?

what would lisbeth do?

twenty-three minutes have passed
since i drafted the email to nandini
(mom's not included on this one)

i read and reread and
reread again, finger hovering
over the send button and then
returning to the keyboard

i pore over those two sentences
study them like a chemical equation
trying to be certain of each word:

although my mom isn't interested
in doing anything media-related
outside of the magazine feature,
i would love to do a tv interview
while i'm in mumbai.

i'd like the opportunity
to share my side of the story.

i hit send and throw my phone
across the bed, heart jumping
when i hear mom humming
in the hallway

it doesn't take long for nandini
to reply, introducing me to taara
a magazine assistant who's ready
to reach out to the press

> *we have a few trusted contacts.*
> *they'll keep things confidential.*

they just want to know if i would be
okay going live on india's largest
news network.

after all this running

i walk willingly into the mouth of a dragon
because the regret of never returning
would have killed me anyways

but joti can't miss work
and aunty jee's back is too bad to travel
and sahaara refuses to stay home

and i tell myself that my daughter
is safest by my side
but, in truth, i think i am frightened
by the thought of facing this battle
without her.

Kiran

the night before the flight

"I've changed my mind. Sahaara, you're not coming." Maasi and I look up from my half-packed suitcase on the floor. Mom is standing in the doorway to my room.

I tuck a rolled-up pair of underwear into my suitcase. "Mom, there's no way you're going without me." Just as the idea of going to Mumbai has wrapped itself around my thoughts like dense vines, it's gotten stuck in her mind as well. Her reasons have nothing to do with mine and everything to do with her mother. "If we're doing this, we're doing it together."

She wrings her hands, that familiar, distant look in her eyes stealing her away from the present. Then she slowly nods before disappearing from the doorway. She is both terrified for me and terrified to be without me.

"Stay with the magazine people at all times, don't take any pangeh, and keep that knife on you at all times, yeah?" Maasi tells me for the fiftieth time, elbow balanced on her knee, hand in her currently blonde hair. She's not happy about the trip but she gets it. "That was a good call from Jeevan, giving you the knife."

My heart clenches at the mention of him. "I still haven't seen him since the . . . you know."

"Has he texted you?" Maasi asks, placing a rolled-up pair of faded jeans in the suitcase.

"Yeah . . . but it's, like, forced. I've been texting first and he'll give me these dead, two-word answers. Tried to video call him last night and he said he was busy." Habitually, I glance over at my phone, hoping that the screen will light up with a message.

"Give him some time. This is . . . a lot."

"That's what I said," I mumble. "Can I ask you something?"

"Uh-huh." She looks up briefly as she unfolds and refolds a striped maxi skirt.

"How'd you know you were supposed to be with your girlfriend? Like, what was it about Aman?" Maasi's been in a relationship with a NICU doctor for nearly nine months now and the joy practically glows on her skin.

"Hmm." She pauses. "I think I knew Aman was the right person because I never had to justify our relationship. Like, I didn't have to constantly convince myself that things were good. Or that I was happy. I didn't have to . . . twist around my personality for the relationship to work. We just came to each other as ourselves—our realest selves—and we fit." She shrugs with a smile that's perpetually young.

"Were you into her from, like, the moment you met?"

"There were definitely instant sparks, but over time, it was less about the sparks and more about the long-term glue. The trust, the affection, the stability. All that is just as important as chemistry."

You're confused, Jeevan had said. He was right. And wrong. That kiss was overwhelmingly beautiful, but where the hell did it come from? His touch was a sea of wildflowers blooming on the ice field of my skin—how did he thaw a body I loathed?

"Lately . . . I haven't felt like myself," I mumble. "Makes it hard to understand this Jeevan thing."

"After all the shit that's happened in the last few months, you need time to process. If I can give you *any* annoying aunty advice, it's that things are gonna be fine. You're nineteen, for god's sake. You might not have it all figured out right now, but slowly things will be clearer. And the boy stuff will smooth itself out."

It's hard to believe that, considering that I may have permanently fucked up my friendship with my best friend. "When Mom was my age, she'd figured out enough to know she wanted to have me . . . and how she was gonna raise me."

Maasi drops my tie-dyed sports bra and cracks up. "Are you *kidding*? She had things figured out? Lemme tell you something. Your mom and I figured out a whole lotta shit as we went along. Most times, we didn't know what the hell we were doing. Both of us were thrust into situations that forced us to grow up way too young. We just handled that stuff because . . . there was no choice *but* to handle it." She holds my gaze with kindness. Certainty. "You're allowed to be a teenager. You're allowed to do normal shit and be confused about boys and make a mess in the process. Okay, don't make too much of a mess, but you know what I mean, right?"

"I guess."

"We done with the suitcase? Anything else you wanna pack?" My pillow-length taichee is filled with just enough clothing and toiletries and art supplies to get me by for a week. Reaching into the canvas bag sitting next to me on the carpet, I find Jeevan's knife and tuck it beneath a coral-colored blazer.

"I think we're good."

mom's rules for mumbai

1. remain at my side at all times.
   i don't care if it's juvenile.
   we go everywhere together.

2. no interviews. no media.
   we go to our events
   and then we go home.

3. when you meet ~~your nani~~ hardeep
   at least *try* to be polite. not for her.
   for me.

4. tell no one where we are
   or where we're staying.
   no tweeting or instagramming
   our live location until we're home.

5. don't lose the knife.

departures

So, I've never actually been on a plane before. I've been to YVR a few times to drop off Bibi Jee and Joti Maasi, but I was always the one hugging my loved ones *goodbye*. Not the one who crosses the security gate and disappears behind the wall that leads to the sky.

Standing here right now, the long line of travelers slowly draining through the airport security gate, the moment is surreal. Mom's Indian passport arrived last month, after we visited the embassy. On a black bench outside the building, I watched as the passport shook in her tight grasp, a million heart-bursting realizations striking her at once. This palm-sized, twenty-eight-paged little book meant she could travel freely again. That leaving Surrey wouldn't mean she'd never be able to return. That this land was no longer a hiding place.

"Got everything?" Maasi asks. "Pillow? Blanket? Earplugs?"

"Knew I was forgetting something," I groan. "Left the earplugs and the eye mask in the kitchen."

"Koi na," Mom says, hoisting her overstuffed duffel bag into her arms. "Don't worry. Just use mine."

From behind her new glasses, Bibi Jee's eyes flit worriedly between the two of us. "You're sure about this, huh?"

"Hanji." Mom feebly nods, and I throw an arm over her shoulder. "Now or never, right?"

"It's gonna be great," I reassure them all. "Everyone's coming back in one piece. I promise."

Bibi pinches my cheek, kisses me hard on the forehead. "Pungeh nahi lainay, teekh aa?" *No getting into any trouble, okay?*

"When do I ever get into trouble?" I giggle.

"Not talking about you. I'm talking about your mother." She surveys Mom, a playful gleam in her eye. I laugh with them, ignoring the seed of guilt sprouting in my stomach. *I need to do this*, I remind myself. *They'll understand why I speak out. Maybe? Eventually?*

"Okay, guys, I think you should head through security," Maasi yawns. "You're cutting it close on time." A seven a.m. flight means we're all exhausted—and that Jeevan slept through my last-minute shot at a goodbye call. Or maybe he ignored it.

We hug for the millionth time and no one cries during this round. All of our tears were drained before we left the house.

"See you guys in eight days." I grin.

"Eight days," Maasi repeats.

"Read Chaupai Sahib on the flight for protection," Bibi solemnly says. "Let's hope you only meet kind earth and skies."

Mom and I head toward the security officer who stands before a translucent glass wall, carry-on and duffel bag in hand. He's wearing a heavy black vest. So very coplike. So painfully familiar. Color drains from Mom's face; fear passes through her full-moon eyes: the residue of a lifetime of trauma.

"Passports and boarding passes, please," drawls the blond, goateed man, towering a foot above us both. I pass him both my and Mom's documents and attempt the smile that every person of color has mastered. The one that reads, *I'm thoroughly nonthreatening. Please don't pull me aside and racially profile me.*

He cannot hear my heart rumbling as he scans our boarding

passes, thin and white and slippery between his fingers. After a quick inspection, they are returned to our hands and we are gestured to the door with an uninterested jerk of his chin. It is always a beautiful exhale when authorities are uninterested in us. So often, invisibility has meant safety.

"How're you feeling, Mom?" I ask as we walk through an opening in the glass wall.

She stares over the diverse sea of travelers in the snaking, endless lineup. At the airport security staff poring over computers that will scan our possessions. At the two CBSA officers in serious conversation with a stout Asian man holding a backpack. Her eyes linger on the officers who we have come to learn far too much about. "I'm okay, puth. I can do this."

the plane builds speed

and we could be on a greyhound bus
until the ground evaporates beneath us.
my chest pounds in panic as loud as the infant
across the aisle until i peer through the window
and let wonder erase my anxiety

there she is
the earth.
small and infinite all at once.

houses and cities and mountains and humans
shrink as we drift higher
and nothing on google maps
could have ever prepared me
for the endless beauty of this jade terrain

mom leans over and watches silently
then she says

isn't it beautiful
the way rising up high
can make all of our problems
seem so small?

my daughter sleeps in my lap

and i am thinking about the last flight i boarded
twenty long years ago
when she was still a bundle of cells
bubbling in my womb

how strange it is
to think of that weary girl with a time-bomb heart
waiting for collisions
she never believed she could survive

i plant a kiss on sahaara's heavy head

if my body is a burial ground for midnight-dark memories
and a thousand open-ended regrets
i can, at least for a moment, bask in the sunlight
of what has bloomed.

Kiran

mom is drifting off against my shoulder

and i am lost in a tantalizing daydream
that's been on my mind for days

jeevan said healing does not require
the listening ears of our abusers
that he had nothing to gain
from sharing his letter with his father

but my machete heart has other ideas

a jagged-edged monster giggles
and dances beneath my rib cage
every time i imagine
the news network interview
where i will confront ahluwalia
before the entire watching world
and make sure my face haunts him
in the same way i cannot escape his.

customs

we land
beneath a hazy morning sky
that is unlike any
that's ever hung above surrey
and i am suddenly overwhelmed
by the way we've been carried
halfway across the world in less
than the length of a day

we follow the signs
and the flurry of passengers to customs

border security.

eyes scarlet with exhaustion
we wait in an airtight maze of humans
itching to flee the airport
and carry on to their next destinations

passports?
a thin, brown man with a giant mustache
says as we finally make it to the front of the line

from behind his desk and a layer of glass
his beady eyes survey our passports
he looks up to compare them to our faces

mom gulps, fear rising in both of us
although we've done nothing wrong

what is your purpose of travel?
he asks.

> *we're guests of nandini rajalingam*
> *at* woman magazine.
> *we're attending one of their events.*
> i reply with the lines i've been
> rehearsing for days. the safest words to use,
> nandini has told us.

are you conducting business
while you are here? are you
working?

> *no. just attending*
> *an event.*

and where will you be staying,
he looks mom directly in the eye,
ms. kiran kaur?

she looks at me and i think we are both
scared of the exact same thing.
she tells him the truth about where we're
staying, though.

> *the taj hotel.*

arrivals

Even if Taara wasn't carrying a highlighter-green sign that read "Kiran & Sahaara," I would've spotted her immediately. Her silky black hair cascades down to her waist in influencer-worthy waves and I can't look away. When I say influencer-worthy, I mean I've only ever seen hair like this in the magical, carefully curated realm of Brown Girl Instagram. Her hair sways with her tall body as she rises from a metal bench and waves at us, practically bouncing on her tippy-toes to grab our attention. A muscly, middle-aged pair of security guards flank her on either side and nod politely. While Taara is wearing a summery floral crop top and a knee-length yellow skirt, they are clad in black pants and T-shirts, plain in every regard but for their silvery earpieces.

"Hello!" Mom yawns, rubbing exhaustion from her eyes. Her ancient suitcase drags behind her in an awkward S shape, halting if she doesn't pull it at the right angle. Between a sleepless twenty-one-hour flight, a long wait in customs, and an even longer wait for our baggage, both of us are ready to collapse.

"You must be Kiran and Sahaara!" Taara says, a smile frozen on her heart-shaped face. "So nice to meet you! Welcome to Mumbai!" She leans into Mom and me for air kisses and hugs. "This is Vidya and Kunal. Your security escorts while you're with us."

Vidya and Kunal extend their hands, in turn, to both Mom and me, curtly nodding and smiling. The gentlest creases frame Vidya's thin lips, beauty marks scattered across her warm-caramel skin. Her T-shirt is tight around her sinewy shoulders and well-defined abs. Kunal stands a few inches shorter than her but looks equally invested in his fitness regimen. The faintest shadow of a beard lines his full cheeks and dimpled chin. "Very nice to meet you both," Vidya says, brushing aside a stray hair that has escaped her neat bun. "You must be exhausted. We'll take your bags to the car."

Mom barely argues when Vidya grabs the handle of her suitcase. Kunal's steely eyes rove the entire room as he grabs my luggage and guides us to the exit.

"The flight was . . . long." I sigh. "Me and Mom tried sleeping on each other's laps."

"But we weren't too successful." Mom yawns once again.

The walk across this arrivals area is a whole journey of its own and I have time to give the internet one more shot (the first thing I did when I got off the plane was try to get online and, of course, it refused to work). A joyful shriek accidentally bursts from my throat when I get bars. My cell momentarily freezes with a sudden, buzzing influx of WhatsApp, Twitter, and Instagram notifications.

Shit. There's a message from Jeevan.

Jeevan: Hey sorry I missed your call. I was knocked out.

You're back in 8 days right? I'll see u when u come home.

we definitely need to talk.

Sahaara: Hey, just landed. No worries lol. Thought u were ignoring me. :/

It's nearly five p.m. in Mumbai, so it's around four a.m. back home in Surrey. There's no way he's gonna respond right now, but I still can't help but stare at the time stamp below his name, hoping it'll miraculously turn into "online." *Snap out of it*, I think. *You're not even ready for his reply.*

I send Maasi a quick text, letting her know we made it here safe, and then shove my phone inside my baggy hoodie pocket. Dressed in saris and jeans and business suits, travelers zigzag around us at a dozen angles, all moving as if they have somewhere to be. When a group of university-aged girls pass by with their suitcases, chattering away in what I think is Marathi, I listen closely, trying to catch a grain of familiarity in their speech. No luck. A man in a black suit grazes my shoulder as he speed walks toward the exit, muttering in Hindi about condo rentals. A teaspoon of excitement jolts through me at my understanding. I've watched enough Bollywood movies and speak enough Punjabi to catch the basics of Hindi.

"So!" Taara begins, more jittery excitement in her voice than I could muster with three espresso shots. "We're headed to your hotel with Vidya and Kunal right now. They'll be staying in the room next to yours just as a safety precaution. I'm sure you two want some sleep, so we'll let you get some rest and if you're up for it, we'll meet up later tonight? Or early tomorrow morning?"

"Sounds like a plan." Through layers upon layers of sliding glass doors, we cross a cool threshold into the sun-drenched world outside. Mumbai punches me in the face with a humidity that the air-conditioned airport had sheltered me from. Hot air, sulfurous and fishy, reaches into my nostrils and envelops every pore on my skin. We're definitely not in Surrey anymore.

We push through an ocean of travelers, trying not to bump into all their suitcases as they jump into their Ubers and Olas and taxis. In the grid of vehicles, there are a spattering of shiny black taxis, distinct with their yellow rooftops. They dot the length of the white canopy-covered roadway as far as I can see.

We're here. We're in the same country as him.

"Is it always this hot?" I gasp, fanning myself as we finally jump in the car. Beads of sweat are already forming on my forehead.

"Believe it or not, this is on the cooler side for us." Taara laughs. She reaches into a humongous checkered tote bag, grabbing a few water bottles and passing them back from the passenger seat. "Here. Make sure you stay well-hydrated, okay?"

Water feels like paradise against my tongue as we enter the queue of honking taxis. My head rests heavy on Mom's shoulder and bluish drowsiness threatens to steal the first glimpses of this city from me.

"OOOOH! Before I forget!" Taara's excited chirp pries my eyes wide open. "I've printed out a few trip itineraries for you both."

Oh, shit.

She hands me a piece of paper and passes one over to Mom before I can grab it. Suddenly, the car is brutally claustrophobic.

"So, tomorrow morning at ten, you have the interviews over at Aasra Shelter," Taara says. "You're okay traveling there with Vidya and Kunal, right?"

"I guess that's okay, but . . ." Mom glances up from the itinerary in confusion. "There's an interview scheduled for Sahaara tomorrow. We didn't agree to any interviews." The AC might as well be off right now, the way sweat is dripping down my armpits.

"Oh, but . . . in the email, we talked about it. I believe you said interviews are fine . . ." Taara rifles through her papers, probably searching for the email where I secretly agreed to a television appearance. She anxiously flutters between me and Mom.

"An email? Sahaara was answering all the . . ." Mom's voice trails off as she turns her attention toward me, eyes ready to ignite.

Hot blood rushes to my ears. My dumb ass was really hoping she'd find out tomorrow, so close to the interview that she wouldn't be able to say no. There will now be three unfortunate witnesses to my homicide. She's gonna kill me. "Okay, don't freak out. I—um—decided to do a couple interviews—"

"*Excuse me?* You did *what*?!"

"Hear me out . . . they're not interviews with *you*. They're just with me!"

The vein in her forehead is throbbing. She snaps her head toward Taara. "I'm sorry . . . Sahaara won't be doing the interviews—"

"But, Mom! It'll be fine. It's with a news network that *Woman Magazine* trusts—"

"It doesn't matter, Sahaara. We'll talk about this later."

"Um . . ." Taara flimsily interjects, "I can see about canceling the second interview, but it might be a little late for the first one . . . INN's already made preparations and, um . . ."

"This is unbelievable . . ." Mom shakes her head, eyes bulging. "Sahaara and I need to talk about this first. I'm sorry. It's not your fault, obviously. *My daughter* needs to remember that we discuss serious decisions like this *together*."

"If I might suggest," Kunal says without taking his eyes off the road, "I think we can find ways to safely do an interview. Kiran, you've done an interview previously, yes?"

"I have, but that was in Canada. I don't want people knowing we're in Mumbai unless they absolutely have to."

"So, what if . . . the interview is set up in such a way that it looks like you're calling in from somewhere else? From Canada."

"What do you mean?" Vidya asks from beside him.

"INN has those correspondent interviews, don't they? Tell them to make it look like she's calling in from abroad. Or else the interview won't happen."

"I'm—I'm not sure if we can ask them to do that, but I can try?" Taara's chirpy tone now sounds like a bird in frenzy. She pushes her long hair out of her face, unlocks her phone, and furiously types.

Mom turns toward me once again, balls of fire now fully formed in her eyes, ready to blaze into me the second we're alone.

I know I could've come here, shut my mouth, and gone home, as if the hurt living beneath my skin will dissolve on its own. But deep down, the pain and I both know that's never gonna happen. So, I mouth the word *sorry* and mean it. I'm sorry that I couldn't tell her, but I don't regret what I've done. What I'm going to do. Then I close my eyes to the hazy, cloudless sky, in history's most pathetic attempt at pretending to fall asleep.

the taj hotel

I knew Mom would have to find out eventually. And I knew it was fucked up to think I could tell her so last minute that she wouldn't be able to say no. But it was the only way I could do this. I feel like shit, but the icy fortress of anger within me is more brutal than the guilt. Or the fear.

So, when the car's sudden stop jolts me awake, I glance over at Mom, hoping the fury has eased from her eyes but still wondering how to convince her to let me speak.

Her head rests peacefully against the tinted window. She's still asleep.

"Mom?" I place a hand on the paper-thin blue cotton of her kameez and gently shake her awake.

"What—where are we—oh . . ." She turns her head toward the impressive sight of the building outside the window. A majestic gray-bricked palace sprawls before us as far as the eye can see. Its ground level is built almost entirely of white, door-sized archways, each one pristine and ivory. Above are several levels of white bay windows that protrude from the walls. I crane my neck to take in the opulent, rust-red domes that mount the corners of the building like minarets. More than a hotel, it reminds me of a grand fortress.

Beneath the golden hour sun, dozens of pigeons fly over the domes and land somewhere out of sight. "Meet the Taj Mahal Hotel," Kunal says as he puts the car in park.

"We're . . . staying here?"

I can't tell if it's exhaustion, anger, or something else, but Mom looks uninterested. I'm willing to bet it's anger.

Between idling taxis, I watch as a gaunt, elderly man with a wiry beard walks along the cobblestone opposite the lavish building, unbothered by the tourists who push past him. He sits down among a flock of pigeons, his graying, tattered shirt fluttering against his skin in the hot wind. The pigeons, just as unbothered by the swarm of tourists, happily clamber around the crumbs he scatters among them. A gray sea sways behind the old man, populated by lazily floating boats that dip past the horizon.

"That right there," Kunal says as he clicks off his seat belt, "is the Gateway of India." He points toward a grayish stone archway sitting to our left, a magnet that tourists gather around. Nearly the size of a baseball field, the boxy, intricately chiseled gate rests just before the sea, guiding people to the water. It reminds me of the Arc de Triomphe in Paris that I painted for Art 11. "Stunning, isn't it?" Kunal beams with pride.

I follow Mom's eyes as they travel from the gate to the bony man among the pigeons. She nods absentmindedly. "Stunning."

i suppose it's beautiful

the greeter wears a maroon sari and a pristine smile
as she welcomes us into the hotel with garlands and tilaks
the porter is perfectly polite as he takes our bags
and guides us up the elevator to our suite

everyone is kind here
because someone has paid enough money

everyone is at ease here
because someone has paid enough money

and i can't help but wonder
whether a restless ocean sits beneath
their happy veneers
just as one rumbles beneath mine

whether they are just as hopeful
that today may be the beginning
of a broken relationship finally mending

whether they are just as frightened
that they have made a dreadful mistake
simply by showing up

nothing about this lavish building
erases the muddy truth of who i am
where i am, where i have been
and where i am going
not for a single moment

after all, a beautiful hotel is a temporary stay

home.
that is messy
and honest
and tumultuous
and forever.

Kiran

please

we climb a red-carpeted staircase that could rival hogwarts
the ceiling is a turquoise sky hanging high above us
and mom's voice is low
while taara walks ahead and security follows behind

sahaara, what the hell has gotten into you?

i need to do this. and i know it sounds
ridiculous and i know you don't want me to
but you aren't the only one who's hurting, mom.

i have a story, too.

miss dhanjal

"All right, ma'ams, this is your room," the dewy-skinned porter declares through a handlebar mustache. The journey up to the fourth floor was filled with details about the hotel and its Jiva Spa and nine restaurants and outdoor pool (or *pools*? I can't remember). I politely nodded a lot, but didn't hear much, to be honest. Mom hasn't said a word to me since we departed from the staircase.

With the beep of a key card, the wooden door glides open and, despite the anvil in my chest, my eyes widen. I catch the light ebbing through the bay windows before I can even take in the ornate queen beds and the rest of the royally decorated room. Mom and our *Woman Magazine* hosts trail behind as I sprint toward the window to soak up the view. The gray Arabian Sea stretches below, its waters shimmering with sunlight, its tide stirring steadily. Contemplatively.

"You didn't bring your paints, did you?" Mom startles me from behind. I glance back to see her frustration cool at the sight of the sea.

"No, just the charcoal pencils. They'll work really well, though. Look at all those grays in the water. . . ."

"As I said in the elevator, ma'ams, room service is available twenty-four hours a day." The porter unloads my heavy suitcase from his trolley and straightens his mahogany vest. "Is there anything else I can do for you?"

"No, no, thank you," Mom says. "This is wonderful. Too much, really." She reaches into her purse in search of rupees to tip the porter but Kunal waves her away.

"You're guests in our city! We pay for everything. Don't

worry." He hands the porter a crisp bill and he bows his head in gratitude.

"Mrs. Dhanjal, Miss Dhanjal, I hope you have a lovely time at the Taj. Like I said, please don't hesitate to call the concierge if you need anything at all." The porter offers another small bow and begins to reverse the trolley from the room.

"Mrs. Dha—" Mom begins, but Vidya discreetly shakes her head. She remains silent until the door closes with a smooth click behind the trolley.

"We have you staying here under the name Anisha Dhanjal. Another safety precaution. Sahaara, I think we named you Divya Dhanjal."

"Affirmative." Kunal glances up from his phone. "Divya Dhanjal it is."

"Divya Dhanjal." I pronounce each syllable, wrapping my tongue around my new identity. "It has a ring to it. Like the lady in a naatak who secretly poisons her in-laws."

"Oh my god. It does, na?" Taara giggles. "Excuse me. I'll just be outside for a moment. Phone call from INN." Taara sneaks out of the room and I take a seat on a velvet gray footstool resting before the bed. The rich red duvet is woven with intricate gold patterns that I'm tempted to sample for an art piece. From the swirling Arabian Sea to the opulent decor, inspiration has somehow kindled an emotion that isn't dread or rage.

"Challo, we'll let you get some rest, but we're next door in room ten if you need anything. You have our phone numbers, correct?" Vidya asks.

I double-check the contacts on my cell. "Yep, I've got 'em."

"We're here to make you feel as safe as possible. That means if you hear an unexpected knock on your door in the middle of the night or see something strange outside the window, you're welcome to call us. No questions asked," Vidya says. "Sincerely, I don't think we'll encounter any problems in this hotel. The Taj takes its security very seriously . . . ever since the 2008 attacks. But you can never be too safe. *Any* concerns and you dial us, theek hai?"

"Theek aa," Mom agrees, taking a seat beside me on the footstool. "It means a lot to me that you're willing to go to all this trouble."

"This isn't any trouble, Kiran." Kunal crosses his arms over his puffed chest as he speaks. "It's the least that we can do. You're raising your voice for so many who aren't heard. It's just an unfortunate truth of our world that the powerful will go to any length to silence their critics."

Mom grimaces, something queasy stalking her features when she looks away.

"I have good neeeeews!" Taara sings, shutting the door behind her. "INN is going to set up the interview so that it looks like Sahaara's calling in from abroad—"

"Just a second," Kunal interjects. "We haven't heard whether Kiran is actually comfortable with going through with the interview at all."

"Oh . . . yes. Right," Taara mumbles with a deflating fizzle. "It would be set up so that Sahaara is in front of a blank background . . . Anu Shergill would be interviewing her from a different room. They wouldn't mention anything about her location. And, um . . . they did say that before I called, they had already started tweeting about the segment, so the news is already out. . . ."

"Taara." Vidya irritatedly clicks her tongue. "Tweets can be deleted. The priority here is Kiran's comfort."

Before I can plead my case, Mom speaks up. "I know you've already gone to all this trouble, but I don't want this interview to go ahead. I need you to just cancel it. I know that it'll upset the news network, but—"

"Don't worry about upsetting the news network." Kunal waves away her concern. "Not for a moment. They'll fill the slot with something else."

My long nails dig into my sweaty palms and I hold my gaze there while I speak. "You're all talking about this like I'm not even in the room." I look up and all eyes are suddenly on me. Mine stare into Mom's without flinching away. The words leave my mouth as if this courage is real. "I'm going through with the interview. I'll be safe and I know what I need to say."

"What you *need* to say?" she scoffs. "You don't *need* to say anything. Everything that needed to be said has already been said."

"No." I shake my head. "It hasn't. And whether you're with me or not, I'm doing this interview tomorrow. If you don't want to help me, I'll figure out a way to get there myself. I'll call in if I have to."

The room holds its breath, Taara, Vidya, and Kunal nervous hostages in my standoff with Mom. She closes her eyes, chin tilted toward the glass chandelier as she rubs her temples. Finally, her eyes blink open and she studies me like a puzzle she cannot make sense of. "Sahaara, what on earth do you want to say so badly?"

motherhood is

knowing that your greatest teacher
looks up at you as if you are the world

watching her grow up too quick
and always wanting to cradle her in my arms

being perpetually frightened for her
and in awe of her

forgiving myself for my failings
on more nights than i can count

gathering a love that overflows
too much to carry in a single body

the most complicated journey
made simple by her joy

wishing i was a shield
capable of protecting her
from the ugly might of this world

accepting that the greatest protection
i can offer her must be instilled
within her. not forced, entrusted.

Kiran

just before sleep steals her away

i ask
are you mad at me?

mom replies without missing
a heartbeat.

> *of course i am.*
> *but i'm also proud.*

the silence is haunting

in the dead of night
while mom is fast asleep
my heart pounds me awake
the nightmare still lingers
in my heaving chest

in the dream
mom stood behind me
and i screamed
and screamed
and screamed our story
but my words were lost
in a mindless crowd
as if i had spoken
them through water

and he walked past
shameless and proud
and powerful
worshipped by all
and unbothered
by the truth.

sleepless, i check whatsapp

my convo with jeevan
is filled with hourly check-ins
to make sure i'm still alive
but all of my attempts to joke and laugh
and ask about his day have gone ignored
save for an
i've been doing a lot of soul-searching.
we've got a lot to talk through when you get back
so you better make it home in one piece.

pause. breathe. recollect.

i drift to twitter
by a twisted force of habit
and type in a name that smells
like decomposing flesh

hari ahluwalia
has responded to growing outrage
and sexual assault allegations
for the first time

my heart stops
the article opens

a single sentence
sends shivers down my spine

*"this accusation is a baseless lie
from a conniving, calculated woman
who's simply trying to distract from
all the good work we are doing."*

a rough start

I rub sleep from my eyes and her dark silhouette, framed by morning light, comes into focus. She stands still as pond water by the window, steam billowing from her cup of tea.

I ease myself out of the far-too-comfortable bed and join her.

"Sleep well?" I ask, certain from her peaceful stance that she hasn't encountered Ahluwalia's statement yet.

"Not at all." She takes a sip. We watch as two ferry boats meander past each other, the hour still early enough that they only appear as black outlines against the misty, golden sky.

"How does it feel to be home?" I murmur, leaning against her shoulder.

"This isn't home, Sahaara. Punjab is home. *Was* home." She pauses. "Sometimes it feels like home was stolen from me, too. When . . . other things were."

"Because you had to leave?"

"Yes, but also because home is familiar. And comfortable. And safe. He took that safety from me when he made me go."

"Do you miss Punjab?"

"Sometimes, but I wonder if I'd even recognize it if I went back. Aunty Jee always says it's changed so much. I wonder if the bazaars and parks and fields would still feel familiar. Or if it would feel like . . ."

"The city grew up without you?"

"Exactly." Her hooded eyes rest on the sea. On these uncommon occasions when she draws down her heavy guards, I leap at the chance to dig deeper, not knowing when the opportunity will arise again.

"Your mom is coming tomorrow."

"She is."

"How are you feeling?"

"I'm feeling good."

"I mean, how are you *really* feeling?"

"I *really am* feeling good, Sahaara." She smiles. "I feel ready. Like . . . a weight is coming off my shoulders."

"Did you feel guilty?"

She nods, understanding me without explanation. "I did."

"But you know you had no reason to, right? You did what you had to do. By leaving."

She shrugs. "It still hurts, puth. It always hurts." Anguish creases below her eyes and between her brows, but she doesn't cry. "I wanted to talk to you about something."

"What's up?"

"Depending on how this meeting with your nani goes—"

"—she's not my nani."

"Okay. Fine. She's not your nani." Mom sighs. "Depending on how this meeting with my mom goes, I'm thinking that, one day, I'd like to sponsor her to come stay with us. In Canada."

In compete disbelief, I stagger backward. "I'm sorry, *what*?"

"Prem said this could be an option—"

"Mom, are you kidding? Why?! Where's she gonna live? We're already crowded at Bibi's house as it is."

"We can start saving up to move out of Bibi's house."

"No. *No. Bibi* is my family, Mom. And Maasi. And Jeevan. And you. *That* is my family. My whole entire family. I don't wanna live with this random person who's never even been here."

"Sahaara, I can't just leave her behind. Not . . . not now that all this stuff is out there in the news. You need to give her a chance. What if—what if she's changed?"

"It's cool that you wanna get back in touch with her. That's up to you and I'm happy you're doing that for yourself. But she doesn't mean shit to me. And she never will. Just consider the fact that she *abandoned* you because of me."

I regret the word *abandoned* as soon as it escapes my lips, but the damage is already done. I catch the sting in her eyes before she turns around and gathers something nonexistent from the coffee table below us.

"Go get dressed," she says with her back to me. "We have a long day ahead."

wrong move

breakfast is quiet
and my small talk doesn't help
mom is lost in the catacomb of her thoughts
and i am left outside
sipping orange juice and eating toast
hoping that tonight
i will prove how much she matters.

hoping that she will let me back in.

aasra shelter

"Main teri hoooooon," croons Dhvani Bhanushali over the radio as we sit idly in a grid of cars and motorcycles. Vidya is driving today and she's a lot more merciless on the road than Kunal. When traffic gets moving, she speedily cuts off a yellow-roofed taxi before making a whiplash-inducing left onto a side street. Something about her quiet confidence makes me certain that we're not about to die. Mom, however, clings on to the headrest in front of her for dear life.

"We're leaving Colaba now," Kunal says from the passenger-side seat. "The Taj Hotel—where you're staying—that's in Colaba. Around the southern tip of the city. We're heading a bit north. To Dharaspuria."

"What's that area like?" I ask.

"Run-down and quite filthy, to be honest," Taara sniffs from beside me, without breaking from her phone. "Make sure you keep your things close when we get there."

"It's a beautiful community, Sahaara." Kunal shakes his head. "I think Dharaspuria has made a bad reputation from those of us outside, but if you actually get to know the people there, you'll realize they're some of the kindest, most giving folks you'll meet in the city."

"But she should still watch her purse there!" Taara retorts with a little less confidence.

"We're in a city of eighteen million people. She should always watch her purse." Kunal chuckles. "Vigilance is important. No matter where we are."

Tall skyscrapers and apartment buildings slowly fade into

the distance of the gray-white sky behind us. Kunal watches the drifting landscape while Mom falls asleep beside me.

When Mom's body slowly and inevitably slumps into mine, I appreciate the closeness. For a moment, I consider softening the statement I've been saving for tonight. I've caused her enough stress as it is. Then I recall Ahluwalia's words.

I adjust the floral backpack squished awkwardly between my legs. Before we left the hotel, I hastily packed a water bottle, phone charger, asthma inhaler, interview consent forms, and a little tripod, hoping I hadn't forgotten anything.

Eventually, we exit the freeway and rejoin a wide road dense with vehicles. Mom's nap is cut short by an alarm clock of car horns that fill the entire street. The noise does little to move traffic, but a few motorcycles manage to slip through the cracks between cars and taxis, trickling ahead.

"Where are we?" Mom blinks away drowsiness, recalibrating herself in time and space.

"Nearly there, now," Kunal replies.

Boxy, apartment-like buildings line either side of the road, the paint on their once-white walls stained yellow like well-loved books. As I follow the path of a hefty russet-brown cow lazily wandering the roadside, I'm startled by a knock on the car window. A girl no older than seven with brown hair lightened by dust presents me with a bouquet of roses.

"Didi, only a hundred rupees for all of these," she squeaks, knocking on the window once more.

"Oh, don't open the window." Taara nonchalantly tries to wave away the girl. "The city's filled with beggars. They'll never leave you alone if you give them money once." Mom flashes me a quick, wide-eyed glance and I can tell she's thinking the same thing: Taara's classism is repulsive.

"Okay, thirty-five rupees, didi. Just thirty-five for the bunch!" the little girl bargains. The blue eyes of Barbie stare expectantly back at me from her threadbare T-shirt.

Vidya rolls down her window and beckons the little girl toward her. "Here. We'll take them all." She practically leaps with joy as she passes Vidya the bouquet and examines the bill with both hands. Traffic starts moving. Vidya throws the bouquet to Kunal while the little girl leaps backward onto the cement divider separating cars on the busy street.

"A gift for the ladies at Aasra Shelter." Kunal passes Taara the bouquet and she reluctantly sniffs them. He turns to Mom. "Kiran, I've been meaning to ask you . . . what gave you the motivation to speak up about Ahluwalia? I mean, it would have obviously been easier to say nothing. And safer. . . ." He shifts his body to see her better.

"I suppose it was just . . . Sahaara."

"What do you mean?" I sit up a little straighter at the sound of my name.

"You . . . wrote something. I didn't mean to find it, but it gave me the courage I needed to stop living in fear."

Fuck. She found my letter. I know I should be freaking out, cringing at the fact that she read something so personal, but right now, I just want to hold her.

"You know, my father was an activist, too." Kunal rests his coconut-brown cheek in his palm. "He was born in Dharavi—it's a neighborhood that's seen as a slum. Even after he left, he fought for rights of people living there. To have access to water and electricity and so on. It was an uphill battle, of course, trying to create change. Even though he moved south, people would look down on him as soon as they found out where he was born." I sneak a glance at Taara and catch a hint of crimson skin. "But that's the life of an activist, isn't it? People will try to tear you down for any reason they can find. And you need to carry on."

"I don't know if I'd . . . consider myself an activist," Mom replies. "I was just trying to do the right thing. So that others wouldn't have to go through what I did."

Kunal smiles kindly. "Sounds like an activist to me."

"Arre! It was my turn to go!" Vidya angrily curses at a gray sedan under her breath and pulls another sharp turn onto a pothole-filled road. A piercing, pungent odor filters into my nostrils.

"What is that?" I sniff.

"Burning plastic, probably," Kunal replies. "In these neighborhoods, people are forced to burn their waste to get rid of it. Government provides no other infrastructure."

Sure enough, we pass by a flaming mound of garbage before the car slows down and comes to a stop on a tiny dirt road bustling with life. To our left, a patchwork of boxlike wooden homes squish themselves against each other, their painted walls chipping and peeling. An elaborate array of shops decorates the right side of the road, some of their roofs made of wavy, rusted sheets of metal, others simply covered in brown tarp. Directly across the street from us, a dark-skinned woman in a yellow sari stands behind a sizzling vat of oil, wiping sweat off her brow and cradling a deep-fried delicacy in a ladle. She stares into our car, studying each of our faces.

I wonder how obvious it is that we're outsiders.

"All right!" Vidya pulls her key out of the ignition. "Kunal will stay in the car to keep an eye on the street. And because they usually only allow cis and trans women inside the shelter, for safety reasons."

Mom's shoulder tenses up hard against mine. "But wouldn't it be better to have both of you there for security?" she asks.

"The shelter's a safe place," Kunal gently reassures her. "And from a security standpoint, it would be best for me to stay here and keep an eye on who's traveling in and out of the gulley."

Mom nods her reluctant agreement and we step outside, hot, sticky air immediately wrapping around our skin. I try to fill my lungs but my inhale is shallow and labored.

As we step carefully along the cobblestone path caked with dirt, my head is grazed by wet T-shirts and chunnis hung out to dry under the raw Mumbai sun, their touch a physical initiation into a neighborhood that refuses to be ignored. Somewhere behind one of the doors, a mother yells mercilessly at her kid in what sounds like Marathi.

"We're just in here . . ." Vidya pushes open a metal door tucked among a ramshackle collection of others that line the lane. Emerging from a dark, tunnel-like alley, we find ourselves in a cement courtyard outlined with a balcony above. Joyful children chase each other on the veranda while their chatty mothers laugh with their whole chests, washing clothes in soapy buckets and hanging sheets on the railings. Without breaking from their conversations, they follow us with their eyes as we walk below.

"This way." Vidya gestures toward a door across the courtyard.

Inside the building, a kind-faced woman greets us from the front desk. She checks our IDs and then guides us to an empty, windowless room with a polka-dotted bedsheet spread across the cement floor. After a few moments, she returns with a curly-haired, chubby woman wearing a white lanyard over her gulabi kurti.

"Sorry I'm late! Got busy with a new intake, otherwise I would've been at the door to greet you. I'm Priyanka. A pleasure to meet you all!" Her smile stretches from ear to ear and she reaches out a hand to shake mine. She wraps Vidya up in a giant hug. "So nice to see you again, Vidya didi. We've missed you at the shelter."

"It's been a busy few months. Promise I'll be back to volunteer soon," Vidya replies.

Priyanka turns to me and gushes about how excited her team has been to host my interviews. She asks if I have my consent forms ready for the women I'll be interviewing and I pass her the documents. My art professor told me that without the appropriate consent forms, I wouldn't be able to interview people on behalf of the university. When Priyanka has read through everything, she glances up at me, resting her glasses above her forehead. "So, tell me a little more about your art project, Sahaara. It says here that it's about empowering victims of sexual violence. What does empowerment mean to you?" She asks the question with kind curiosity, but with all eyes suddenly on me, I'm just as nervous as I was when Rhonda grilled me about the assignment.

"Well . . ." I begin, not entirely certain where my sentence is going, "to me, empowerment is about helping victims realize that they *do* have voices. I want victims to know that there are people who will stand with them as they tell their stories. Empowerment is about guiding women away from fear."

As I speak, Priyanka surveys me thoughtfully, lips pursed.

"Sahaara, as you get into allyship work in spaces like this, just be mindful of two things: listening and centering."

"Oh, um, what do you mean?" I ask.

"Just a sec," she says. She quickly slips out of the room and returns a moment later with a pink book in hand. Black cursive across the cover reads *It's Not About You: How to Be a Better Ally to Survivors of Sexual Assault.* "I want you to check out this book. We've got a ton of copies here, so please do take it home. It's all about how to actively listen to survivors. Sometimes, if we aren't careful, we can slip into the habit of thinking we know what a survivor needs. A well-meaning ally might insist that their friend go to the police or that there's *only* one way to deal with a tough situation. Usually, life's a lot more complicated than that, na?" I nod, doing my best to absorb her words.

"You're doing beautiful work and your efforts are deeply appreciated. Just remember, love, we need to be learning *from* survivors. Not guiding them." Priyanka moves on to Mom and asks for permission before grasping her hand in both of hers. "Kiran. I have to say, it's such an honor that you're here with us. *Truly.* Thank you so, so much."

"For what?" Mom shakes her head in confusion.

With a crescent of light in her eye, Priyanka says, "For making it easier for all of us to tell our stories."

the interviews
trigger warning: sexual assault

portrait i: priyanka

downturned eyes
upturned mouth
that's only smiled since we arrived

priyanka sits down before me
while my phone clicks onto a tripod
to save a conversation
i've anticipated for weeks

i begin with the question
i've wondered ever since
we met over email

what made you want to work
at a shelter for survivors
of sexual assault?

she doesn't hesitate
before she speaks

i went through things
that no child should ever
experience

i was privileged enough
to have community support
a family that held me close
a circle of friends that lifted me up

but i was chased by the thought
of those who weren't so
well-favored by chance

i wanted to do something—
anything—to undo the ugliness
of this world

portrait ii: khushi

khushi filters into the room with reluctance in her gait
i follow priyanka's lead and put the camera down
for fear that it will become a wall between us
my broken hindi is as useful as punjabi
before a woman who speaks marathi

> understanding fumbles between us
> until priyanka says
> *why don't you speak in english?*
> *i'll be your translator*

> khushi's first question is for me:
> *what made you want to talk to us?*

i reply
i'm sick of the unfairness of this world.
your stories deserve to be heard.

> *but why?*
> she presses
> *what good do you think*
> *my story will do?*

somewhere behind me
mom exhales.

portrait iii: saima

she sits down with a frown
and a baby against her breast
four months old
she says
and his father didn't want either of us
after he found out that my izzat was taken.

izzat. honor.
a word all of us understand.
just like that, her storytelling begins
and i pause her only to remind her that
the recording will only ever be seen by us
my husband's cousin came to live with us
just after we got married
and that's when all the trouble began
i hadn't moved far from home
but this house was the farthest thing from it

never enough for my mother-in-law
although her son was a drunk
she forgave me when i gave her
a grandson

but when i told her about the rape
she named me a worthless whore
pushed me out of the house
and tried to keep the baby

i ran and i ran and i ran
ahmed in my arms
and collapsed here
the only place
that still wanted me.

portrait iv: radhika

i was a sex worker for thirteen years
and a sex slave before that for five
you had better know the difference
if you're going to talk to me, child

i came to pay off my mother's debt
but i stayed, even after i got free

kamathipura was home
sex work was the only trade i knew

and the men always came
from the north and south
the desire to fill their lonely nights
didn't discriminate by class
or caste or religion or wealth

the men always came
even after they vowed to never return
even after they promised themselves
to their wives again and again

the key was to find the ones in suits
willing to empty their pockets

but sometimes
even when i knew they came from money
they would use my services and refuse to pay

my breaking point
was the lawyer from colaba
who came with his well-to-do friends
to have his way with me
with a hand around my throat
like a noose i never welcomed
and then walk away
like my body only existed
to be taken.
like he believed himself too good
for an equal transaction.

an afterthought

radhika remains seated after she tells her story
she gazes into my phone's camera
without smile or scowl
gold koka glistening below a single lightbulb
as i snap a picture
a reference for the painting i will craft
to capture her spirit of flame and lightning

i snap another
and her eyes wander past the lens
they come to rest on mom

i've seen you on tv
she says in hindi that i understand
but cannot speak
watched the whole interview

she pauses only for a heartbeat. a breath.

you're lucky, you know.
you got to leave. you got to run away.
that's what you did, didn't you?

ran off to canada to escape
all your problems
like only a rich girl could

you come here now
and take your pictures
and do your interviews
and then you go back
to safety.

women like me
don't end up on tv
like heroes.

we hide ourselves away
but we're never out of reach

friendship

at indian news network
they search our bags as a safety precaution
but do not search my body

a black blade rests against my breast
and enters the building with me

a small safety that i know
i won't need here

but somehow
keeping this promise to jeevan
eases a weight off my shoulders

we've hardly spoken
since *the day*
a folding knife keeps him close.

sahaara is getting
her makeup done

and i am seated across from her
in a tall director's chair
in a quiet dressing room
in a high-rise building
that houses india's largest news broadcaster
trembling in a way that no one notices
but me

in forty-five minutes
she'll go live on the air
before millions of people

and i am scared
for countless reasons

but i shake
because of the truth
in radhika's words

why should we be here
greeted with excitement by staff
guarded by vidya and kunal
going to sleep at the taj hotel
while so many others
were never even invited
to the conversation?

with highlight across her cheekbones
sahaara's face is ready for television
and i think i'm going to be sick.

stick to the points we discussed
i tell her
you just want to say
that we're speaking out
because no one else should
have to go through this.

for the millionth time
she nods.

Kiran

now or never

Until Mom got her PR card, butterflies in my stomach were a daily occurrence. They whirled and flapped against my insides with wings sharpened by anxiety. By fear of the unknown. By fear of what would happen if our secrets became found out. It seems only fitting that they would make their return right now, as I sit before two giant computer screens in a cramped news studio, waiting for a red light to flicker and a cue to be given that it's time for me to speak. Mom refused to let me enter the studio alone, although she knows that she must remain completely quiet and out of the camera's view. She stands just behind me next to a tinted-glass wall, where the show's producer and tech person are seated.

"Good evening," Anu Shergill begins, the somberness in her voice in stark contrast with loud red lipstick. "We begin our report tonight with an exclusive interview with Sahaara Kaur, daughter of Kiran Kaur, who has grabbed headlines in recent weeks—as well as the attention of the entire nation— when she revealed allegations of sexual abuse against the well-admired People's Party candidate currently running in a tight race for chief minister of Punjab. Most recently, Mr. Ahluwalia has released a statement dismissing the allegations, and student organizations in Punjab that have protested at his events have been disbanded for 'defamation and creating civil disharmony,' according to the spokesperson of Chandigarh University. Counterrallies have also taken place, led by Ahluwalia's loyal supporters, who believe that he is bringing honesty and accountability to Punjab's political scene."

Anu disappears from the right side of the computer screen and the broadcast cuts to footage of a pro-Ahluwalia rally. Hundreds of supporters dressed in yellow, the color of the People's Party, carry signs and banners celebrating the rapist like he's a misunderstood political revolutionary.

Ahluwalia appears and my heart balls up into a fist at the sight of his chiseled face. He's flanked with women on either side who carry signs that read *WE BELIEVE HIM!* "This accusation is a baseless lie from a conniving, calculated woman who's simply trying to distract from all the good work we are doing. A single charge has not been filed against me because the person making these ridiculous claims knows that they are nothing more than fabrications. Because justice has always been on our side!" He says it all with a shadow of a smile reaching into his dimples—*my* dimples. With a sneer in his voice that I needed to hear aloud: a reminder of why I'm sitting in this room. A reason to set the butterflies ablaze and release them from the tip of my tongue.

Don't look back, I tell myself. *Eyes on the screen, like the news people told you.*

This is the first time Mom is hearing Ahluwalia's statement. Every bit of me is filled with worry and all I want to do is glance back to see if she's okay, but I'll be live any second now.

"Good evening, Sahaara. Thank you for joining us tonight," Anu says, and my heart thumps. The sweaty tips of my fingers grip the table and I try to stare directly into the camera like the tech guy told me to.

"Thank you for having me!" I reply far too quickly. *Calm down. Slow down.*

"Let's get right into it, shall we? After evading the media's questions on this issue for several weeks now, Hari Ahluwalia has released a statement rejecting your mother's accusations of sexual assault. How do you respond to that?"

"I, um, I'd like to say that his statement is a lie. But, honestly, I don't think I expected him to take responsibility for his actions, so I'm not surprised by his lie. Over the last twenty years, it's been my mom who's had to pay for his actions—not him."

"As of tonight's report, no charges of sexual assault have been filed against Ahluwalia. Why is that? Is your mother planning to file a report?"

"I h-haven't talked about this with my mom yet so I'm not sure if that's something that she's planning to do but, like, we have to discuss it still and . . . decide if that's the direction she wants to go in and—"

Anu cuts me off as I ramble. Oh god, this is not going as planned. "And what do you want to say to those who suggest that these accusations are very well-timed, given the upcoming election? There have been multiple reports that your family has been paid by the HJ Party to sabotage Ahluwalia's success in recent polls. Ahluwalia is the first member of the People's Party to stand a chance against the far right. What do you have to say about that?"

Her words sling a noose around my heart. I feel nauseous.

"I—all I can say is that we're telling the truth. The only— the only thing we have on our side is the truth. Nothing about my mom's story has to do with an—an election or anything like that. It's not the fault of a victim—of a survivor of sexual assault—that her abuser decided to join a political party that's doing good things. That doesn't change the reality of what happened. *That's* what I want people to know."

Anu nods, looking impressed, and I exhale. "If you could speak directly to Hari Ahluwalia right now, what would you say?"

I've fantasized about this moment for weeks. The thought of it has been tantalizing. Overwhelming. It has given me the motivation to wake up every morning and continue living in this birdcage of a body. All I need are ten seconds of courage, just like I once told Mom. "I would say, stop hiding. Stop hiding from the truth of what you did. I don't care how important you are or how highly people think of you. Look me in the face and take responsibility for your crimes. I exist, I was born, because of the monster that you are. If I have to be haunted by your face every time I look in the mirror, you should be haunted by your actions. Despite what you might tell yourself to fall asleep at night, you are a rapist and you deserve every consequence that's coming to you."

that which is etched into my bones

"What *on earth* were you thinking?!" Mom breathes. "What went through your mind and compelled you to feel that of all the things in the world you could've said, exposing your connection to him was a good idea?" We're standing in the studio, inches apart. Her angry whisper inches dangerously close to tears.

"I had to, Mom. I had to."

"What do you mean you had to?!"

"It was the only way—"

"—to get his whole family after you?!"

"To shake him up. To make him realize he can't hide from the truth. I'm literal evidence of what he did."

"You have no idea what you've done, Sahaara. There's a reason why I've never said anything about him being your—your—"

"He created me." I bring those three ghastly, haunted words to life through gritted teeth. I render them visible and naked and unavoidable in this room. "He made me out of his own violence. And emptiness. And what does that make me if I came from something as twisted as that? As twisted as *him*? Doesn't that make me a monster as well? He needs to stare me in the face and feel the wrath of what he created—" My words dissolve into sobs and my body slumps into the fierce grip of Mom's hug, my head held tight between her trembling hand and caving chest.

She cradles my head in her warm hands and tilts my chin up toward her, wiping my tears with her thumbs while hers flow freely. "You are never—*never*—a reflection of him. Do you hear me? You are your own person, Sahaara Kaur. Who you are has nothing to do with him—"

"—His jaw. His mouth. His cheekbones. I know you can see it, Mom. I know that's why you—you don't look at me when you're upset. I never understood before, but I get it now. They're all—they're all his."

Just as quickly as shock registers across her face, she blinks it away. "And what about your heart? Your bravery? What about those beautiful paintings you create because the earth inspires you? The way you want to stand up for what you believe in? Hm? Who do those things belong to, Sahaara? Because they sure as hell don't belong to that—to that piece of shit. I'm sorry, Sahaara—I'm sorry for the way my mind plays tricks on me. But he doesn't define you. He *does not* define us."

you are not your dna

i know better than most
the feeling of your body not belonging to you
the feeling of being snatched from yourself
at the hands of a monster

for twenty years
i held her like a promise
close and guarded
praying she would never know
a hurt like mine

little did i know
the anguish
that can be
hidden in plain sight

right there in our bones.

Kiron

dear universe

please tell me
please tell me
please tell me
please tell me

that i am more
than my conception.

hardeep

"But it's nearly been an hour. Shouldn't she be out by now? She should definitely be out by now." For what seems like the dozenth time, Mom checks the alarm clock sitting on the night table and then continues to frantically pace the hotel room. Her cell phone trembles with her wrists as she places Kunal on speaker.

"There's a chance her phone is just dead and she's looking for her luggage. Let's try not to panic." Kunal attempts to reassure Mom over the phone, but it does little to mask the worry in his own voice. He's been waiting at the airport with no sign of my mom's mother. Hardeep hasn't answered any of Mom's texts or calls since yesterday evening when we were at INN.

"I'll try her phone again." Mom bites her nail and hangs up. Returning to the window, with her back to Vidya and me, she runs a trembling hand through her hair as if she's trying to steady it. After a few deep breaths, she places the call. The phone rings for a moment, a desperate shout that could be echoing in a desolate place none of us dare to imagine. Then the dial tone goes silent.

My throat is barren. Constricted. This could all be my fault. This *is* my fault. Back against the headboard, I draw my knees up to my chest and try not to think of the news report Jeevan warned me about. The politician who killed someone because he was accused of rape.

"There are any number of possibilities, Kiran," Vidya says, seeming to read our minds. "We mustn't jump to any conclusions." She rises from the edge of the bed and begins to pace the room, just like Mom was.

Mom says nothing. Instead she continues to watch the water. The sea outside is restless and unforgiving.

"I'm sending a message to one of my contacts in . . . in . . ." Vidya halts by the night table, gaping at her phone.

"What?!" I gasp, and Mom swivels around.

"Turn on the news," Vidya whispers.

Vidya whips the remote from me as I fumble with the buttons. Anu Shergill is on the screen, her signature red lips forming the last words I expected to hear this morning: "We bring you a live broadcast from Chandigarh, where Hardeep Kaur, mother of Kiran Kaur, is about to deliver a statement responding to her daughter's sexual assault accusations against Hari Ahluwalia."

Anu Shergill's somber face is replaced with Hardeep Kaur standing behind a podium, next to an older woman who can only be Ahluwalia's mom and a middle-aged man who shares his sharp cheekbones.

Mom drifts toward the TV screen, shock and relief registering at the same time: her mother is safe.

Hardeep clears her throat and I'm stunned by the sight of her wheatish-brown, weather-worn face. By her round eyes that are so similar to Mom's and mine. Mom once told me that we shared her eyes, but she didn't have a single picture of the woman in her possession. I somehow imagined her taller, a figure that would tower over us with her lofty expectations. To see her now, barely a head above a podium, on TV when I'd been anxiously hoping that she'd walk through the door at any moment, is dizzying.

She begins to read from a piece of paper resting before her.

"In regard to the allegations made by my daughter against Hari Ahluwalia, I would, unfortunately, like to state that they are baseless and absolutely untrue to the best of my knowledge." She pauses to look up at the camera, staring into each of us before she continues. "Regretfully, I cannot vouch for Kiran Kaur's account of events, but I would like to say that the Ahluwalia family has shown integrity, respectability, and resilience in the thirty-plus years that I have known them and throughout this ordeal. I sympathize deeply with my daughter's mental health struggles and, presumably, the delusions that they have created within her own child. I appeal to my daughter to seek psychological support for those issues. I and the Ahluwalia family would also like to ask supporters that my daughter be given space to address her issues. . . . We wish her all the best. This statement was not written because of my political affiliations—I've actually been an HJP voter for many years. Instead, I have shared this today because . . . I *must* stand on the side of truth and hope that this drawn-out ordeal receives an amicable ending for all parties."

Anu Shergill returns to the screen and Vidya turns off the TV with the remote still held within her grasp. For several few moments, we are all silent.

Then Mom's phone vibrates. "It's her," she whispers. She opens the message, face unreadable.

"What'd she say?" I croak.

"*Please call me in an hour.*"

At the end of one of the tensest sixty minutes of my life, Vidya leaves the room and Mom dials the number.

"Kiran?" Mom's name is a strangled rasp on Hardeep's lips.

"What do you want?" Mom replies, no feeling in her tone, no emotion on her face. In the hour since the broadcast, I've watched her sit wordlessly by the window, most of my questions ignored, some of them greeted with a shake of the head. She's elsewhere right now. "Hello?"

"I'm here. I'm here." Hardeep sighs. "Did you see—"

"Of course we did."

"I have to explain—"

"What is there to explain? You made your feelings about me crystal clear—"

"*Kiran!* This isn't *just* about you!" she shouts. "You two want to run around making a scene, saying whatever the hell you want as if *I'm* not the one who's going to have to pay for it. I've lived through the embarrassment of you leaving . . . the humiliation of you not showing up for your own father's funeral. Now I'm supposed to live through your face plastered all over the news and to top it all off—your daughter claiming that Hari is her father?! Did you ever stop to think about what all this means for me? Did you?!" Hardeep hisses. Mom stays silent. "Do you have any idea what the Ahluwalias said to me after your daughter's little speech?"

"My *daughter* is sitting right here," Mom coldly retorts.

"Good. I hope she's listening. They came over to my house—"

"Hari?"

"No. His mom. And brother. They said if I didn't discredit your lies, they'd make my life a living hell. They said they'd make sure I lose my home and—and everything I care about." Mom and I lock eyes and I think we're wondering the same thing. "But . . . they said if I made the statement, they'd leave me alone. Permanently. They said no matter what else happens, I'd have done my part."

Mom says nothing.

"You can't blame me for this," Hardeep continues, almost pleading. "I've been through enough in my life. I just want to live the rest of my days in peace."

"You're right," Mom whispers, "I can't blame you." I look up to see anguish force itself into her features like a cracking sheet of ice. A tear spills down her cheek. "I can't blame you . . . but it still hurts."

"I'm . . . sorry, Kiran. I did the best I could do for you. I never told them that you're here—they still think we haven't spoken in decades. They think you hate me so much you wouldn't show up no matter what happened to me." She pauses for a breath. "I told them to leave you alone because of your mental health—"

"You thought you were doing me a *favor*?! By telling people I made this all up because of my mental health?" she smolders. "Since when have you ever known a single thing about my mental health?"

"But—but why else would you run off—"

"Are you kidding?! I don't know if you told yourself that to feel better about yourself or—or if you didn't want to feel like a bad parent, but you've known the true story for *twenty years*. And you made a choice—a conscious decision to ignore it. To dismiss my words. No, I don't blame you for protecting yourself, but don't you *dare* claim that you're doing me a favor by telling the world—by telling ME—that I'm a liar. Not when I've lived with the guilt of not being there for you, every single day since I last saw you. Not when you've probably never felt the same. Don't you dare."

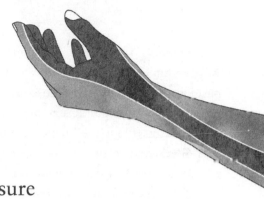

closure

amid all the new hurt
that a single conversation
places upon my shoulders
one weight is lifted:

i did my very best
i reached out a hand

a hand that, perhaps,
she was never meant to grasp
in this lifetime.

lotus & bee café

The *Woman Magazine* team, Mom, and I file down a long wooden table, sitting down on tree stumps topped with black cushions. A thick, leafy canopy of orchids hangs over our heads, an acoustic guitar strumming over the stir of dinner-time chatter filling the rustic restaurant. Vancouver could only dream of a vegan joint so hipster.

It's adorable, but god, I want to go home.

"Ah, I just cannot *wait* to style you both for the gala tomorrow! We are *just* going to have so much fun in the *Woman Mag* closet tomorrow," squeals Jaanvi, a magazine stylist who I met a few moments ago. Her chocolate brown hair is drawn into an elegant fishtail braid that complements her Tiffany-blue blazer. Her glossy lips look like they were crafted by Kylie Jenner herself. "By the way, that skirt is to *die* for, Sahaara. Florals look fabulous on you!"

Taara leans into Jaanvi, appraising me through her thick falsies. "Doesn't it just look lovely on her? The yellow was made for her skin tone. I'm way too pale to pull that off. . . ."

"Thanks." I politely smile, unsure how else to respond. The sun hasn't yet set but this day has already worn me to the point of exhaustion. All I want is to banish Hardeep's face from my memory. To unhear her bullshit excuses.

Vidya and Kunal form a protective wall around Mom and me, Kunal the only man at the table among a dozen fashion-forward women—writers and editors and executives and stylists who eagerly grabbed our hands and air-kissed our cheeks as soon as we met at the door. Kunal quietly roves the room with his eyes, always on guard no matter the relaxed mood of everyone else. Cheerful chatter fills the table like a hearty meal, but Mom and I are quiet, smiling when we must, responding to questions when we must.

"How've you been enjoying the city? Have you hit all the touristy spots?" a gazelle-like woman in a jumpsuit asks from the far end of the table.

"It's been really nice—hot, but we've been enjoying it." I smile.

"Oh, you must hate the heat! You probably have layers of snow in Canada right now, na?" an older woman with a bob cut chimes in from the other end of the table.

"No, um, we only really get snow in December in Surrey. Some years we don't really get any."

"Really?!" She rests her head in her palm, studying me in fascination. "I find that so hard to believe—"

"Oh, no, it's true, Shivani!" a stout woman next to her begins, her elaborate earrings and loose topknot swaying as she animatedly speaks. I lose track of the conversation, relieved that I'm no longer being spoken to.

With a quick glance at Mom, I catch an all-too-familiar distance in her glazed eyes. She's not here right now. My hand finds hers under the table and after a moment, she squeezes back.

"You okay?" I murmur.

"How long are we here?" she whispers through her teeth. I squeeze her hand a little harder.

"Kiran," comes Nandini Rajalingam's wispy voice from directly across us. "I'd like to tell you again just how grateful we are for your presence." Nandini's demure tone matches her diminutive stature but she commands the attention of the entire table. Conversations slowly go quiet all around us as the magazine's editor in chief clasps her manicured fingers together and rests her pointed chin upon them. She surveys us through precisely lined, feline eyes framed by a perfectly straight set of bangs. Seeing her here in the flesh—real as can be and no longer confined to flawlessly curated IG posts on my phone—is a little trippy.

"It meant a lot that you asked us to come," I reply for both Mom and me. "Really and truly. Your email came at a time when we really needed some hope."

"I heard from Vidya and Taara that your interviews at Aasra Shelter went well?" Nandini continues.

"Well, they mostly did." Taara grimaces. "There was that one lady who was quite rude, wasn't she? The sex worker . . ."

"I didn't think she was rude at all." Mom speaks up, to my surprise. "She was sharing the truth of her own experiences. I think we needed to hear it. There are so many women who don't get to tell their stories—who don't live to tell their stories—because of their status in society. Because of the place they were born, or the way society looks down on them."

Taara pours herself a glass of mint-infused water, quickly taking a sip and diverting her eyes from Mom. The rest of the table watches Mom intently, collectively mesmerized by her unfiltered honesty.

"Radhika was right," Mom continues. "I'm *extremely* lucky. I have privileges that she doesn't, just because of my distance from . . . him."

Nandini slowly nods and continues to survey Mom through her long bangs. "Right. You're absolutely right." She turns her head to Taara. "Priyanka from the shelter is joining us at the gala, na? I wonder if the women staying there would join us as well. Will you send Priyanka a message?"

"On it!" Taara practically whistles, eyes reverentially glued to Nandini while she unlocks her phone.

Mom shakes her head. "I think . . . an invitation to the gala is a start, but—"

"Kiran," Taara croaks. "Kiran. You need to—you need to check your phone. He's made another statement."

"W-what?" Mom breathes, and hushed whispers ripple across the table, every hand reaching for a phone. Mom leans into me as I tap a link that Taara's just texted me.

He stands before a beige wall, camera shaky like he's recording on his cell phone. "In response to statements made by Kiran Kaur's daughter, I would like to challenge her to speak for herself instead of having a *child* speak on her behalf. Open dialogue and discourse are important in any democracy and as a candidate for chief minister of Punjab, I welcome frank and honest conversations. If Kiran Kaur is not afraid of being confronted—of being challenged—with the truth, I would invite her to join me tomorrow on INN for a public conversation about the allegations she has presented."

"My god . . ." Jaanvi whispers.

"What a shameless bastard!" Vidya spits.

A few phones seem to ping and vibrate at once. Taara's eyes bulge. "Aaaaaand, we just got an email from INN. They're asking if Kiran will come on TV tomorrow." She looks up at Mom. "Hari will be calling in from New Delhi. They want to do a live broadcast with you."

My skin is numb as a corpse. Mom's hands grip a cloth napkin, trembling.

She glances at me, opening her mouth to speak and then closing it. I watch as a whirlwind of emotions play out behind her eyes—fear, disgust, anger, shock, and fear, once again.

Then Nandini speaks. "I think you should do it, Kiran. Between this pathetic pretense of concern for democracy and that *disgusting* stunt they pulled with your mum, you should be given a chance to challenge him. Head-on." I'm surprised that this ridiculously important woman has an opinion on a situation that feels so utterly and bitterly our own.

All heads seem to shift toward Mom in eager anticipation of her response. She clears her throat. "So much has already been said on our part. *Too* much. And honestly . . . where's it gotten us?"

"What do you mean?" Taara shakes her head, genuinely confused.

"We've spoken twice now," Mom sighs, "and the Ahlu-walias turned it all against us. They got my own mother to come on television and call me a liar, for god's sake. Even if I speak, even if he somehow doesn't get elected, what good will it really do? Who's to say his opponent is any less horrible than him? Who's to say this will actually fix anything?"

"Oh, your voice won't fix everything, Kiran. I'm under no illusions about that," Nandini steadily says, "but what it *will* do is frighten a lot of very powerful men."

"Frighten them?! How could I possibly . . ."

Nandini leans back. Without looking away from Mom, she says: "Of those of us sitting at this table, how many have been harassed by a man . . . this week?"

Nearly all the women raise their hands, some shaking their heads, others responding with an irritated eye roll or a sigh.

"And how many of us sitting here," Nandini continues, "have experienced abuse from men that . . . goes beyond words called out to us on the street?"

Most of the hands remain raised, some women lowering

theirs but subtly nodding to themselves. Taara grips her glass with both hands and doesn't glance up.

"And why do they get away with it?" Nandini asks the table, eyes drifting across each of us.

"Patriarchy," someone replies to my left.

"Because men have more power in society," Shivani replies to my right.

"Money. Wealth. Men control money, so they control the world," the gazelle-like woman says.

"Because sexual harassment is normalized. Abusers make mistreatment of women seem like something that's to be expected!" Jaanvi fumes.

"People don't believe women when they tell their stories," Taara sighs.

"I agree with all of these reasons. But also . . . izzat. Honor," Nandini states, and the table erupts in a low murmur of agreement. "This patriarchal idea that a girl's honor—a woman's honor—depends on her virginity . . . and who she gives it to. And what happens to girls when all their lives, they're made to believe that their worth depends on this thing between their legs? When they're made to believe that if they are raped, their dignity is forever stolen as well? When their reputations become the most important garment they wear?"

When she pauses, no one takes their eyes off her and no one speaks.

"What happens is . . . abusive men revel in the power of *shame*. They revel in the fact that shame can keep women in line, just like violence can. The men in suits—the ones who want to keep their hands clean—use shame as their weapon of choice."

I shiver at the word *shame*: the reason why a mother could turn her back on her own daughter.

"Isn't that what Ahluwalia's trying to do here?" Nandini locks eyes with Mom. "Shame you into shrinking—shame you into silencing your own voice—so that he comes out looking like a hero of the people. But what would happen if shame no longer kept us in line? Would that not frighten men like him?"

A white petal quietly drifts down from the canopy, landing on the white napkin still strangled within Mom's grasp. It rests there. She loosens her grip.

amid darkness, a glistening moment

i walk into a white marble room
that's accessorized with more mirrors
than anyone could possibly need

mom steps in a few moments later
wearing heels i already know she hates

there she is, in a glittering midnight gown
that could put a starry sky to shame

here i am, in flowy white chiffon
that could reflect the sun

here we are, the night to the other's day
the balance we both so desperately need.

the city is in motion

From a balcony on the seventeenth floor of Indian News Network, Mumbai looks formidable and endless, a city with far more stories to tell than time to stop and listen. Hundreds upon hundreds of skyscrapers and concrete apartment buildings fill the landscape before me, as far as the eye can see. The farthest of the buildings disappear behind a pale yellow haze of city smog, blurring the line between land and sky. Black-roofed rickshaws and yellow-topped taxis move mercilessly on the streets below, the sound of their horns reaching us all the way up here.

Her hands haven't stopped shaking since we got here, but her face is oddly serene. "You know, this sky reminds me of Punjab." She lightly crosses her arms and surveys the sunset from her black chair. "Without all the skyscrapers, of course, but the haze . . . I almost forgot about it."

"Who knew smog could create such a beautiful sunset?" I shrug. The setting sun is a fiery orange that I've never seen back home, casting marmalade onto the smog and golden light onto whitish buildings below.

"Aren't we familiar with toxic fumes masked as beauty?"

"Shit, Mom. Touché," I gasp. On an apartment rooftop a block away, I spot a little girl with an older man, perhaps her father. They guide an ornate white kite through the evening sky, the kite swaying in the wind and then nose-diving into their arms. "I, um, I've been meaning to tell you something."

"What?" Mom pivots toward me in her black chair faster than I can take another breath.

"I kinda did something that I didn't mention before—"

"Sahaara, what the hell did you do? I thought we agreed on no more surprises!"

"Oh, no. It has nothing to do with this trip. It's, um, Jeevan." Warmth ripples across my torso, jitters in my knees. "I sort of . . . kissed him."

My words slowly register on Mom's face and her anxious, furrowed brow relaxes, giving way to a grin. She begins to laugh, her shoulders heaving with her chest.

Totally confused, I crack up as well. "What—what are we laughing about?!"

Her laughter unrelenting, she reaches out a hand and grasps mine. "I'm not laughing at this, puth! It's just—of all the things I've heard this week—I thought it was going to be something like"—she wipes a tear from her eye—"*Mom, I killed someone.*"

"I might as well have," I mumble. "We haven't really been talking."

"Hold on. When did this happen?!" Interest sparkles in eyes that have dwelled in sorrow for far too long.

"Why aren't you freaking out? Aren't you supposed to be, like, mad?"

"Oh. Well"—she pulls back slightly—"Jeevan's such a nice boy. I know that he's . . . *good*, you know? He has a good heart. And I know you're growing up, Sahaara. I always knew you'd have to grow up, eventually. I just wasn't . . ."

"Ready?"

"Willing to let you," she sighs.

"You've been talking to Maasi, huh?"

"She's helped a lot, I'll admit. But also, if these past few weeks have taught me anything, it's that you're not a little girl anymore. And that's perfectly okay." She nods, as if she's reassuring herself.

I study her dark, tender eyes, unsure what to say. Eventually, I whisper, "Thank you."

"So, are you going to tell me more or am I going to have to wait until your maasi fills me in?"

I roll my eyes. "It kinda happened outta nowhere a week before we came here. And, um, it got really awkward after . . ."

"Why? Did he—did you not want to—"

"I *wanted* to kiss him. At least, I thought I wanted to, but, um . . . I don't know if I was ready."

"Yeah?"

"Yeah." I swallow, not sure how to say this. "I've felt fuzzy, lately. And kissing Jeevan felt right but it also felt like . . . I was trying to escape my head *through* him. Does that make sense?"

Mom's gaze drifts from me to the city spread before us. "Hmm. I think I've been there before." She purses her rose-tinted lips.

I tilt my head to survey her. "You know, sometimes I wonder what goes through your mind when you're quiet."

With a raised brow, she glances at me for a fleeting moment and then returns her attention to the kites fluttering within the haze. "You're better off not knowing, Sahaara."

"You sure? Talking about what's going on in your head has worked out pretty well, so far."

"Has it?!" Her laughter solidifies into seriousness. "What time is it?"

"Four fifty," I say, checking my phone.

She nods solemnly.

"You're going to do fine, Mom. You know what you have to say. All you're gonna do is tell the truth."

"Before March, I hadn't seen his face in twenty years. But now, with the videos and the news articles, I've seen it four times."

My hand grips hers tight. "Are you sure you're ready for this?"

Her chin jerks in the slightest of nods. "The first time, in March, I was shaking after I saw his picture. I couldn't breathe."

"What?! You didn't tell me. . . ."

"I was okay. I handled it on my own. The second time, my heart started racing but I could still breathe. Same with the third time, in the studio. And then we watched the video at the restaurant—"

"Shit! I'm so sorry it played in front of you—"

"No, Sahaara. When I watched it, my heart was pounding, but it wasn't from fear. It was from anger. I wanted to face him. I want him to look me in the face, just like you said. I'm ready."

the physics of my honesty

high school was a lifetime ago
and i don't remember much
of what i learned

but i do remember that
potential energy is stored up
in an object, waiting to be used
and kinetic energy is that very
same force set in action

a floodgate broke within me
when i spoke the truth
and he tried to call it
nothing more than
a fairy tale

all the rage
stored quietly beneath my skin
pushed my fear over the edge

Kiran

checkmate

"Kunal, my friend! So nice to see you!" booms a balding, hook-nosed man in an off-white suit. He strides purposefully toward us, down an otherwise empty hallway, a younger man trailing slightly behind him. He's left the top buttons of his purple shirt open, exposing a hairless chest. Somehow, I feel like he's just missing three gold chains and a cigar.

Kunal politely shakes his hand. "Mr. Mukherjee—"

"How many times do I have to tell you? Call me Varun." He heartily pats Kunal on the back.

Kunal places a fraction of distance between himself and the INN exec. "Right, Varun, you've met my wife, Vidya. And this is Taara. I believe you've been in touch by email—"

"Yes, yes, of course," he says, nodding at Vidya and Taara, who silently stand beside me. He turns his attention to me and Mom. "But you two ladies, I haven't yet had the pleasure of meeting. Although it seems I *see* them nearly everywhere, these days." He exposes a toothy smile.

Mom tries not to grimace. Unease painted across his face, Kunal makes the introduction. "This is Kiran Kaur and her daughter, Sahaara."

"*The* Kiran Kaur." He extends a hand to Mom from across the small circle that has formed in the middle of the hallway. "A pleasure to meet you. Glad we could have you on the show tonight—oh! And this is Ajay, our new *co—executive producer.* The lucky bastard just got the promotion." Varun pats the waifish, goateed man standing next to him and he nearly topples into us with the force. Ajay, irritated and red in the face, nods at the group as he regains his balance.

"Congratulations, sir." Kunal coolly nods at Ajay. "We're looking forward to participating in a quick and *professional* dialogue, tonight. As we discussed, it will look like Kiran's calling in from Canada, correct?"

"Yes, yes, Kunal, of course." Varun adjusts the sleeves of his close-fitting jacket. "You know we run a tight ship here at INN and I'm sure the segment's going to be quite enlightening for viewers. It's not every day that we host a debate like this. The ratings shall be phenomenal! Really—we can't thank you enough for joining us tonight, Miss Kaur." He flashes Mom another toothy smile, a gold incisor gleaming at us.

"I'm not sure if we're looking for a debate, per se." Vidya crosses her arms over her chest. "More like a simple laying out of the facts."

"Yes, of course, of course." Varun crosses his arms as well, appraising her. "But there are many versions of facts, na? Truth comes in many shapes and alternatives."

"Well . . . it was, um, it was very nice to meet you all," Ajay says, "but I've got some business to attend to. Looking forward to your interview, ma'am." Mom weakly smiles at him and then he turns around, swiftly marching down the never-ending black marble hallway in his navy-blue suit. In the distance, I watch as he briefly glances back at us and then takes a left, disappearing into another hallway.

Raveena, a cheerful assistant who we met earlier, steps through a tinted glass door to my right, a yellow cup of coffee in hand. "Are we ready to get Kiran into the booth?"

"Yes, yes," says Varun. "Let's get her set up in there." He opens a heavy black door behind him that leads to a video-recording studio. With a desk equipped with computers and microphones, and a long, tinted window running across the back wall, it's almost identical to the room where I did my interview. Varun holds the door open for Mom, Vidya, and Raveena as they step inside.

Before I can enter, he stops me. "Only two guests in the booth at once. We find that it's best for recording quality that way."

"Oh, um . . ." Mom glances back at me.

"It's okay, Mom. I'll wait outside."

Vidya rests a hand on Mom's shoulder. "She'll be fine," she says, and I'm not sure whether she's trying to reassure Mom or me. I offer Mom one last smile that she attempts to return.

The door lazily shuts as Raveena explains the recording equipment to Mom. When Mom can no longer see me, my grinning mask falters. Completely oblivious to my quavering chin, Varun guides me, Taara, and Kunal, almost giddily, through the door across the hallway.

"And this is the greenroom!" Varun grandly gestures toward the narrow room filled with black leather sofas, coffee tables, and several TV screens mounted along the left-hand wall. The wall on the opposite end is made entirely of glass, revealing another hallway where two employees appear to be in deep conversation.

A stern-looking older woman and a younger man glance up from their game of chess. "All set?" the short-haired woman asks Varun.

"Ready to go. Should be any minute now." He grins, practically bouncing on his feet as he pours himself a glass of chardonnay from a black marble table filled with a decadent array of snacks and drinks. He chugs it back in one gulp, thin lips still curled into a smile. "This is going to be epic. *Epic!*" he booms. God, I want to gag.

INN's familiar news-intro tune suddenly fills the room. A dozen TV screens snap on at once. Anu Shergill smiles in sync on each one. Here we go.

"Take a seat, everyone, take a seat. Grab some coffee and snacks." Varun gestures toward the marble table but none of us move from our place below the TVs. I can't sit through this.

Our eyes are collectively stuck to the screens when Raveena walks in. "It's showtiiiime!"

I glance over at Taara, who twinkles with just as much excitement as the gaudy news exec.

"It'll be fine," Kunal whispers to my left.

Nervously, I look up at him. "Let's hope."

"Good evening," Anu Shergill declares. "We begin our newscast tonight with a live, moderated discussion between Hari Ahluwalia, candidate for chief minister of Punjab, and Kiran Kaur, a woman now well-known across India for the allegations of sexual assault that she levels against Mr. Ahluwalia. Good evening to you both."

"Good evening," Mom and Ahluwalia reply almost simultaneously. They both appear in tiny boxes on the screen, to the right of Anu. The sight of his face, although sickeningly familiar, vacuums the air from my lungs, as it always does. Here he is, staring smugly into a camera as though he's looking directly at me. Through me.

The feeling is repulsive.

With violent difficulty, I pry myself from his jaw, his cheekbones, his sharp, beetle-like eyes. Mom's expression is difficult to decipher: she could be completely focused, or, like me, she could be shivering inside.

"Let's begin by giving Kiran the floor. I'd like to ask that no one be interrupted while speaking." Anu pauses, and

Ahluwalia nods. "Kiran, you are, presumably, speaking to Hari Ahluwalia for the first time in years. What would you like to say right now?"

Mom blinks several times but doesn't break from the camera. She swallows. The room fills with tense silence and finally she begins to speak. "Over the past twenty years, the thought of facing you has . . . horrified me. Shackled me. And as I'm sitting here right now . . . my heart is pounding but I refuse—I *refuse* to be trapped by my fear of you. You don't deserve to have that power over me—or any woman. No abuser, no predator deserves that power. You can try to defame me, you can try to turn my own family against me and question my credibility, but the truth will always be the truth and you *cannot* run from it."

Holy shit. She just did that. Air finds its way into my lungs once again, and I exhale.

"Powerful words, Kiran," Anu states as Ahluwalia tries to force down the edges of a smile. "Mr. Ahluwalia, you've been running a political campaign over the last several months that has continued full force despite sexual assault allegations from Kiran Kaur. How do you respond to her?"

"Well, first of all, Anu, I'd like to start by saying thank you so very much for having me on the show today," he drawls, faux politeness wrapped expertly around his voice. "I think that Kiran Kaur, although accusing me of *complete* lies, has sparked a very important conversation about sexual assault—one that we, as politicians, need to be having! Young women have made their voices clear: they feel unsafe. Our party, the People's Party, is committed to changing that."

"Well, I'm curious about the sincerity of that, Mr. Ahluwalia," Anu says, "when university groups were disbanded in Punjab because they raised their voices against sexual assault—against you."

"That—that really had nothing to do with me or the People's Party. You'd have to take that up with the universities. Returning to the topic, though, I'd like to say that while Kiran Kaur has sparked important conversations and has just delivered a *stirring* speech, there is no credible evidence for her allegations. First and foremost, why did it take so long for her to come forward with this story? Why now, during the election? Why have no charges been filed against me? Why did she never report this to the police?"

Mom's laugh is tinged in fury. "It should be pretty clear why I never approached the police. You *were* the police. Who could I possibly ask for help when I was"—she takes a deep breath—"when I was sexually assaulted in a police station *by* a police officer?"

"Holy fucking shit," Taara breathes beside me.

"My god . . ." whispers Raveena. The serious-looking woman stands up from the leather sofa and inches toward us, lips parted and eyes on the screen.

Fire kindling in Mom's eyes, she presses on. "When you are violated and victimized by the very system that people claim will protect you—why on *earth* would you expect justice there? How could I press charges in a system that has completely failed me and so many other women when, for twenty years, I've simply been trying to survive? You ask why it took so long for me to come forward when you knew—"

"This is absolutely—" he interrupts.

"No! I'm speaking right now! You ask why it took so long for me to come forward when you saw the fear in my eyes that day. And you laughed. You can stand here today dressed up as whatever you want, but you cannot—*cannot*—look me in the face and simply pretend that never happened."

No one in the room breathes. Not even the news anchor, who simply gapes at Mom, stunned. Ahluwalia coughs. "Another rousing speech, no doubt," he begins, the faux politeness slipping away with each word. "But before the public casts any judgment simply based on this emotional venom, I'd like to share a few images with you all."

Mom, Ahluwalia, and Anu shrink to the bottom of the screen and a black-and-white image appears before us. A man and a woman lean toward each other from across a table. Black rectangles cover their eyes, but I'd recognize the woman's mouth and chin anywhere. The dark-skinned man, I've never seen before.

"This is a picture that I took with my own camera," Ahluwalia proudly exclaims. "Although the eyes are covered, it was no question who—and what—I was looking at that day. It's quite a shame to say, but it's common knowledge back home in Chandigarh that Kiran Kaur was engaged to my brother for some time—"

"H-hold on a second!" Mom stammers, eyes wide.

"No!" he thunders. "You had your turn to speak and now it's mine! When I discovered that she had—allegedly—been cheating on my brother, I was deeply, deeply hurt by the thought of it. I had to uncover the truth for myself—"

"But this is—"

"*I confronted her directly*"—he drowns out her voice—"and, as you can imagine, she was defensive. Just as defensive as she is today. So defensive that, perhaps, she left for Canada and decided to never return? Not even for her poor father."

Another picture appears on the screen and all blood drains

from my face. Mom's hand is placed atop the man's.

From behind me, Raveena gasps. "What. On. *Earth*."

"Did not see that coming," the other woman scoffs.

"Sahaara, it's going to be okay—" Kunal begins.

"They need to—they need to end the interview," I croak, burning at the sight of Varun beaming next to Kunal.

"Where'd they place him?" Raveena quietly murmurs from behind me.

"This floor, I think. East wing," the other woman replies.

Slowly, I turn around, the room spinning. "Place . . . who?"

"Oh, um." Raveena gulps, glancing nervously over my shoulder.

I swivel around fast enough to catch Varun furiously shaking his head at Raveena.

"Place *who*?" I repeat, moving toward him.

"No one—I—I'm not sure—what they're—uh—" Varun stammers, edging backward toward the wall, glancing from me to the TV screen before he can stop himself.

Kunal's gaze moves from me and Varun as understanding sinks in. "Is he . . . here?" Within a second, he drags Varun toward him by the scruff of his neck. "Is he?!"

"No! What! That's ridiculous—I—"

"THE TRUTH! I want it right now!" Kunal roars, inches from Varun's face.

"He's a good man, Kunal!" Varun pleads. "He means no harm—"

Kunal pounds Varun's large body against the wall and Taara shrieks. My ears ring and in the split second that Kunal's back is toward me, I make a decision.

"We trusted you!" Kunal shouts as I silently escape from the room. "I would never have brought them here if I knew—WHY IS HE HERE?!" I look left and right down the long hallway and obey the instinct in my gut: Ajay went right. Heart pounding, blood rushing, I race down the hallway, as fast as my heels can carry me, praying that I can run faster than Kunal's razor-sharp attention. I skid to a stop at the hallway where Ajay turned left and kick off the pumps. They're slowing me down.

Continuing barefoot down the hallway, I reach into my bra, grasping hold of the folding knife that my best friend entrusted to me. Without breathing or thinking, I slip it into the black sleeve of my top. A door suddenly creeks open to my left and I all but run into it.

Papers scatter across the floor and an unfamiliar man in metal glasses emerges from behind the door. "Shoot—shoot—sorry—didn't mean to run into you!"

"Sorry!" I gasp.

"You, uh, lost, or something?" he asks, gathering his papers.

"No, just, um, just looking for the washroom," I nervously laugh.

"Right . . . uh . . . down that way . . . end of the hallway . . ." He points in the direction I was walking.

"Thanks," I dizzily breathe, grateful that my long maxi skirt covers my bare feet.

I speed walk down the cold black marble, reading each door in adrenaline-fueled desperation. *Good Morning, India!* reads one. *Greenroom* reads another. My stomach lurches when I hit another hallway to my right, a gold plank glistening on the wall: *East Wing.*

I exhale with purpose. My bare feet move precisely and silently. Portraits of celebrity guests line either side of the empty hallway, punctuated by an occasional black door.

Fear finally begins to crawl through my skin, but my body continues forward: he hurt her. He violated her. He stole her safety.

Voices echo against the walls. "Excellent interview, sir! You smashed it . . . destroyed the lying bitch." I can't calibrate where the words are coming from. They seem to be everywhere.

"The best way to crush opposition is with the facts. So glad we could have you with us, sir! Truly an honor," comes another voice. I slip into an empty doorway and listen to shoes clack louder and louder against the floor.

"All in a day's work," laughs a familiar, snarky voice.

"Hopefully we can have you back on the air sometime soon."

Several men in black suits suddenly whoosh past me, moving as a unit around a navy-suited man and the one I've come to see. They look straight ahead, not even noticing my body pressed into the corner of the doorway.

My heart pounds as loud as their voices. Here we go.

"Hey, kutheya." I step into the center of the hallway. Like robots, every head turns toward me at once. All heads but his. "I'd like to have a word."

Slowly, he glances over his shoulder, no shock or fear on his face. Instead, a bemused grin. "Kutheya? Now, that's a bit rude, isn't it?" His whole body swivels around. He folds his hands and smiles serenely from behind his security guards. Frigidly.

"I call 'em like I see 'em." I shrug, inching forward.

"Sir, I'm—I'm so very sorry. I'm not sure what's going on—I—" Ajay sputters, rattled by the sight of me. The security guards shrink their protective circle, closing any gaps.

"No need to apologize." Ahluwalia laughs. "And why the panic, my friends? It's just a little girl." Some of the guards snigger and curse under their breath. Ahluwalia brushes one of them aside, stepping out of his cocoon. When he moves toward me, a security guard follows and he brushes him away.

Taller than Jeevan, he leans down to meet my face and rests his hands on his knees. "What were you saying, again, young lady?"

Only if I need it. Only if I need it. Only if I need it. Remember what Jeevan said.

"You don't scare me," I whisper, despite the pounding in my chest that could drown out my voice. "Your lies won't shut us up."

"My *lies*?" He cackles. Just loud enough for me to hear, he says, "Maybe you and your mumma need to have a little chat. Find out where you're really from, you feisty little bastard. Hopefully she kept track—"

"Go fuck yourself," I spit.

The smile slides off his face. "A word of advice: next time you think to make a trip to my country, don't. My eyes are everywhere. Next time, I might not catch you in a building like this, where you and your whore mother get to hide behind cameras. Randi ki bachi saalee." He straightens his back and raises his voice so that everyone can hear. "That's the beauty of a democracy, isn't it? We all speak our minds freely and, in the end, only truth prevails." The knife slides down my sleeve, into my hand.

"SAHAARA?" Her voice reaches me before I see her at the end of the hallway, chest heaving and fear painted across her face. "GET THE HELL AWAY FROM MY DAUGHTER!"

Ahluwalia's sharp jaw snaps toward my mother just as Vidya, Kunal, and Raveena, the INN assistant, catch up with her. Breathless, Vidya becomes a wall in front of Mom, and Kunal barrels through the cluster of security guards.

"DON'T TOUCH HER!" Kunal shouts as he grabs me around my shoulders. The knife almost slips through my fingers as he pulls me past the guards. I glance up to see moisture in his eyes. "Let's go, Sahaara. NOW!"

The five of us are silent as we race down the hallway, following Raveena's lead as she takes each turn. We take a right and run into Taara, who's holding an elevator open with her body.

"Hurry up!" Vidya shoves Mom and me inside. As soon as we're all in, Raveena slides her ID through a card reader, hits a button, and we're moving down seventeen floors.

"Are you—are you okay?!" Mom wraps her arms around me and our breathless chests heave against each other.

"I'm fine—I'm fine—"

"What the *hell* were you thinking?!" Kunal roars.

"I—I wasn't—I just had to—"

"Had to *what*?! Put yourself and all of us in serious danger?!" Kunal yells. I grip the metal bar behind me. "You and your mom are the single greatest threat to his political career. Did you think you were just going to have a nice chat over tea? Do you understand that these politicians play by their own rules?"

I shiver as I recall Jeevan's words. "I'm sorry—" I begin just as the elevator dings and the doors open.

Speeding across the marble lobby, a receptionist frantically shouts at us from behind her desk, "Excuse me! *Excuse me!* Where are you all going?! You need to return your tags!"

Kunal rips off his ID tag, throwing it on the ground behind him, and all of us do the same.

"The car—where's the car?" Vidya asks as she holds the heavy glass door open for all of us.

"Just over there," Kunal replies. Humid air immediately seals itself around every crevice of my skin as we run across the street.

"Here!" Vidya throws Kunal her keys and we jump in the car.

"I'm so sorry! I didn't know—I didn't know that you all didn't know he was here. I didn't know it wasn't safe—" Raveena cries as she closes the car door behind me.

"Not your fault," Kunal cuts her off as he starts the car. "Let's just get the hell out of here."

He tears through the parking lot, just barely scraping through a metal gate that's closing past another car. "Hey!" shouts a security guard sitting inside a white security booth at the entrance. Kunal speeds through traffic, cutting off drivers before traffic gets so dense that we can't move.

"Okay." He takes a deep breath. "Let's hope they aren't following. Vidya, look for the next flight to Vancouver."

"On it," she replies, pulling out her phone.

"But—but the gala. They can't leave—"

"Taara," Kunal fumes, "I'm going to say this once. Fuck the gala. Nandini will understand. They need to leave immediately. We drive back to the hotel, grab their bags, and get them the hell out of here."

"But my mom. We can't—I—I can't leave her behind," Mom stammers.

"We won't. We'll figure something out. Can you call her?" Vidya asks.

Mom dials but the call goes nowhere.

"Try texting her?" I croak.

Mom fumbles with the phone as she tries to type but before she even finishes, it vibrates. "*I'm fine. What do you want?*" Mom reads the message and looks up at us.

"Get her mom on a flight to Canada as well," Kunal tells Vidya as he makes a sharp turn. "Will she go with you?"

"I don't know. I'll—I'll ask," Mom says, calling again. "Hello? Hello, are you there?" She places the call on speaker.

"I'm here."

"Mom—I need you to come to Canada. It's not safe—"

"I'm *fine!*" she hisses.

"You don't understand—you could be in serious danger—"

"And whose fault is that?"

"We need to get you to Canada—"

"Listen to me. I've been on my own for six years. I've handled my affairs without you for twenty years. I do not need your help now. I'll figure something out with your chacha." Hardeep cuts off the call and we sit in silence until we reach the hotel.

"In and out as quickly as you can, okay?" Kunal says as he pulls up in front of the palace. Vidya waves away the valet as she steps out of the car and we follow her. Kunal and Taara remain seated. Taara's satin hair is in wild disarray and her blue glasses are so askew, she looks like she could've just been through a storm.

In the elevator, Mom struggles to stand still. She begins to wring her hands, pacing back and forth until we're released.

"Sahaara, I need to explain . . ." Mom whispers as we walk down the hallway.

"It's okay." I place a hand on her shoulder. "We can talk about it later."

"No—you don't understand. Those pictures—they're not what they look like."

Vidya swipes a key card into our room door and it swings open. "I'll stay out here," she says. "You two pack."

In seconds, Mom and I are shoving clothes into suitcases. I run to the bathroom and throw all my makeup and Mom's into a single bag.

"I wasn't cheating on Prabh. I just—there was a boy—a boy from secondary school. And I met with him once—I never knew that Hari saw—I just—" I look back to see her fumbling with sweaters, trying momentarily to fold them and then simply squishing them into an overflowing suitcase.

"Mom, don't worry, we can talk about this after," I gently say as I zip up the makeup bag and shove it into a suitcase. My dresses get haphazardly thrown into Mom's suitcase and her shirts get pushed into mine.

"I don't understand—I don't understand how he saw"— Mom whisks our passports off the night table—"and how he found me." I shove my laptop in my backpack and scan the room for anything we've missed. Mom picks up a suitcase sitting near the window and accidentally trips backward, landing on the bed.

"Mom!" I gasp, taking hold of her hand to help her up. My heartbeat slows as I take in her current state: fear etched in her eyes, hair strewn from her bun, body shivering.

"Sahaara, please believe me."

I hold both of her trembling hands in mine as I say, "I do believe you. Always have, always will. And there is *nothing* that you could have done that justifies what he did to you. This isn't your fault."

When we make it back to the car, Kunal is on the phone with someone. He hangs up the call to hoist our suitcases into the trunk. Then he proceeds to drive to the airport, just as hastily as he drove to the hotel.

"That was Nandini on the phone," he says. "She said she's sorry about all this—and she understands why you have to leave."

From the back seat, Mom asks, "Do you have some paper?"

Vidya rifles through the glove compartment and emerges with a white napkin and a pen. "Does this work?"

"It'll do," Mom says as she begins to write something I can't see.

"I've booked you for the next flight out. It's leaving in five hours. Airport's not far so we'll get there in time." Vidya looks back at us. She smiles in that way that Mom would when I was young and scared.

Despite my hatred for her, I pray that Hardeep is also headed to an airport right now.

We reach the drop-off zone, a narrow road where cars fight for space to unload suitcases. When we step out of the car to face each other, we breathe a collective sigh: we made it.

Taara is the first to speak. "You know," she nervously laughs, "I had no idea working for a fashion magazine would be so exciting."

Kunal shakes his head, passing me my suitcase. "I think you two have given us enough excitement for a lifetime. All right." He claps his hands together. "We need to get you on your flight. Vidya will go inside with you two. I can't leave the car here. So, I suppose, this is goodbye."

Mom shakes his hand. "Thank you for everything—oh,

and please get this to Nandini." She passes him the napkin and he skims the message, nodding before he slips it into his pocket.

Heart finally close to a normal pulse, I hug Taara and then shake Kunal's hand. Mom adjusts her suitcase handle and heads toward the door with Vidya. "Let's get going," Mom says, glancing in my direction.

"I'll be a minute," I call after her, and I look up at Kunal. "Just wanted to say thanks for being here for us. My mom . . . she doesn't usually feel comfortable around men, but you made her feel safe. That's a big deal."

Eyes shut to the bustling world around us, he smiles peacefully. "Good. I'm grateful."

"I wanted to ask you something, though."

"Shoot. But make it quick—I don't want you missing your flight."

"Why were you crying?"

"What? When?" he asks, genuine confusion on his face.

"When you grabbed me . . . from Ahluwalia. Your eyes were kinda wet."

"Oh," he says. "Do you want the honest truth?"

I nod.

"It was because"—he swallows—"I saw his face next to yours. Same chin. Same jaw. Same cheekbones."

"Oh," I whisper.

He pats me on the shoulder. "Takes a lot of courage to do what you did, beta. *Completely* irresponsible, mind you, but still . . . courageous. Now, please, go the hell home."

420 ❧

on the napkin

dear nandini,

thank you for the courage that your words gave me today.
i faced him today for millions of reasons—you were one.
my daughter was another. nirbhaya was another.

the women at aasra shelter were another.

although i cannot attend the gala, there are four women
who i hope will accept woman of the year on my behalf:

priyanka. khushi. saima. radhika.

it is an act of bravery to live through hell and run from it
when we have been made to believe
that running is far more dangerous than staying

i beg for a world where we all have the resources
to seek safety. to find shelter. to find refuge. to run.
but moreover, more than anything,
i beg for a world where all the reasons to run
are washed away.

Kiran

breaking free

There's a relief that rises into the air with us. When Mumbai becomes a twinkling galaxy below our bodies, for a moment, I am as light as the sky that welcomes me into its weightless embrace. Right now, I do not touch the same earth where he dwells. Right now, we are out of his reach. But the moment of comfort is just that: a moment. A short-lived spark that dies, forcing my eyes to adjust to the darkness. I live in a world where powerful men can have the truth of their actions shined bright in their faces only to smile. Only to live comfortably in their bodies as if they cannot remember the violence. Only to teach the masses how to forget.

"It was all because of Charan?" Mom whispers. We lift our eyes from the glittering midnight landscape below and find each other's.

"The man in the picture?"

"Hanji. The man in the picture." She rests a clammy hand on mine. Squeezes. "I was sixteen when I befriended this boy in my English class. He . . . he made me feel special. Heard. Important, I suppose. He made me feel like I wasn't a complete screw-up. Mom never made me feel like that." She pulls the blue fleece of an airline blanket closer to her chest.

"*You* liked a boy?" I tease. "Scandalous." She lowers her eyes. "Sorry, just trying to make you smile. Go on. I'm listening."

"I got . . . attached to him. Charan. Charanpal Chawla. I would sneak out from my bedroom window to go see him. We'd go to the park and eat smoked corn or catch our favorite Kajol films at the cinema or sit for hours watching the moon at Sukhna Lake. We'd only meet in places dark enough to not get spotted by our parents . . . or watchful aunties and uncles who would report to our parents." She shakes her head and laughs. "I thought I was so clever. Of course they were going to find out."

"How did they?"

"Mom caught me climbing out of my window one night. And Dad . . ." She sighs. "He caught Charan."

"Shit."

"Yup. My dad roughed him up. Scared him into never talking to me again at school. He acted like I didn't even matter. And I was devastated." She shrugs, resigned to the way this story played out.

"But he came back. The picture . . ."

"Yeah," Mom sighs, "he did. I hadn't spoken to him in years. Hadn't seen him since school ended. But, of course, he had to show up after Prabh Ahluwalia came along. I knew Prabh since I was a kid. He came from a well-off family so, obviously, my parents wanted us together. And he was . . . nice enough. Kind enough. Didn't seem like the kind of guy who would just disappear on me like Charan. So, I did what my mother wanted and got engaged to him."

"Did you meet up with Charan while you were engaged to Prabh?"

"I did. I was young and stupid and I thought—I thought that if I saw him, just that once, I'd know for sure what I felt for Prabh. What I wanted. Because, when Charan called me out of nowhere, after all that time, I still felt something. And it wasn't . . . what I felt for Prabh. It was different. Denser."

"Where'd you meet?"

"A restaurant. I remember I chose it because it was on the

other end of the city. Far enough from home that my family and Prabh's wouldn't run into us. I sat down with him and he told me all sorts of garbage. Said he felt bad for cutting me out of his life when we were in school. Said he wanted me back . . . that I should just drop this thing with Prabh and forget about going to school and marry *him*. Like that would make everything better."

"So, let me get this straight." I laugh. "This guy ditches you because he's scared of your dad and then shows up one day, tells you to forget about school and your fiancé and just asks you to get married?"

"Yeah." Mom shrugs again. "Maybe he thought he was being flattering but it only made me feel more suffocated. Alone. And I held his hand and I said thank you for lunch and then I left. I never should've held his hand."

"You were my age, right?"

"I was."

I squeeze her palm a little tighter. "You were a teenager. And you were scared and confused about a huge decision that you weren't ready to make. Holding someone's hand doesn't justify what Ahluwalia did. Please believe me."

"I'm trying." Her chest slowly rises and caves. "It makes sense now . . . what he said."

"What *who* said?"

"Hari. When I was sitting in his car before—before it happened. He went on this whole speech about how I wouldn't get away with embarrassing his family. I thought he was talking about my outfit. About my midriff showing. Really, he was talking about Charan."

"So, that whole thing on TV where he said he confronted you about it—"

"The rape. That was the confrontation," she murmurs.

"Why didn't you tell me about this?"

"That night when I was telling you the story, I didn't think to mention this because I didn't even know the two things were connected. You know how hard it is for me to talk about things I bury away. Charan was someone I buried."

"I get that."

"My mind is strange, I think. Packed up tight like a suitcase. And if I have to dig for one memory, all the way at the bottom, I make a mess of all the other stuff as well. Everything comes out. Spills onto the floor. So, I try to just . . ."

"Keep it all in."

"Hanji."

Mom strokes my hand with her thumb. "There's, um, something that's been on my mind."

"What's up?"

"It seems like you're beating yourself up over this thing with Jeevan. You're feeling guilty because of your confusion, because of what happened. Am I right?"

"In a way, yeah."

"This world makes us feel like our stories begin and end with men—the ones who want us or don't want us or hurt us or love us. But if I've learned anything, it's that happiness doesn't need to hinge on the boy you end up with." She touches my cheek. "You can choose yourself, too."

"I don't think I know how to choose myself, Mom." I sigh. "Self-love is hard when your body feels like . . . it isn't really yours."

Her saucer eyes meet mine. "I think I know what you mean, puth. But you are so much more powerful than you think you are. I meant exactly what I said at INN: who you are has nothing to do with him." She pauses, reaches for my hand, and holds it in her warm grasp. "You know, when you wrote me that letter, it changed everything for me—*everything*. Maybe it's time you wrote another letter. To yourself. To your body."

dear body

it's fair to say we haven't been on the best terms.
god, i've been angry at you.
i've hated you.
i've wanted to erase you.

and you dripped water at my rage.

of course, there will always be a piercing hurt
when i remember how you were formed
but you deserve so much more than punishment
for a crime you never committed.

you are my first home
the only place i will ever dwell
the vessel that will carry me to the end
the source of my voice
and an ocean overflowing with love
and kindness
and creativity
and bravery.

i don't know what tomorrow will bring
but, today, i'm begging myself to believe
that you are a new canvas
and i can color you in the paint
of *my* choosing.

while mom sleeps

i crack open my sketchbook
and let my pencil fill the holes
that this trip has cut into me

the painting blooms in my mind
five women sitting together
four who i just met
one who brought me into this world

they huddle close
spilling their truths
over cha

in this beautiful oasis
among their sisters
khushi
saima
radhika
priyanka
and mom
are finally
and unequivocally
safe

him

It's nearly ten in the morning when we leave Vancouver Airport. If we'd come home on the day we were originally meant to, Maasi would've been waiting outside for us with chocolate Timbits and hugs. Instead, she's working a twelve-hour shift at the hospital. So I sucked it up and made an extremely awkward phone call.

Without missing a beat, he said he'd skip his morning lecture to pick us up.

The drive home is quieter than the forest behind my house. Mom is knocked out in the back seat. My eyes are bloodshot from exhaustion but so very relieved by the sight of him.

"Glad you're back," Jeevan softly says, glancing in his rearview mirror to make sure that Mom is still asleep.

"Really?" I murmur. "Didn't exactly seem like you wanted to talk. . . ."

For a moment, he pulls his gaze from the sparsely populated freeway and rests his gentle eyes on me. "I needed space to figure things out, Sahaara. Doesn't mean I stopped caring. Still checked in on you to make sure you were okay, didn't I?"

"Well, you'd be a bit of an asshole if you didn't even bother making sure I was alive."

"No . . . I'd be Sunny."

"Oh. Shit." I can't help but burst out laughing. "That was cold, Jeevan. Accurate but *cold*." I place my arm on the center armrest, my fingers dangling just over the edge. Jeevan shifts gears and then rests his arm next to mine. Our hands almost graze.

When we reach home, I pop Mom's suitcase out of the trunk and place it in the driveway. Then I try my best to calm the scarlet growing in my cheeks as I ask her the question that I've been dreading the whole way home. "Can I, um, have a minute in the car with Jeevan?"

She glances from me to the back of Jeevan's head. He's sitting in the driver's seat scrolling through his phone. "Of course. Just remember what I said."

I return to the passenger seat and toy with my phone case, unsure what to do with my hands. "So . . ."

"So." Jeevan and I look everywhere but each other. When we accidentally make eye contact, we don't look away.

I cough. "I don't—"

"I'll wait for you."

"—know if I'm ready for a relationship."

"What?" we both say at the same time.

For a moment, we are silent, absorbing the impact of our words, studying one another's features. Jeevan rests a hand on his steering wheel, pulling off his glasses with the other. He stares down at his feet, square jaw clenched. "I'm such a mess," I finally say. His face falls out of focus as tears blur my vision.

"Aren't we all?"

Mom's words rush to me. "I know that something beautiful can grow between us. I can see it. I can feel it humming under my skin. But these past few months have been some of the toughest in my life. I've learned things about myself that I can never unlearn. I've seen things in me that I've never seen before. I need to take the time to get to know me before I meet . . . us."

His grip loosens around the steering wheel. "You know you don't have to learn to love yourself on your own, right? You can lean on others."

I smirk. "Thanks for the reminder. But I think this one's on me."

"I respect that. Just know that I'm not going anywhere."

The selfish creature inside me wants nothing more than to lean over the armrest. It wants to rest my hands on his scruffy cheek, nuzzle into his warm neck, and fall into the safety of his embrace, into the kind lightning of his mouth. "I want you to be happy."

He shakes his head, laughing to himself. "Happy? The happiest days of my life usually involve you being right here next to me."

"Am I even wor—"

"Always. *Always*. How is that even a question?"

"What if this messes everything up? What if our friendship falls apart 'cause of all this?"

"I know it could hurt." He winces. "Really fuckin' bad. But nothing good in life comes without that risk."

I think of every peril I've welcomed in the last seven days that felt both heart-poundingly frightening and completely necessary. I can't help but agree.

Jeevan shifts in his seat to face me directly, softness in his brow, stillness in his hands. Our chests fall toward each other, the heat of his body magnetic against my suddenly thrumming skin. He lifts my chin and we hover inches apart. Just as they did the last time we were this close, the only things that exist are his saltwater eyes and his parted mouth.

With a slight shake of my head, my lips accidentally graze

the soft skin of his. "Not yet," I whisper. "Only when I'm completely ready. You don't deserve any less. *I* don't deserve any less."

He nods and sadly smiles, thumb still touching my skin. "Appreciate it, bud."

"So, um . . . I almost used your knife." I sniff.

"The fuck?!" He pulls back in shock. "What happened?"

"Long story." I laugh. "We're gonna need to sit down at Bear Creek for this one."

jeevan

is the safest, warmest place i've ever been

is not a coat to be taken off
and pulled on whenever i'm cold

is a steady current when all i've known
are the intensity of tidal waves

is not an answer
but a question of what could be

i've been poring over priyanka's book

and i find myself rereading the same lines again and again

> *to be an effective ally to survivors of sexual*
> *assault, you need to be prepared to listen more*
> *than you speak.*

i highlight the words in fluorescent blue
that make my chest seize

> *to push your own ideas of healing or justice*
> *onto a survivor may be to traumatize them again.*
> *remember that they have been through a storm*
> *that has likely felt uncontrollable, outside of their*
> *power to contain.*

> *remember that the abuse may have left them feeling*
> *as if the power of choice was stolen from them*
> *in all aspects of life.*

> *power is reclaimed every time they are reminded*
> *that they have autonomy, that their loved ones*
> *and acquaintances will not be making every*
> *decision for them.*

> *how can you play a role in returning the ability*
> *to choose?*

the rest of the painting

comes to me like a thud
when mom hums a boli
as she unpacks her suitcase

mein vi kunda naa kholeaa
ni aageaa kand ttappke

mein vi kunda naa kholeaa
ni aageaa kand ttappke

and i know the folk song
is lighthearted. i know that
it's about a woman whose
husband goes to the movies
while she's waiting for him
at home

but the words still chill me
to my core

i didn't open the door for him
he just jumped the wall and entered.

with a single lyric
the parts of my art gala painting
that i didn't even know were missing
appear, fully formed
and ready to meet canvas.

election day

There's a centuries-old tradition of storytelling from my motherland of Punjab. From grandmother to mother to daughter, bolis have seldom been written down. Instead, the rhyming verses that are sung before weddings are memorized by heart, as if to say that we carry each other within our bodies. Some of the bolis are carefree and joyous—celebrations of beautiful marriages that are to come. Others are carefree but painful. Tales of strained relationships with mothers-in-law and men sung aloud as a release. As a way of saying that hurt exists within us but that we will still find celebration in each other's arms. In our laughter. In our chorus of voices and clapping hands.

My black heels clack against the wooden gallery floor as I step backward into the half-moon of my family to admire my painting. In the meter-long tapestry, dozens of South Asian women gather around in a circle to sing bolis, some dressed in brightly colored salwar kameezes and saris, others in hoodies and jeans, others yet in mini-shorts and crop tops. Each of their heads are draped in bright red chunnis bordered by shimmery, crinkly strips of gold. All of them are brides. All of them are being celebrated. Despite today's date—a day I've dreaded for weeks—the only thing that matters is their wedding day.

"So, they're getting married?" Standing to my right, Jeevan removes his glasses and takes a closer look at the metallic gold strips that I hand-stitched onto the red scarves in the artwork.

"In a way," I reply.

"Who are they marrying?" Maasi asks from the left.

"I could tell you, but I'd rather you told me what you think."

Maasi rests her oversized purse between her legs and continues to survey the artwork. Crossing her arms over her metallic-blue cocktail dress, her eyes follow the Punjabi text that borders the entire painting, her head tilting to the left as she reads the words scribed vertically along the side. Bibi, standing just beside Maasi in her brightest yellow salwar kameez, mumbles the words to herself in Punjabi.

"Are those bolis?" Mom asks from behind me, resting her chin on my shoulder.

"Uh-huh. But I wrote the lyrics myself."

"Oh, Mother," Mom begins to translate the text at the bottom, "I met a world that tried to steal me from myself. My body, a glass pot in their hands . . ."

"Thrown away, smashed against the tiles when they were done . . ." Maasi continues.

"But I held my own hand and held yours. I made it to my wedding day . . ." Bibi Jee nods her head.

"And here I am, oh Mother," I finish the sentence. "Here I am marrying myself."

"Hai rabba, child." Bibi shakes her head, her round cheeks filled with a smile. "When did you become a kavi?!"

"Been writing since I was a kid." I shrug. "When you and Mom started reading poetry to me. Usually just kept the poems to myself. But when I interviewed the women at the shelter, I knew I had to paint something that . . . spoke. Wasn't sure how until Mom started humming that tune."

"What tune?" Mom asks.

"When we came home from Mumbai, you were unpacking your suitcase. You were humming mai vee kundhaa naa khu-lia ni ageya kandh tapke."

"And that was it?"

"That was it." I smile. "Inspiration hit."

"That's them, isn't it?" Mom points to the women painted at the forefront of the warm gathering of women. Seated comfortably on cushions, elevated from the harshness of this earth, four familiar faces smile and laugh and whisper into each other's ears.

"That's them. Radhika, Priyanka, Saima, and Khushi." I've dressed each of them in the saris they wore to their interviews. To their left, sitting cross-legged next to them, is the person I love most in the world. In the painting, she throws her head backward and laughs unashamedly, without the usual restraint of her worries.

"Do the butterflies mean something?" Mom asks, pointing to the spattering of violet monarchs that flutter above the women. They are arranged purposefully, moving upward as if they are trying to break free of the canvas.

"When I'm anxious, it feels like there are butterflies in my stomach. It's like they're trying to escape. Butterflies also symbolize migration. Mom migrated to Canada, but the other women we interviewed fled from traumatic situations as well. They just didn't get to go as far."

"Damn." Jeevan's eyes widen as he rests his glasses on his long nose. "That's deep." Mom slowly wraps an arm across my chest and holds me close.

With a quick glance at me, Maasi taps Bibi on the shoulder. "Hey, why don't we go take a look at the other art?"

Bibi nods and Jeevan trails behind them. The three of them meander toward a wiry, geometric sculpture in the crowded Daphne Odjig Gallery. Then they turn a corner and disappear.

"How're you holding up?" I ask.

She takes a step closer to the tapestry and lingers on her painted reflection. "I'm . . . good. More reasons to be happy than sad, right?"

I check the time on my phone: nearly eight p.m. That means it's almost eight thirty a.m. in Punjab. The election results should be out soon.

"How are the nerves?" Mom studies me with concern.

"The election nerves will be better once they just announce the damn thing. Whatever comes of this, I just wanna know, you know?"

"I know."

"I think it's the same with the performance nerves. I'll be fine once it's over with." My hand instinctively reaches for my purse, where a poem rests, waiting to be heard aloud for the first time.

"You'll do great." She rubs my arm. "We're celebrating *you* tonight. Nothing else matters."

When Mom and I sit down for the part of the evening that I've been dreading for days, my professor slips into the seat beside me.

"Impressive work, Miss Car."

"Kaur," I correct her. "Like core."

"Right. Glad to see you applied my advice to your project," Rhonda whispers, her typically disheveled black hair curled into tight locks and her paint-splattered apron set aside for a glittering purple evening gown. Under the dimming lights, her dress gleams as she shifts her body toward mine. "And great choice of attire. Very *cultural*. Were you trying to connect your outfit to the painting?"

I smooth out the bottom of my burnt-orange kameez,

heavily embroidered with black and blue flowers. My matching phulkari chunni hangs down my shoulder, unapologetic about the way it cascades around me, taking up space. "Not exactly. Just trying to be myself, even in a place like this."

The audience lights hush low and empty seats slowly fill up. Maasi, Jeevan, and Bibi shuffle into our row, offering me pats on the shoulder and smiles of encouragement as they take their seats. When the lights are finally out and only the stage glows, the audience goes pin drop silent.

The dean begins with a speech, but I hear nothing save for a buzzing in my ear, a nervous murmur in my chest that slowly reaches into my fingertips. There are far too many people here. Far too many eyes that will soon be on me.

There are two pieces of paper trembling between my sweaty fingers: one with a short introduction and the other with the poem I completed just before sunrise this morning.

"Breathe," Mom whispers into my ear. The audience explodes into applause and Rhonda rises to take the stage.

She reaches for the mic on the podium and my heart taps a little quicker. Dress shining before the velvet black backdrop, there's nothing onstage to distract us from the sight of her. Nothing that will distract from the sight of me.

"I'd like to thank you all for attending our spring art show. I've watched my freshman students this semester create truly awe-inspiring works of art and I could not be prouder of their growth—"

"Look!" a Punjabi dad seated behind me whispers loud enough for me to hear. "The results are in!"

"It has been my absolute pleasure to curate such a fine exhibit—"

"Jit gaya?" a woman behind me whispers to the man.

"He won! Oh my god, he won!" Suddenly, a man I've never met before taps Mom and me on the shoulder. "Vadhaiyaan! Congratulations! Ahluwalia won—oh, uh, sorry." The cheer on his face goes rocky and somber when he recognizes Mom.

"And I'd like to welcome our first artist, Sahaara Kaur, to the stage!" The room roars with applause and my ears ring. My feet carry me forward, but my head is a staticky river of rushing water. Somehow, I float to the podium, blinking at the bright stage lights that cast the entire audience into a starless night. My family is seated in the third row, but I see no one.

I stare into the haneri, the darkness that transports my body across a sea where I only imagine the two people who need to hear these words. I seat my mother in the audience of my mind, taking in her never-ending abundance of love. I place myself beside her, refusing to see my face as anything but my face. Refusing to hate myself for my bones when my heart and thoughts have always been mine, just like Mom said.

Mine. I am mine.

"Hi . . ." My voice echoes through the room, reverberating in my ears. "My name is Sahaara Kaur. I'm a first-year visual art student at Daphne Odjig. I painted *If I Tell You the Truth*, which is a mixed-media mural that captures South Asian women singing traditional Punjabi folk songs called bolis as a statement about sexual abuse and liberation. I, um . . ." The mic screeches with feedback. "I had a speech prepared but I think I'd like to just recite my poem, which speaks to the artwork."

Amid the hushed room, a few invisible bodies snap their fingers. I concentrate on the image of me and Mom, holding Mom close, holding me even closer. With a deep breath,

I imagine myself growing younger, returning to the little girl who would look in the mirror and only see wonder in her blinking eyes and beating heart and smiling mouth. For her, I free the very last butterfly—the one that calls me a monster.

She smiles into her sweet dimples. My heart slows its pace.

I begin.

to be read aloud

our hearts are a boli
an echoing chorus of beings
too loud to be shaken by the dark
a song bottled in the unbreakable glass of a new world
where power does not mean violence
and violence does not force us to run from our skin

my mother's bravery is a boli
passed down through generations of women
who have worn too much patience in their braided hair.
on their callus-covered hands. on their exhausted feet.
a battle cry that casts away our haunted nights
and frees us from the ghosts of trauma at daybreak

my body is a boli
a sweet psalm i am still learning how to chant
off-key and flawed, at times,
but sung loud in the face of power
that cannot force me to disappear

because even if i run out of words
even if i lose my train of thought
even if i tell you the truth only to lose my breath
i am surrounded by women
who will pick up where i left off.

covid-19

In the year 2020, our way of life shifted dramatically. Written prior to the global mobilization against COVID-19, some sections of *If I Tell You The Truth* were unable to account for the significant changes that we lived through in this year. Sahaara graduated from high school in June of 2020 and Kiran was arrested by Canadian Border Security agents in September of the same year. With countries across the world closing their borders, shutting down their commerce, and enforcing stay-at-home orders in unprecedented ways, Kiran's lack of safety and security would have only increased in the year 2020. Although the public health care system in British Columbia has made great strides in recent years to prevent reporting of undocumented immigrants who come to hospitals for emergency medical care, this was not always the case, and there are still gaping holes in the system. Deeply frightened of accessing public services for fear of her undocumented status being exposed, Kiran would have avoided medical care unless completely necessary, feeling much safer, instead, getting help from Joti, a registered nurse. At the time of writing this note, arrests of undocumented immigrants have continued in the United States, even during state and national lockdowns. The Canadian government has slowed deportations and new detentions during the COVID-19 crisis. We have seen prisoner hunger strikes take place in detention centers across North America, in protest of deplorable living situations amid a public health crisis. The structure of detention centers does not allow for social distancing in any healthy regard. Incarcerated people are often at higher risk of illness than the general population, due to enclosed living spaces, lack of medical care, and a lack of basic sanitation supplies.

pg. 120 / grade eleven
This poem refers to the term *Turtle Island*. Many First Nations communities recognize the land known colonially as "North America" to, instead, be Turtle Island. In this poem, Sahaara honors her understanding of decolonization as she reflects on her classmates' racist belief that Canada was built by and belongs to European settlers.

pg. 205 / the last days of august were slipping through our fingers
In this poem, the news report describing the arrest of an international student was inspired by the real-life case of Jobandeep Sandhu. Mr. Sandhu was arrested by Canadian police in 2017 for working more hours than his student work visa permitted. His story sparked powerful conversations about the plight of international students who struggle to remain financially afloat while paying extremely inflated fees for their educations.

pg. 225 / beneath a moonless sky
On the night of August 31, 2020, Kiran is arrested by Canadian Border Services agents and taken to a detention center at Vancouver International Airport. In 2020, British Columbia's primary detention center for undocumented immigrants moved from Vancouver International Airport to Surrey, BC. The closing of the original detention center at the airport was

sparked by immense community pressure. In 2014, Lucía Vega Jiménez, a Mexican migrant escaping domestic violence who was detained at the Vancouver Airport center, died by suicide. Her death triggered outrage from community activist organizations who demanded that CBSA explain why the agency did not independently report her death until the media covered it. Ms. Jiménez's death has often been cited as the reason why the Vancouver detention center was shut down: no detention center is conducive to the health and wellbeing of detainees, but this center offered extremely little natural light, limited ventilation, and no outdoor spaces or health services.

pg. 258 / the letter
Although Kiran's application for permanent residence in Canada is accepted quite quickly in the story, in real life, the wait time for application processing is often much longer. Prior to COVID-19, it would have been likely that Kiran would wait for between twenty to twenty-four months to find out whether or not permanent residence would be granted in her case. After COVID-19, the wait would have been even longer. While Kiran received her permanent residence approval much quicker than we would see in the real world, the barriers she faced in finding help were painfully true to life. Kiran's history of trauma, particularly at the hands of police officers and authority figures, had a pivotal impact on her ability to seek professional and ethical counsel. Kiran, a young woman of color, was violated by men who used their positions of power, trust, and influence to get away with their brutality. Kiran's struggle to find trustworthy support is a reminder of how justice is often out of reach for marginalized peoples.

pg. 420 / on the napkin
When Kiran mentions the name "Nirbhaya" in this poem, she is referring to the brutal 2012 gang rape of Jyoti Singh (known publicly as Nirbhaya, meaning *fearless*) in New Delhi. The Nirbhaya case triggered a wave of #MeToo protest and activism across South Asia, centering around demands for justice, accountability, and respect for women.

i am forever grateful for

deepak ahluwalia
damanpreet singh
daniela carolina
ishpreet kaur
pardeep kaur
rajan dhaliwal
gurpreet bains
sukhpreet singh
gurjit singh
gayatri sethi
prabhdeep singh kehal
harnidh kaur
parneet malhi
rick gill
tajinder kaur
ishaval gill
ishleen chahal
sahibajot kaur
vickramjit singh
nikki shahi
sarah homer
tara weikum
katherine latshaw

without whom
this work wouldn't have been possible